FINALES AND OVERTURES

Also by Jeanne McCafferty

Star Gazer
Artist Unknown

FINALES AND OVERTURES

Jeanne McCafferty

For Kathy,

With salutations for
your new New York home,

Love, Jeanne

HEADLINE
FEATURE

First published in Great Britain in 1996 by
HEADLINE BOOK PUBLISHING

A HEADLINE FEATURE hardback

10 9 8 7 6 5 4 3 2 1

British Library Cataloguing in Publication Data

McCafferty, Jeanne
Finales and overtures
1. American fiction - 20th century
I. Title
813.5'4 [F]

ISBN 0 7472 1501 4

Typeset by Avon Dataset Ltd, Bidford-on-Avon, Warks

Printed and bound in Great Britain by
Mackays of Chatham PLC, Chatham, Kent

HEADLINE BOOK PUBLISHING
A division of Hodder Headline PLC
338 Euston Road
London NW1 3BH

I am indebted to a number of people for generously sharing their time and expertise with me. My thanks to:

Jeremy M. Steinberg CPA for providing background on the financing of theatrical productions;

Diane F. Krausz and her colleagues for giving me a glimpse into the dynamics of the theatrical producer's world;

David Hurwitz for providing helpful information and suggestions regarding New York real estate;

John O. Phillips for his information regarding the Union Square district and the City Planning commission;

Patricia Shannahan for sharing memories of bus and truck tours of the Oberammergau Passion Play in the South;

Lynne M. Curtis for her detailed review of drug interactions and medical protocol;

Marie Simonetti Rosen, publisher of *Law Enforcement News*, a publication of John Jay College of Criminal Justice/CUNY, and the Honorable William Giovan, Judge of the Wayne County Circuit Court, Wayne County, Michigan for enlightening conversations on the state of the criminal justice system;

John T. Green, for his continuing assistance and information, especially regarding the City University of New York; and

the research librarians at the Central Library, Los Angeles, California and the Frances Howard Goldwyn Library, Hollywood, California.

While all these people were enormously helpful to me in my research process, the responsibility for any errors is, or course, entirely mine.

My thanks, as always, to Brian McCafferty for his assistance in polishing the first draft and to Julia McLaughlin for her early reading, helpful suggestions, and the fountain of information on the actor's life in New York; to Leonard J. Charney, Esq. and Wendy Schmalz for their continuing support and professional guidance; and to Kay Davis and Carol Sheffield and the various individuals making up the networks of prayer that have sustained and encouraged me.

While I thoroughly enjoyed my research in a number of books dedicated to the American musical theatre and to New York theatre in general, for anyone with a particular interest in the history of theatre (and theatres) in New York City, I am pleased to recommend *The City & the Theatre* by Mary C. Henderson, published by James

T. White & Company of Clifton, New Jersey.

One final note: readers familiar with New York City's Union Square area will note that, while I have faithfully recorded many details of the neighborhood, I have taken a number of liberties as well, especially in describing the subway station. This was done both for the purposes of storytelling, and as a reminder to me and to readers that this is a work of fiction; hopefully the story's events that take place in the subway station will remain safely in the world of fiction.

J McC

Dedicated, with love,
to the memory of my father,
E. F. McCafferty.
I can still hear the silence on the other end of the
phone when I told him that my college major would be in theatre.
I trust he would be pleased that I finally found
a (somewhat) practical use for my studies.

PROLOGUE

Before Buratti's phone call – a phone call that would turn her world upside down – the only thing on Mackenzie Griffin's mind when she got home that Thursday night was that her feet were cold.

It had been a long day and she was tired and, in fact, she couldn't remember the last time her feet weren't cold. It had been a bitter winter in New York – bitter in many ways – and the spring, which had officially started almost three weeks ago, was remarkable so far only for being the wettest on record, and one of the coldest.

Her tiredness, too, was of long-standing, and of the type that an extra hour's sleep here and there wouldn't cure.

She tried to put her still-open umbrella down in the hallway to dry, but managed only to get large drops of rain all over the hardwood floor. Sighing, she headed for her bedroom, but when she heard the squishing sound her shoes made when she walked, she stepped out of them and left them by the umbrella. She looked at them, realizing that they would be the third pair to bite the dust in the last few months.

Eliot was right, Mac thought, as she padded in her stockinged feet toward her bedroom, April is the cruellest month, or it can be when it's like this one. It tries to fool

1

you into thinking it's spring, but it's really late winter under another name.

She was just shrugging off her soggy raincoat when the phone rang. It was probably Peter. She'd half expected him to be at her place even before she arrived, since they'd planned on an early dinner. So it was a double surprise when the voice she heard was a familiar one, but not Peter's.

'Mac, is that you?' Lieutenant Mario Buratti snapped. The first part of the surprise was that it was Buratti, not Peter. Mac had spoken to the lieutenant only a few times in the past six months, and not at all in the last two. The second part of the surprise was that he was calling on her home line. While their relationship had evolved into a professional friendship a long time ago, it had remained in the professional realm, and Buratti, when he called her, always called on her office line.

'Mario?' Mac's voice made it a question, even though she was ninety-nine percent certain she had the voice right. 'What is it?'

'Sylvie Morgan. She a friend of yours?' Buratti said bluntly.

Images flashed into Mac's mind of the reasons police call people asking about other people. Images of accidents, robberies, muggings – the general stuff of the eleven o'clock news. 'What's happened to her? Is Sylvie all right?'

'This is strictly between us, Mac, and falls into the realm of favour – the big kind of favour.' He paused, and Mac realized that he'd been speaking very softly. 'You know that new theatre over on the south side of Union Square?'

Yes, of course she did. That's where she'd met Sylvie when they'd gone to dinner just a week ago. 'Yes. Mario, tell me—'

2

'You might want to get over here, Mac. Your friend's being questioned about a suspicious death over here, and it looks like we're gonna be taking her in.' In the background, someone interrupted Buratti, and he cut them off with a 'Be right there' and then came back on the line to Mac. 'Make it quick if you can, Mac,' he said and then the line went dead.

Mac stood there staring at the phone in a daze. Then the droplets of rain that had collected on the belt of her trench coat started dripping onto her feet and she snapped out of it. Sylvie? A suspect in a murder? That's what 'suspicious death' usually turned out to be, after all. Sylvie? Not possible. Was it?

Mac changed into heavy knit pants and top, a kind of dressy sweatsuit whose main virtue tonight was that it was warm and dry, and put on socks and running shoes to complete the outfit. She wrote a note to Peter, grabbed her shiny yellow hooded slicker that made her look like a crossing guard and was walking out the door within five minutes of Buratti's call. She knew she'd be able to make good time on foot since the theatre was only a few blocks from her apartment. She jogged past the surprised doorman in front of her building and headed toward Union Square, the exact same route she'd travelled eight days ago to meet Sylvie.

As Mackenzie headed west on 15th Street, she realized that Buratti hadn't told her – and she hadn't had time to ask – just who it was who was dead. But she knew from her visit to the theatre that night just a week ago that there was enough tension among the members of the show's company to suggest a few possible deadly combinations of victim and killer.

CHAPTER ONE

When Mac had walked this same route the week before, it was under much more pleasant circumstances. Given the whimsies of New York weather, the temperature that date had soared briefly, and for a few hours a person could actually believe that flowers would be blooming in Union Square in the near future. She'd been eager to see Sylvie, and was looking forward to hearing about her friend's experiences of the last five months.

Mac was also thrilled to get a preview look at the theatre that was bringing so much attention to her neighbourhood. The construction of the Century Theatre had been heralded in the New York press when it was first announced last year. Much of the early press coverage had taken the slant of how the Century was reviving one of Manhattan's original theatre districts. Once the Union Square area had, at least as far as concentration of theatres was concerned, been the Times Square of the late 19th century.

The architect and developer had been lauded for the exterior design, as well. The theatre's look echoed the late 19th century style that had surrounded Union Square in its heyday.

The owner of the theatre, Simon Wexler (who, rumour said, had grand plans for developing the blocks adjacent to his new enterprise) was a savvy public relations man, and was literally keeping the building under wraps. To every extent possible, given the needs of the construction crews, the building was draped in canvas; the canvas would be removed when a crew was working on an area, and when they finished it was re-draped. Mac had no idea how effectively one could hide a four storey building by draping it, but the publicity Mr Wexler had gotten out of the effort certainly made it seem worthwhile.

Mr Wexler did seem to have a certain showman's sense about his development. In fact, he was also one of the producers of *Reunion,* the show that would be the Century Theatre's inaugural production. It was the show that, fingers crossed, would be Sylvie's big break at last, and Mac couldn't wait to hear the details about the show, and about Sylvie's part in it.

She also wanted to find out if the buzz was true. Word had it, if one believed the columnists in the New York papers, that *Reunion* was going to be a smash. That kind of advance word was rare on a show that had suffered post-ponements, and *Reunion* had had its share of those. Originally announced late last year for a mid-March opening, it was now scheduled to open April 30th.

Mac assumed the delay in the production was part of the reason that the recent press on the show appeared to be a goofy attempt to maintain public interest by in-sinuating that there was a 'ghost of the Century Theatre'. Mac had read only a few of the news stories, which had recounted tales of construction workers and actors hearing strange noises, or claiming that they felt a presence in the theatre, but she had trouble figuring out how a brand new theatre, especially one that sat on a lot most recently occupied by a supermarket and a bowling alley, could be home to a ghost of the theatrical persuasion.

As she crossed Irving Place to head onto the last stretch of 15th Street before the square, Mac realized that, as eager as she had been to see Sylvie that night, there was a part of their upcoming conversation that she wasn't looking forward to. Mac hadn't seen Sylvie since she'd left the last week of November, which meant Sylvie hadn't been here when The Bombing happened. While there was a lot the friends would catch up on that night, there was a lot they would never catch up on, simply because Sylvie hadn't been here when it happened, and it was one of those experiences that simply could never be explained.

It wasn't just Sylvie, of course. The Bombing was simply one of those events. Even Mac's colleagues and neighbours, some of whom were travelling when it happened, thought that because they had returned within a day or two of The Bombing, they had been a part of it. Her family, living up in Connecticut, thought they had lived through it, too. And certainly they had, in a way. But nobody who was outside New York that day could fully appreciate what getting through those hours had meant, and nobody outside the Union Square area could fully appreciate what living through those minutes had been like.

It was one of those dividing lines we've come to accumulate, she'd realized, experiences that unite people who lived through them and separate them from those who haven't. For her parents' generation, it was where they were when they learned John Kennedy had been assassinated, or Martin Luther King, Jr. For another generation it was learning that John Lennon had been shot dead outside his home. For the current generation, those markers also took on the form of witnessed tragedy: Were you watching when the Challenger exploded? Too frequently, the markers were acts of terrorism: Were you downtown when they hit the World Trade Center? Remember those first eerie images out of Oklahoma City, filled with smoke and silence? And now, in New York, for a city that so frequently calls itself The City, it was The Bombing. Were you in Union Square during The Bombing? If the answer was 'yes', you were a member of an exclusive club, and the other members were the only ones who really understood that look in your eye.

As she headed down Park Avenue South to cross at 14th Street, Mac glanced back up the east side of Union Square. There they were, still. The orange and white barriers that rimmed the east boundary of the Square, and confined the traffic to one north-bound lane, were vivid, daily reminders for the area residents of the events of the week before Christmas. She shook her head to clear the remembered images from her mind, and waited for the traffic light to cross the street.

Looking at the still-draped facade of the Century Theatre, Mac realized she was, in fact, excited at the prospect of glimpsing a musical as a work in progress. She'd been a fan of musicals since her parents first took her to see *1776* when she was ten years old. The following year she'd seen *Purlie* and then *Godspell* six months after that, so by the age of twelve she was hooked. A trip to see *A Chorus Line* when she was sixteen had been the first time she'd travelled into the city with friends, without any parents chaperoning. It marked a coming of age for her, and it was the show for which she still had the greatest affection.

Her experience with musicals had only been from the audience, however. And while in the last several years she'd gotten backstage glimpses of various productions that Sylvie had been in, some of which came under the heading of *very* experimental, none had been an authentic Broadway musical. Or was *Reunion* an off-Broadway musical? Even though the theatre sat at the corner of Broadway and 14th Street, it wasn't in the neighbourhood usually associated with quote Broadway theatre unquote. She'd have to ask Sylvie when she got a chance.

Mac entered the theatre from the furthest right door, as Sylvie had instructed her, and was stopped before she made it through the lobby by a tired and very aggravated man in his late thirties. Even as she was admiring the details of the black and white lobby floor and the sconces adorning the walls, a weary voice that had gotten its character from too many cigarettes had stopped her before she made it to the interior doors. 'Where do you think you're going?'

Mac stopped, looked around, and realized the voice was coming from the shadows on the far side of the lobby. The glow of the tip of a cigarette told her that she'd been right about her assessment of the voice; she'd probably interrupted a surreptitious smoking break. She couldn't believe it would be kosher to smoke in an area still littered with construction materials as this one was. Not that it was kosher to smoke indoors in that many public places in New York City anymore.

'I'm meeting Sylvie Morgan here. My name is Mackenzie Griffin.'

'That's *Doctor* Griffin to you, Larry,' she heard Sylvie say in a loud whisper behind her. 'She's my shrink. You people are making me so crazy, I had to request a house call.' There was just enough edge in Sylvie's voice that Mac couldn't tell if she was joking or not, but when she turned and saw the wink first, and then Sylvie's arms about to encircle her, she guessed there was no emergency.

'Mackenzie,' Sylvie said in a low voice as she wrapped her friend in a bear hug. '*God*, it's good to see you!'

9

Sylvie's hug had pinned her arms, so Mackenzie was prevented from returning the embrace, but she could still talk. 'Good to see you, too, oh star of tomorrow.'

'We'll see about that,' Sylvie muttered. 'We're just going to duck in the back here, Larry,' she said to the man now finishing his cigarette in the corner. 'Don't get your shorts in a knot or anything.' Turning Mac by the shoulder and pointing her toward one of the six doors that led to the theatre auditorium, Sylvie whispered in a softer tone, 'He's the stage manager and just got yelled at bad, so he's sulking out here. But everybody's getting yelled at tonight, believe me.'

In fact, as Sylvie opened one of the heavy doors leading to the theatre, Mac heard the sharp tones of at least two male voices talking over one another. The door closed silently behind them, and Mac saw that they were at the back of the auditorium area, in the wide aisle that crossed the entire theatre behind the last row of seats. The house lights were on, as were a number of stage lights.

'We picked a good night for you to be here, Mackenzie. The whole bunch of coconuts is here.'

Mac glanced around the theatre, surprised that it was smaller than she expected. The newer theatres she'd seen in New York over the last ten years seemed immense in comparison to this. They were mostly in high rises, of course, and had more room to work with, she guessed. This was more the size of some of the smaller playhouses on Broadway. The Booth Theatre maybe. Or the Golden.

Even with the rising volume of the voices from near the stage, Mac found that the interior design of the theatre held her attention. Though the interior was obviously not finished, it promised to be very inviting. The walls were wainscoted with large panels of a dark wood; inside the wood panels were fabric panels that had a tapestry look to them. At the seams where the wood panels met were sconces similar to the ones in the lobby. Actually the sconces were evident only on the first seams up from the stage. The other seams had holes where additional sconces presumably would be placed. Mac took a closer look at the seats directly in front of where she and Sylvie were standing; two of them, the two closest to the aisle, were uncovered (the other seats in these last rows were still wrapped in a heavy plastic), allowing Mac to see that the upholstery picked up the deep rose that was the predominant tone in the tapestry panels. That the theatre interior was a work-in-progress was evident everywhere. In the left aisle were strips and scraps of the carpeting that covered the aisle ways, a few large tool boxes with locks on them, and a pile of the plastic wraps that had been taken off the orchestra seats that were uncovered, which included the first six or seven rows. While it was apparent that this was a new building, especially from the scent of fresh wood, new materials, and somewhere, fresh paint, it seemed to Mac that it had an old feeling to it, a very comfortable old feeling. The effect was akin to being transported in time: she was looking at a new 19th century building.

Mac's concentration was pulled away from the theatre and toward the stage when the volume of the voices grew suddenly. 'And I don't give a good goddam what you say, this show is going to open April 30th!' a red-faced man standing on the edge of the stage shouted, apparently directing his opinion to a man standing in front of the first row of seats on the right side of the auditorium.

'Ah, it's Quigley's turn to get yelled at,' Sylvie said softly, looking intently at the stage. She looked over at Mac. 'Bruce Quigley. He's the architect.' She looked back at the man

11

who was speaking. 'One very nice looking architect. And single, too, do you believe it? Only slightly damaged from his divorce.'

'I'm trying to help, here, Simon, not piss you off,' Quigley was saying calmly.

'Well, it pisses me off to hear about this kind of a delay at this point!' barked the angry silver-haired man standing centre stage, whom Mac now recognized from his newspaper photographs as Simon Wexler, the gentleman who was both one of the producers of the show and the owner of the theatre. His navy dress pants were held up by bright red braces that looked like they came from the Larry King Collection, and he held an unlit cigar in his right hand, which he used to punctuate his words effectively. There was no doubt that the April 30th he had referred to had an exclamation point after it.

As Mac looked toward the stage to identify the other people involved in this discussion, she felt her heart speed up slightly when she spotted the man lounging against the proscenium arch on the right side of the stage. It was Gil Richardson, *Reunion*'s famed director.

If truth be told, as pleased as Mac was to be seeing Sylvie tonight, she was equally excited that they had agreed to meet at the theatre because she knew she might get a chance to meet Gil Richardson. She was still enough of a groupie, even at her age, to be thrilled by the prospect. And he was every bit as attractive as she thought he might be.

Richardson slouched against the proscenium arch, tall and lanky and elegant in his signature black turtleneck and dark grey trousers. Thinner than she had imagined, but incredibly elegant in his posture, he reminded her, as he always did, of a taller, darker Fred Astaire. Just watching his head move as the conversation moved from Wexler to

12

Quigley and back again, you could sense that this man still had his stage presence about him. Even leaning against the proscenium, he knew he was on stage, even if he was only an audience to the argument currently underway.

'And all I'm saying, Simon, is that if you want to make that date, we have to get the cast out of here, get them rehearsing someplace else, let me bring in the people who can finish the interior. We finish up the balcony seating, the carpets, the lighting, the lobby. Two, three days max, they'll be out of your hair. If not, you'll be opening without the building looking as good as you want it to. But remember the opening of the play is going to be the opening of the building too, and that means the opening of the whole Century Redevelopment.' Quigley paused, expecting Wexler to reply. When he didn't the architect continued. 'Two, three days, and then we can get out of your way until the undraping. I'll still need the building for thirty-six hours before the opening so we can get the draping off and finish the marquee. But like I said, Simon, I'm trying to help here, not piss you off.'

Mac leaned over to Sylvie and whispered. 'He's involved in the interior *and* the exterior?'

Sylvie whispered back, 'He designed the whole thing. Outside, inside – even the ladies rooms, as far as I know. He's very talented. And did I mention single?' She barely finished when the sound from the stage erupted again.

'What pisses me off is seeing money leaking out through a goddam sieve, when we don't have any coming in!' Simon Wexler responded, again using his cigar the way a symphony conductor uses a baton. He stopped, looked over at Richardson and said, in a calmer voice, 'What do you think?'

Before Richardson could reply, a voice from the first row

13

of seats to the right piped in. 'If the construction people are going to be running around when the actors aren't here, on what is supposed to be my time, I'm screwed.'

'Manny Erickson,' said Sylvie, like a sports commentator. 'The show's designer.'

Wexler look down at him. 'So this is the theatre, Manny. Everybody gets screwed on time. Grow up.'

Manny evidently took umbrage at the remark, and stood. 'Look, Simon, you said you wanted me to simplify the act two—'

Wexler interrupted. 'No, I said those two drops that are hangovers from the California set look cheap, and we have to come up with something to replace them.'

Sylvie leaned toward Mac while Wexler was still talking. 'One designer bit the dust already. Richardson brought Manny in just about a month ago.'

'Think simple,' Wexler was saying. 'Think elegant. Think no money.'

'Simple sometimes costs, Simon,' Manny replied. 'Elegant almost always costs. If not in money, in time, and you're telling me time is what I don't have right now. Unless you want to postpone the opening.'

'No!' Wexler stormed. 'We can't postpone the opening again! How many times do I have to tell you! We're going to open April 30. It's a Thursday and I need those Friday morning reviews and the Friday press. The next week, you have the new Sondheim show opening, and then that revival of *The Music Man*. We can't go head to head with either of them, and there's no more time left before the Tony eligibility date.'

'As it stands now, is the Tony date a factor?' piped a woman's voice from a few rows up, where the lighting wasn't as strong. Mac strained to get a look at her and turned to Sylvie. 'Joan Henley Byers,' Sylvie said. 'One of the producers. Loaded.'

'Maybe not for a nomination, Joan, but like I said before, we can play the hell out of it in our press campaign.' Wexler's voice was considerably more subdued when talking to this woman, Mac noted.

Wexler examined his cigar and turned to Richardson again. 'You never told me what you thought.'

Richardson pulled himself from the proscenium, as elegantly as if it were a choreographed move. 'We'll do what we have to do, Simon. We just got the last of the new costumes in, and it would be best if we could work here, but maybe this is what you get for dealing with amateurs.' There was an audible gasp from the small assembly, as Richardson looked pointedly at Bruce Quigley, then utter quiet as everyone froze in their respective positions.

'Whoa,' said Sylvie in a soft aside to Mac. 'Score a direct hit, why don't you?'

'What!?' Quigley shouted, taking a step toward the stage. 'Amateur? Where the *hell* do you get off calling me an amateur?'

'Well, then, tell me Bruce, how many theatres have you designed before?'

'You know damn well this is my first theatre, Gil. And you also know that theatres aren't exactly springing up like weeds all over the country. The delays that we're experiencing have nothing – absolutely nothing – to do with the fact that this is my first theatre.'

'If you say so, Bruce,' Richardson replied, and then turned to Wexler. 'Let's see if we can find some space for us to work in through Wednesday of next week. That will put us back in here for a week before the first preview. It's not my preference, but it'll have to do.'

'Actually, this might work out well,' said another man's voice. 'We'll have time to work up the "Like It Used to Be" number.' Mac recognized the speaker this time. 'Isn't that Ben Wheeler, the songwriter?' she asked.

'Bingo. Here it comes.'

Richardson stood away from the wall, pulled himself up to his full height and, eyebrow raised, seemed to smirk at the composer. 'Ben, I told you, that number doesn't need to be replaced!'

'Well I think it does,' Wheeler replied, and turned to walk up the aisle.

'It's working beautifully!' Richardson yelled at the composer's back.

'I think it could be better!' Wheeler called back over his shoulder.

'Not bloody likely!'

There was silence for a moment. Wexler broke it. 'Lenny, what do you say?'

Sylvie got in her identification before the man replied. 'Lenny Yarnevich. He wrote the book.'

Mac didn't have a clear view of Yarnevich, given where he was sitting, but she noticed when he replied that, despite the tension that had built noticeably in the auditorium, his voice sounded remarkably relaxed. 'I say I stay out of Ben's songs, and he usually stays out of my scenes.'

Wexler had obviously been expecting Yarnevich to back up Richardson, and looked surprised. But before he got a chance to reply, Richardson cut in again. 'Lenny, you're a nice guy, but let's face it, you have just about as much experience in this as Ben does, so basically, I don't care what the fuck you say.' Yarnevich has turned slightly in his seat to look at the director, and there was just enough light from the stage that Mac and Sylvie could both see the nonplussed expression on his face. But just as Sylvie was trying to elbow Mac to make sure she saw it, Richardson turned on Wheeler again. 'Just why is it you want to replace a perfectly good number, Ben?'

Now it was Wheeler's turn to glare, and he did before replying, 'Let's just say it doesn't feel right.'

'Ben, this is not a therapy session,' Wexler interrupted this time, the cigar back in full swing again. 'This is a goddam musical we're putting on here. A musical that's costing a lot of money! *My* money.'

There was a slight 'ahem' in the audience. 'Well, some of it's my money,' he clarified. 'Some of it's Joan's.'

Wheeler was adamant, and took a few steps toward Richardson. 'Well I'm the composer, and that's my name out on the signs, and I say the number needs to be replaced! In fact, I checked with the guild today, and I formally withdraw "Remember When" from the score, so it can't be used.' He stepped back toward his seat, then turned to Richardson again. 'The "Like It Used to Be" number is the replacement for the hole that will be left in the second act.'

Even from the back of the house, it was evident that Richardson's eyes were fiery as he stared at Wheeler. The assembled group was quiet, and the tension level ratcheted up in the silence. Those gathered knew they had just seen Richardson play his high card and get trumped by Wheeler. From the look on his face, Richardson was not happy.

'How much time do you think it would take to work in a new number, Duran?' Richardson asked after a few moments, still staring at Wheeler.

The young woman – the choreographer, Sylvie identified her – had been sitting in the shadows on the working stairs that led from the auditorium floor to the stage, and she stood and looked toward Richardson. From her body language, one could tell that this discussion was news to her. 'A whole new number? I'd have to hear the music first, see how much of a change we're talking about. And we're replacing "Remember When"?' She turned to Wheeler with a shrug of her shoulders. 'I thought that was working pretty well.'

Richardson gave Wheeler a hostile 'I told you so' look.

'I don't think you'll have to change the choreography all that much, Duran,' Wheeler said, trying to mollify her. 'I'll try to keep a lot of the same structure.'

'Let's get Larry in here and see what space he can find for us for the next week,' Wexler said. 'Then you and I, Jonathan, are going to have to have a look at the cheque book.' Wexler looked down at the first row, where a young man, in his early thirties, sat holding his head in his hands.

'That's Jonathan Humphries, Wexler's co-producer,' Sylvie explained. 'It's his first big show. Lately, he's been looking like someone hit him over the head with a two by four.'

A man slipped in the door behind Sylvie and Mac and proceeded to stride down the right aisle. 'While you're getting your cheque book out, Mr Wexler, don't forget the first contract payment to the Technician's Union.'

'Christ, who let him in?' Wexler said. 'Isn't there somebody watching the door? Larry!'

'Who's this?' Mac said, surprised.

'Howard Goldman, some union guy. The whole union thing on this show is *facakte* – I'll tell you over dinner.'

'*Larry! Larry!*' Wexler looked toward the back of the theatre where Mac and Sylvie stood, and the stage manager finally appeared on the third call of his name. 'Would you be so kind as to show Mr Goldman out the front door?'

'You can't get rid of me that easy, Wexler. You have to

come to the table at some point,' Goldman said as he was being escorted up the aisle.

'It's my table and I don't have to make any offers I don't want to make, Goldman. And I can get rid of you any way I want. Because this is *my* theatre!'

Mac suddenly noticed a young man sitting on the aisle in the last row of seats, directly across the theatre from where she and Sylvie were standing. She noticed that he pulled a very large-sized bottle of antacids from his suit coat pocket and popped a few, just as Mr Goldman was being escorted past him. 'Who's the guy with the Rolaids?' she whispered to Sylvie

'Max Osgood, the press agent for the show and for Wexler. I don't think he has any stomach lining left, or if he does, he won't by the time the show opens.'

Wexler watched from the stage until Goldman made it into the lobby. 'Okay, I need to see you, Jonathan, and you Joan, for a brief conference. We'll leave these creative types to finish their rehearsal.'

Gil Richardson moved from the side of the stage. 'Oh, rehearsal is finished for today – it's almost eight o'clock. Curtis, ladies?' he said, peering toward the back of the house and shading his eyes. 'There you are,' he said when he spotted Sylvie standing at the back of the theatre. 'Tomorrow regular time. We have full chorus in the morning, so please be prompt. Here until further notice,' he added pointedly.

'Got it, Gil,' a man's voice replied from one of the front rows, as he stood and reached for his coat. A woman's light voice came from the same area, with the same words. Sylvie waved that she'd heard the instructions as well. 'Here comes Curtis,' she said to Mac. 'You've got to meet him.'

Curtis Leland ambled up the aisle, a handsome white-haired gentlemen who looked to be in his mid-sixties. When Sylvie introduced Mac as one of her oldest, dearest friends, Curtis was almost courtly in his response. 'A pleasure, Doctor Griffin, I'm sure. And may I tell you that it has been one of the delights of a long career to work with your friend here.'

Sylvie positively glowed. 'Did I tell you he was a sweet-heart or what?' she said to Mac.

Mac nodded. She found the older actor very appealing. 'It's a pleasure to meet you as well, Mr Leland, and I'm looking forward to seeing your performance. This must be an exciting time for you – being in a new production, in a new theatre.'

'Yes, yes it is. Especially being on this new stage – It's a privilege.' He turned to Sylvie. 'We must turn this building into a theatre, mustn't we, my dear?' He looked back at Mac. 'It's much like consecrating a church, I would think. A theatre isn't a theatre because you call it one. It has to become one.'

As they were talking, Gil Richardson walked slowly up the aisle. As he neared them, Mac noticed he look older than the forty-nine years a recent article had claimed him to be. Or perhaps it was just the fatigue that was visible in the slump of his shoulders and the grey around his eyes.

He approached them just as Curtis had finished his good-byes, and Richardson put his hand on Sylvie's shoulder. 'Good work, today, kid.'

Sylvie beamed at his approval. 'Gil, I'd like you to meet my good friend, Dr Mackenzie Griffin.'

'Doctor?' Richardson said, extending both his hands to capture Mackenzie's. 'Now why don't I ever get to see doctors as attractive as this? I probably should make an appointment.' Mac knew he was just flattering her, but she loved every second. This was Gil Richardson, after all, the subject of a feature story in the *Times'* Arts & Leisure section the Sunday before last, a man whose bio she'd been reading in theatre programmes for fifteen years now, and the man responsible for some of her best nights in the theatre in that same span of time.

'Not unless you want your head shrunk, Gil,' Sylvie teased. 'Mackenzie's a psychologist.'

Richardson's eyes lit up with interest. 'Doing a psychological study of the theatre, doctor?'

'Why, do you think one is necessary?' Mac replied.

'Well, I've often wondered why – no matter how bad a show is, if you put in a scene where people start kicking in a chorus line, the audience goes crazy applauding. Do you think there's some deep, dark, psychological explanation for that?'

'I've often wondered about it myself,' Mac said with a smile.

'Actually, Gil, Mac is on the faculty up at John Jay College of Criminal Justice,' Sylvie added, 'so a psychological study of the theatre might be a stretch.'

Richardson looked at Mackenzie with renewed interest. 'Oh, I don't know. I've seen any number of performances in the theatre that I thought were a crime against the audience. And God knows, we have enough criminals in the theatre, although,' he leaned toward the two women conspiratorially and then gave a nod of his head to the assembled producers standing down at the front of the right aisle, 'most of them are behind the scenes, if you know what I mean.'

A young man, tall and blond, approached the group from the aisle, carrying a heavy grey-green storm coat. 'Your dinner appointment is at eight-fifteen at Tavern on the

Green,' he said, as he started to assist Richardson into the coat. 'The car service is waiting for you outside. You can just make it.'

Richardson gave him a playful salute and an 'Aye, Aye' and turned back to Mac and Sylvie. 'Thomas is one of those people who is never late, and has made it his mission in life to make sure that I'm not either. I'm afraid it's a losing a battle.' Thomas took the teasing with a small bow and a smile, and handed the director a leather briefcase, and then Richardson turned back to Mackenzie. 'Dr Griffin, it's been a pleasure. Can I assume that we'll be seeing you on opening night?'

'Yes, you can,' Mac said. 'I'm really looking forward to it.'

He leaned toward Sylvie with a 'Ciao' and was out the door. Thomas offered a shy wave to them and headed back down the aisle as soon as Richardson left. 'I tell you,' Sylvie said to Mac 'if we all had assistants like Thomas, life in New York might actually be manageable.'

'So was it me, or was Gil Richardson hinting that the producers or one of the producers might be a criminal,' Mac said, looking toward the group of three still talking down in front of the stage. 'Is that the Byers woman you mentioned?' she asked when she took a clearer look at the group. The woman was on the short side, less then five foot four, even in heels, and very round.

'Yes, that's her, and I think Gil was just teasing,' Sylvie said. 'Don't you?'

'Probably,' Mac said. She was distracted by the sight of a stunning young woman with dark red hair standing in the aisle talking to a man still seated. 'Who's that?' she asked.

'Oh, that's Rhonda. Rhonda Deveraux, doncha know.' From the sing-song of the rhyme, Mac guessed that the actress was frequently referred to that way. She also guessed that the actress was referred to that way behind her back.

'Rhonda?' Mac said with a chuckle. 'As in help me, Rhonda, help, help me Rhonda?'

'Exactly.'

'Do we think this is the name her mother gave her?'

'Let me put it this way,' Sylvie said. 'We think her name is as much a part of Rhonda's natural heritage as the colour of her hair and her breasts. Do we get the picture?'

Mac nodded her reply, since she had to stifle a laugh.

The trio of producers was breaking up their conversation. Joan Henley Byers headed up the aisle and, from the expression on her face, she was none too happy when she saw Rhonda Deveraux standing where she was. 'Matthew? If you'll get my coat, I think we're ready to leave.'

A very tall, slender man unfolded from the seat next to where Rhonda was standing, picked up the coat from the seat next to his, and headed toward Joan Byers. 'That's her husband,' Sylvie whispered. 'I just hope that they haven't found out that everybody in the company calls them the Sprats.'

Mac looked at her, squinted until she came up with the reference. 'Oh, yeah.' Jack Sprat could eat no fat, his wife could eat no lean. Unfortunately, it fit the couple perfectly, especially when you saw them standing together, as they were now, Mr Sprat – or Mr Byers – assisting his wife on with her coat.

'Oh, shit, Rhonda's heading this way. I'll have to put on my cheesy grin,' Sylvie said in a barely audible tone. 'Then I'll get my stuff and we can get outta here. I'm starving!'

As Rhonda Deveraux approached, Mackenzie was again struck by how attractive she was. The dark auburn hair – natural or no – was gorgeous with a creamy complexion and blue eyes that looked almost teal. There didn't seem to be a lot of light in those eyes, but they sure were beautiful.

'Hi, Sylvie,' Ms Deveraux said as she cruised toward the lobby door. 'Bye, Sylvie. See you in the morning.'

'Right, see you,' Sylvie said. When Mac looked at her she did, in fact, have a cheesy grin on her face. 'And that's what passes for a witty conversation with Rhonda,' she said to Mac once her face resumed it's natural expression. 'Let me get my coat.'

As Mac waited for Sylvie, she was wondering how the show on opening night was going to beat what she'd seen already. Being with Peter for the last two years, she had grown familiar with the high incidence of large egos and strong personalities in the entertainment world. If a high tension level meant a successful show, *Reunion* was indeed going to be a smash.

CHAPTER TWO

As they walked around the west side of Union Square enjoying the unexpectedly mild evening, Mac and Sylvie caught up on the news of their mutual friends and acquaintances from college. One of the joys of seeing Sylvie was that she was an old friend – or friend of long-standing, as another of Mac's old friends had insisted she be called – and there was a shorthand of communication that came from those years of friendship.

She and Sylvie had met their freshman year at Connecticut College, in Mac's first brief phase of quiet rebellion. Her parents both taught at the venerated Riverside University, some twenty-five miles north of their home in Registon, Connecticut, and both her mother and father were Riverside alumni as well. To Mac's adolescent sensibilities, it seemed entirely too predictable, too pat that she would attend Riverside, and so, at the age of seventeen, when making her decision about college applications, she had opted instead for the nearby and equally admired Connecticut College.

She met Sylvia Morganstern the first week of school, at a freshman orientation seminar, when they were seated next to one another and discovered they had both indicated an early preference for majoring in psychology. Sylvie's interest in psychology was not quite as long-lasting as Mac's; her major changed at least two more times, maybe three, by the time they ended up graduating. It was Riverside they had graduated from; Mac had transferred at the end of their freshman year, and Sylvie followed her, once she was able to convince her father's company, who had sponsored her scholarship, to allow her to transfer it.

Three months after graduation, as Mac was about to head for New York University for her graduate work, Sylvie announced she was going to be an actress, and enrolled at the American Academy of Dramatic Art. Not long after that she decided she'd be known as Sylvie Morgan.

The last twelve years hadn't been easy for Sylvie, partly because, as she realized early on in her career, she was a character actress. That allowed for longevity in a career once it was established, but it made establishing the career a bitch, because there weren't a lot of character parts for twenty-five year olds. Things had gotten better in the last few years, and she was able to cut down on the number of temporary jobs needed to sustain her. Sylvie was, she had joked to Mac, probably the only woman in Manhattan who had been thrilled to turn thirty.

The maitre d' at Hudson's, Mackenzie's favourite neighbourhood restaurant, smiled his greeting to one of his best customers, and ushered them to the back room, where he knew she preferred to sit. The restaurant's decor – wood-panelled walls, leather lined booths, faux Tiffany lampshades – seemed cozy tonight, and the welcoming fireplace on the one brick wall that adjoined the kitchen held a small glowing fire.

'That was quite a scene at the theatre,' Mac said as they took their seats in the booth. The waiter set down a bread basket and handed them their menus. 'Is Gil Richardson always so . . . mercurial?'

Sylvie shook her head. 'He's been out of sorts for the last several days, he's been fighting off a cold, but I've never seen him the way he was tonight. Of course, we – the actors – don't usually get to see him with the producers and the architects and the designer, either. This was a special thing tonight, when Wexler walked into our rehearsal just about six o'clock.' She opened the napkin covering the bread basket. 'Warm rolls, I think I'm in heaven,' she said, tearing one open and watching the puff of steam escape. 'Don't get me wrong, Gil's a tough taskmaster, but he's professional all the way. He seemed to be going for the jugular on a couple of those guys, though.'

The waiter reappeared with a water pitcher and asked for their drink orders. Sylvie, not usually a wine drinker, surprised Mac by asking for a big glass of red wine. 'Medicinal purposes,' she explained when she saw Mac's surprise. 'I just got rid of – knock wood—' she said, reaching under the table to rap a few times 'the company cold that we've been passing around for two months now – the one that finally got to Gil. Curtis has finally sold me on the preventative qualities of strong red wine.'

Before she started on the second half of her roll, Sylvie leaned toward Mac. 'I tell you, Mackenzie, this is the best thing I've ever done. This show is the best thing that's ever happened for me, but it's the tensest – or most tense or however you say it – company I've ever been around.' She leaned back and shrugged, as though trying to come up with an explanation for herself. 'Maybe it's because I've never been in a production this big before. Big as in dollars. Because I gather that they've got a lot riding on this.' Her face softened as she leaned forward again. 'I've never worked so hard, but it's been fabulous too. And when it works, Mac, the audiences, I mean at least the audiences in California, it's just magic.'

The waiter brought their glasses and delivered his spiel on tonight's specials. Mac smiled that they'd need a few minutes before ordering. 'So tell me about it. How did this all come about? When you left – was it in November? – it all happened so fast.'

'Actually, it goes back to last spring, when I heard about it. They had done a few backers' auditions, and one of the people helping them out, singing the female parts, was a friend of mine, Sally Michaels, who goes to the same voice coach I do. She's the one who told me about the show. So I nosed around, and found out when they'd be auditioning. I actually tried out for them last summer, and was turned down. Too young, they said, like where have I heard that before?'

'They turned you down last summer?'

'Yep. They started some rehearsals here, with the principals, but after a few weeks, they decided that both Miss Goodwin, the role that I play, and Curtis's role, the professor, needed to be recast before they headed for California, where they were physically putting the show together. Miss Goodwin had to be younger and the professor had to be older. So, boom, the two of us – Curtis and I – got calls on Thursday and had to be on a plane the next Sunday.'

'So tell me about the play, or the show, or whatever you call it,' Mac said. 'Can you tell me about it without spoiling it?'

'Think *Same Time, Next Year*, but with a group of friends instead of a couple. It starts with their graduation from a small college in the late Sixties, and the next scene is their

28

fifth reunion, then their tenth. The second act is their twentieth reunion and then their twenty-fifth for the big last scene.'

'And who do you play?'

'I'm Miss Goodwin – also called Miss Good Wind, the women's athletic director. Your basic female jock.'

'And at which reunion do you appear?'

'Actually, I'm in it throughout. All the characters are.'

'You mean you age twenty-five years?'

'No, the students do, but we don't. One of the twists of the play is that Miss Goodwin and the Professor look the same age all the way through. The students think we're old geezers at graduation, and at every reunion, we look younger to them.'

'So is it a good role for you?'

'Mac, this is the kind of role you'd eat somebody's laundry for. It's not the lead – there really isn't a lead in this show, although Rhonda thinks she is – but Miss Goodwin is the character that people are going to remember. Like the Ado Annie role in *Oklahoma!* Or Adelaide in *Guys & Dolls*. She's funny, she sort of holds the show together, and she's got a dynamite song in the second act.' Sylvie sat back and twisted the stem on her wine glass. 'I tell you Mac, it's magic.'

Mac hadn't seen Sylvie this excited in years, if ever, and she knew she was thrilled for her friend. But watching the expression on Sylvie's face, she felt a twinge of something else she wasn't willing to identify just yet.

The waiter came and took their orders, and Sylvie batted her eyes at him to get another basket of bread.

'So tell me about it,' Mac urged as she started on her own warm wholewheat roll. 'You were out in California for the winter, right? In Los Angeles?'

29

'No, down closer to San Diego. And let me tell you, for as much fun as I've made about California over the years, spending the winter out there is better than a poke in the eye with a sharp stick. It rains some, sure, but basically it's mild and usually sunny and gorgeous. Although I think it would make me crazy all year round. But we had this great playhouse to rehearse in and get the show up on its feet, and we were only there maybe five or six weeks when Simon Wexler got involved and everything went into high speed. That's when it got tied in to the theatre opening, and the time crunch hit, and then this union stuff came up once we hit the city.'

'What's the union stuff?'

Sylvie heaved a sigh. 'It gets complicated and I'm not up on all the details – on purpose. But it's basically this. In the actors' union, we have a couple of different kinds of contracts – Broadway and off-Broadway are the main types that apply in New York. Outside New York, you have regional theatre contracts and maybe one other. I assume the other creative unions have the same kind of breakdown, but it gets confusing.'

When the waiter placed the fresh break basket in front of her, Sylvie reached for another roll – her third! – and she continued. 'So, in New York the dividing line between whether a show is a Broadway show or off-Broadway show isn't the geography but the size of the theatre that it's playing in. More than X number of seats – I think it's five hundred – it's a Broadway house. Under that, it's off-Broadway. So the Century should technically be considered a Broadway house, since it's gonna have, I think, seven hundred seats. But it's not in the theatre district, and Wexler had this whole pitch about how he's reviving the old Union Square theatre district, and how opening a new theatre means expanded opportunities for theatre people, et cetera, et cetera.'

'So?'

'So the creative unions – the actors, designers, costume people – agreed to a special form of contract with the *Reunion* producers, for the next two years, and they'll re-evaluate after that.'

'So the union problem was solved,' Mac said as she leaned back for the waiter to serve her dinner; it was her favourite of Hudson's specialties: coq au vin.

Sylvie paused while the waiter put her plate down in front of her. She inspected the pasta primavera special, then looked over at Mac's dinner and sniffed an appreciative whiff of the coq au vin's aroma. 'I should have gotten that,' she said. 'Oh, well.' Mac smiled in recognition of the syndrome: Sylvie was never happy with what she ordered. Then Sylvie resumed her explanation. 'Sounds like it, but here's where it gets confusing. The creative unions' contract is with the producers of the show, but some of the unions have their deals with the theatre directly, and Wexler is both a producer of the show and the owner of the theatre. The musicians' union agreed to a show-by-show contract, amazingly, because, from what I've heard, everybody thought they would be the real problem. But Wexler won't sign the contract that the technicians' union has proposed on the theatre, because the union wants to classify the Century as a Broadway theatre, and that means that for this show or any other, he has to hire the number of people the unions tell him to, in very specific job functions. Off Broadway, some of those jobs aren't unionized, and they aren't separate. So you can have a prop guy who also moves scenery. But Wexler says he'll go down fighting on this, take the union to court even, because as the owner of the theatre, on future shows, they could come in and tell him how many people he's got to hire, whatever he or the director of the show or the producer of that show thinks.'

'And that fellow that was in there tonight?'

'Howard Goldman. He's some *über* union guy from the union council, negotiating for the Technicians' Union. He was brought in when the original negotiator and Wexler apparently came this close,' she held up her thumb and forefinger, approximately a millimetre apart, 'to getting into a fist-fight at one session. Goldman and Wexler have been going at one another pretty good, too, and Goldman's threatening to pull all the union people out, but I don't think that's gonna happen.'

'And what was the Tony Award conversation? Is there a chance I'll be seeing you on television in a few months, thanking all the "little people"?' Mac teased.

'I wouldn't count on it – although I've been practising my speech for years. As it stands now, we won't be eligible for Tony consideration because the Tony Award is for Broadway shows only. There has been some griping about that, and some pressure to change it, to make it more of a New York Theatre award, but there's some big hoo-haw behind the scenes. Anyway, from what I gather, Wexler wants to be able to make a point of it in the ads, along the lines of "New York's hottest show, *not* nominated for a Tony", that kind of thing. That's assuming we get good reviews, of course.'

'Of course,' Mac said. 'I have no doubt.' She reached for the bread basket, and found a lonely piece of garlic toast that Sylvie hadn't gotten to yet. 'Anything to report on the ghost of the Century Theatre?'

'No, I think it's just Max's way of getting something into the papers, although a few people have reported some oddball things.' She paused over her pasta, and pointed with her fork, 'This is very good, by the way. But enough about me. What's going on with you, Mackenzie? Everything okay between you and Peter? If I can be blunt about it, you don't look as good as you usually do.'

If Mac hadn't known Sylvie as well as she did, she might have thought that was a *non-sequitur*. But she well remembered a conversation with Sylvie in the spring a year ago, some ten months after she'd met Peter Rossellini, and about six months after they'd officially become involved. It was one of the first gorgeous, unusually warm spring days, and she and Sylvie were treating themselves to Sunday brunch at an outdoor cafe. Sylvie had looked at her over the rim of the mimosa glass and said, 'You look fabulous, Mac. If only the cosmetic companies could bottle the same thing that regular sex gives a woman's complexion.' At that point, Mac almost choked on one of the large fresh strawberries she was eating, but Sylvie continued. 'And when it's good sex – you know, when you're in love and all that stuff, well, that accounts for the twinkle in your eye. But I suppose it's too much to ask for the cosmetic companies to market eye-twinkle, too.'

Mac had sat at the table, dumbfounded. Six months earlier, Sylvie had been amazed that her friend Mackenzie Griffin had become involved with Peter Rossellini, one of the country's hottest pop music stars. The combination of the academic if attractive psychologist and the popular singer had surprised Sylvie, and the celebrity-driven press as well. Mac and Peter had made a concerted effort to keep their private lives private. It must have worked, because now even Sylvie was inquiring about Peter as if he were any old boyfriend. This seemed like progress.

'Peter's fine, we're fine. I'm . . . okay.'

'That "okay" took a while. What is it?'

'You know that I've been on leave from the school this year and—'

'I forgot, Mackenzie. You've been working on that study, right?'

'Right. But being away from teaching has been a big difference, and the last few months, I've been working with some of the rescuers from The Bombing – the 16th Street Bombing – and that's been more difficult that I thought it would be.'

'My God, how did you get involved in that?'

'Well, I had been doing a lot of interviewing of police anyway on the stresses in their professional and personal lives, and then I think there was some consensus that I had an unusual qualification in that I was there when it happened.'

'God, Mackenzie, you didn't tell me you were *there*? When it *happened*? Tell me about it!!'

CHAPTER THREE

A question had been asked in Mac's group session just last week – as to whether anyone had difficulty in sorting out the details of The Bombing, in differentiating what they'd read, or what they'd seen on television, or what they'd heard in group, from what they'd actually experienced.

Mac, for one, didn't have that trouble. Her real experiences, as opposed to those that were secondhand, were carved in her mind, distinguished by the quality of light that day, and the sounds. Those sounds still echoed in her mind.

It was about three o'clock in the afternoon, the Wednesday of the week before Christmas. Mac had attended her regular meeting with Dr Harold Parsons and Dr Annabeth Gershon, colleagues on the study she'd been working on since last summer; the meeting started at noon, but they'd finished up earlier than usual, no doubt because Annabeth pleaded for a break so she could get in some emergency shopping before her son's Christmas party at school, which was the next day.

It was just past two-thirty when Mac got to her apartment, but she went in only to drop off her briefcase, give Peter a quick call, and head out the door again immediately for the supermarket. It wasn't a big shop she had to do, but she was low on a few essentials – milk for her coffee, the tea that Peter found soothing for his throat, juice, a few other odds and ends – and then she'd be able to get back here, take a bath and be ready when Peter arrived. He was due at five-fifteen, and then they were heading to a small Christmas party being given by Rachel Bennet, Peter's manager.

Mac even remembered her walk to the supermarket which was just east of Union Square on 15th Street. The day had been one of those dazzlingly bright winter days, when the air and even some of the buildings in New York seem to sparkle. But the short rays of the almost-winter sun let you know, even at three o'clock, that darkness wasn't far off.

The supermarket wasn't too crowded, and Mac realized while standing in the express check-out line that she had time to stop over in the Square to see if there were any poinsettias for sale. She wasn't sure if she'd be getting a Christmas tree for the apartment this year, but she wanted some touch of the holiday season to brighten up her decor. Heading out of the market onto the sidewalk a few minutes later, she stopped to make sure she had enough cash for the plants before walking the additional block and a half up to the north end of the Square. As it turned out, she did have enough money on her, but she'd have to stop at an ATM on the way home. She had just started west on 15th Street, heading directly toward the Square when it happened.

As she remembered it, she heard two noises: a distant, loud bang! and then a BOOOOOOOOOM that grew and echoed as it moved down the canyon of 15th Street. The noise was like nothing Mac had ever heard, or felt. The explosion had a reverberation that seemed to go on and on, and a power that made you feel you could almost see the sound waves rippling down the street.

Mac was thrown to her knees by the force of the explosion, and her grocery bag ripped out of her hands. Finding herself on all fours on the sidewalk, she had felt the force of the noise in her entire body, picking up vibrations like a tuning fork, and she could still sense the vibrations that passed through the cement below her. Her breathing was shallow and her heart was racing faster than she'd ever felt in her life, and even knowing that it was adrenaline surging through her body didn't help her control the trembling that overtook her. Hearing the glass that started to descend around her, she buried her head under both her arms.

The sound of glass hitting the street and sidewalks followed the first big boom, but it seemed part of the explosion's noise as that continued to reverberate down the streets. The glass came first in crashes, and then in softer, almost tinkling sounds. When the noise lessened, Mac chanced peeking out and saw that one of the huge glass windows on the grocery store she'd just left had shattered onto the sidewalk not more than ten feet from where she was crouched; another was being held in place by the large paper sheets announcing the store's weekly specials.

It later came out that where she had been standing was less than a block from the point of the detonation of the bomb.

The eeriest part of that whole day had been the silence in the seconds right after the reverberations of explosion and the tinkling of the glass had ceased. It was an absolute quiet, a quiet she'd only heard in New York in the midst of a huge snowfall. It lasted only a few seconds, she later realized, but those seconds seemed elastic and to stretch on forever.

In that silence, Mac struggled shakily to get up, the knees of her pantyhose snagging on the cement, and she started edging her way toward the corner of 15th Street, toward the direction of the explosion, needing to see what had happened. As she got to the corner and looked north, she saw a large hole in the street on the west side of Park Avenue South, just south of 16th Street, and some smoke or dust or steam coming from the hole. Large chunks of debris were spread in a pattern on the street, and on the sidewalks on both sides of the avenue. It was utterly silent.

Looking at where the chunks of debris lay, Mackenzie was stunned by the capriciousness of fate or the providence of God, however one wanted to describe the force behind the most minute of details in our lives. If she hadn't decided to check her cash supply, she might have made the light to cross 15th Street heading north, and she would have been at a point in the sidewalk very close to where chunks of cement now lay. The idea of it caused a different kind of trembling, one unrelated to adrenaline.

Suddenly the noise started to creep back in. First it was shouts, then some horns honking, and then the beginning of the sirens, some in the distance, one coming from 16th Street on the west side of the square. Mac spotted a uniformed policeman in a flat-out run across Union Square Park, heading for the portion of Park Avenue South that now had a huge hole in it.

Mac of course didn't know what had happened as yet. It was still just an explosion at that point, probably a gas main, she thought. But she already knew it was something big. Mac edged away from the corner, and walked back to where she'd left her bag of groceries. The bag was now a soggy mess on the curb; her carton of milk had broken as had the bottle of fresh orange juice, and the two liquids were flowing together as they quietly pulsed into the gutter.

She was still standing there when the sirens started converging; every emergency vehicle in Manhattan seemed to be headed for Union Square, and Mac knew that she would never hear one again without thinking of that cold, clear December afternoon, and the sight of an empty 15th Street filling with flashing red and blue lights.

First it was police cars, one right after another. She looked east toward the corner and saw that two police cars had blocked the north-south traffic on Irving Place, and the squad cars were streaming across 15th from Third Avenue. Within three minutes of the first police car's arrival, she heard the distinctive sound of fire engines' sirens, and plugged her ears as first one, then a second, then a third, streaked by her, braked, and then edged their way around the barricade that the police cars had created at the corner of 15th and the Square, to join the fire trucks converging from the west.

As the emergency vehicles got into place, the sirens were cut and in the midst of the new quiet, she heard the wail of a small child's cry. She looked across the street to see a woman bending down, trying to comfort the toddler who clung to the bottom of her coat; with her other hand the woman was trying to keep a baby's pram rocking as well.

Mac felt compelled to help, and cut across the street. She walked up to the woman, whose back was toward her. 'Can I lend a hand here?'

The woman turned around, startled to hear Mac's voice. Her eyes were large and looked teary. When she focused on Mac, the tension in her face abated a bit, but her voice was tight as she asked. 'Do you know what happened?' The little boy tugging on her coat cried out louder, annoyed that he'd lost his mother's attention.

Mac shook her head no. She heard a healthy cry from

the baby buggy and looked in to see a beautiful baby, a girl if the pink snowsuit was any indication. The baby looked directly at her and then screwed up her face to come out with an even healthier yell.

'The noise terrified them,' the young mother explained.

'Understandable,' Mac said. 'It scared me, too. Can I help you?'

The woman stood, moving her son so she could rub his head when she talked to Mac. 'I was just heading home,' she said. 'Over on 17th and Third.'

'That's not far from me,' Mac said as she took control of the buggy. 'Let me help you.'

The young mother picked up the toddler, and they started walking east. By the time they got to the corner of Irving Place, the Emergency Medical Service wagons started careening around the corner, headed for the same knot of vehicles where the police cars and fire engines were. The little boy whimpered at the sound of these new assault of sirens, and his mother tried to calm him with long strokes down his back.

As they waited to cross the street, the mother whispered to Mac. 'What do you think happened?'

'I have no idea,' Mac said. 'But it was some enormous explosion that's left a big hole over in Park Avenue South.'

They were at the woman's apartment within a few minutes, and the doorman for the high-rise came running outside as soon as he saw her. 'Mrs Weiss? Are you all right?'

'Yes, thanks, Jimmy. Can you take the baby's buggy for me?'

'Sure,' the man said, grabbing the front of the buggy and hoisting it up the two shallow steps that led to a mini-plaza in front of the building. Once the buggy was level again, the doorman smiled at Mac and reached for the handle. The woman turned to Mac and said 'Thank you' with a shrug of her shoulders, as though she didn't know what else to say.

Mac just nodded her head and started to turn away. The young Mrs Weiss reached out and stopped her, gave Mac a quick half-hug; it was awkward with the toddler now sliding down her left side.

Mac was surprised, then looked at the young mother. Their eyes caught and the two of them just nodded. They knew they had shared, however briefly, one of those experiences that would stay with them forever.

It took Mac less than five minutes to walk to her own apartment building from where she'd left Mrs Weiss. Billy, the doorman who had the afternoon-into-evening shift at her building, had come on duty since she'd left. 'Dr Griffin!' he called out when he saw her crossing from the small park across 15th Street. 'Are you okay? Are you just coming from the Square?'

'I'm fine, Billy. Does anybody know what happened yet?'

'Just that there's been a big explosion in the subway station over there.'

'In the subway? Oh, God.' She hadn't even thought of that when she'd seen that smoking hole. The subway.

'Mr Rossellini just walked in a couple minutes ago, looking for you. Seemed pretty upset.'

She hurried down the hall, and before she got to the door Peter opened it, his eyes wide and his face taut with tension. He spotted her and closed his eyes, and she could see, and then feel, his sigh of relief as he embraced her. 'Thank God.'

'I'm okay, I'm okay,' Mac said, but as she said it, she started to tear up. She knew that it was just the after-effects of the adrenaline that had been coursing through her body since the explosion hit, but knowing it didn't stop the tears from forming.

'Where were you?' Since she'd told him in their brief conversation less than an hour ago where she was heading, she knew that his question meant where was she when the explosion happened.

'I'd just left the market when whatever it was exploded.'

Peter's eyes widened. 'Oh my God, you were right there.'

Mac nodded, and gave him a brief description of the immediate aftermath, ending with walking Mrs Weiss home. 'And then I came here,' she said as he held her tighter.

'Do you need anything? Do you want me to get you anything?' Peter asked, setting her back from him so he could see her face. 'All that glass. Did you get cut?' He looked her up and down, his eyes widening when he saw her legs. 'Mac, you're bleeding!'

She looked down, startled to see little rivulets of blood on her shins. She'd cut her knees when she'd fallen. Funny, they didn't start to hurt until she saw the cuts and abrasions. 'I'm fine,' she assured Peter. 'I'll change and get cleaned up in a minute. Right now I just want to find out what happened.'

They turned on the television, just as the rest of the city and much of the country did, and they watched the live news coverage. The reports were sketchy at first, and those initial reports were given to the requirements of the moment. Traffic was re-routed, subway trains were diverted, and information was delivered to get people around the city and home in a way that wouldn't interfere with the rescue efforts going on at Union Square.

The reporters covering the scene at 16th Street had a double duty. They were relaying information on what had transpired – a massive explosion, cause yet unknown – with details of which hospitals the victims were being taken to, with requests for blood donations and where to go to give them, with information about a check point and a telephone number for people trying to contact their relatives who may have been in the subway at that hour.

In the next hour, information started to dribble out about who was on the train that had exploded, about how many people were in the station at the time. And when the reporters learned from one of the police officers that one of the subway cars most affected was loaded with a class of third graders from St Stephen's elementary school in lower Manhattan, the news coverage suddenly had a focus. The reporters pressed for more and more details, and more came out over the next few hours.

Sister Margaret's third grade class had been on a special Christmas field trip to Rockefeller Center to see the tree, the first report announced. Then it was learned that they had attended the Christmas show at Radio City Music Hall. Next it came out that a benefactor, himself a graduate of St Stephen's some forty years prior, had arranged for the class trip and the Radio City show. The man, interviewed in front of the church where he had hurried immediately upon hearing the news, was now tortured that he'd brought children to their deaths. For many of them were dead, and many more probably wouldn't make it.

Peter and Mac sat transfixed in front of her television throughout the evening and into the night; Rachel's Christmas party had been cancelled, except for a few early arrivals who stayed to watch the television coverage of the news with her.

Mac's parents called to talk about the news coverage since they knew, of course, that it had occurred in her neighbourhood. They were stunned when they realized how

43

close Mackenzie had been to the actual scene of the bombing. Fifteen minutes after Mac put down the phone from her parents' call, her brother Chad was on the line, demanding to know if she was all right, and insisting that he was going to drive down to the city to see her himself. He finally relented when Mac put Peter on the phone to back up her testimony that she was, indeed, in one piece. Not long after Chad was talked out of his trip, Mac's sister Whitney called from Boston, in tears. She'd been watching the news; it was bad enough that these babies were dying, but now Chad had just told her that Mackenzie was on the scene of this horror? This was unbelievable!

It wasn't until mid-evening that the first police reports of the bombing were aired. Police and fire officials confirmed that it was a man-made explosion, not attributable to gas leaks or any similar occurrence, but apparently a bomb carried into the subway station, or on one of the trains.

That's when the theories started flying, reported by the local media under the guise of man-in-the-street interviews. It was terrorists, of course. Had to be. After years of believing themselves blessedly immune from the scourge, Americans had now accepted their vulnerability to terrorism. So maybe it was Arab terrorists, like in the World Trade Center bombing. Or maybe Israelis, angry at the success of the peace initiatives. Could be a disgruntled faction of the IRA, another group unhappy at the prospects of peace. Or maybe Quebeçois, angry at the US support of a united Canada. Or maybe it was one of the newer breed of domestic terrorists, a breed many Americans were still loathe to admit even existed.

But why bomb a subway station in New York? Of course they'd bomb in New York, came the answer from the same reporters who asked the question. New York was the capital of the world, wasn't it? If you want media attention, New York is the place to hit.

The news over the next few days was divided between both the details of the survivors and the tales of the victims, stories both awe-inspiring and heart-wrenching, and the likely theories of who was responsible and the possible motives. Details kept coming about the St Stephen's class, feeding an impatience that the newspapers and television reporters trumpeted over the fact that the police didn't yet have a theory on the bombing, much less a suspect. They did, however, have a type of explosive: it was a common one used in clearing building sites, most commonly used for blowing up foundations of old buildings that were being demolished.

It wasn't until early the next week, five days after the explosion, that the first stories came out about a possible bomber, a man who was himself one of the victims of the explosion. Police and fire investigators had sifted through every square foot of the bombed-out station, and come up with identification on most, if not all the people who had been travelling on the car where the explosion was centred. They traced some identification back to a man, John Golander, who was last seen wheeling what looked to be a salesman's large sample case, toward the Lexington Avenue subway at 86th Street, not far from where he lived.

As the police back-tracked to Mr Golander, they found he was the last tenant in a five storey walk-up on 89th Street that was scheduled for demolition in January, to clear the block for a high-rise. In fact, most of the block had already been demolished, but Mr Golander was the last hold-out in his building, living in the rent-controlled apartment he'd moved into in June of 1967.

A merchant on Lexington told police he'd seen Golander wheeling his suitcase down Lexington just after two o'clock. A survivor of the explosion, a young woman who'd been in the car next to the one carrying the St Stephen's children, told investigators she'd seen Golander struggling to get his suitcase through the connecting door of the subway just before the explosion.

So the story came down to this: a man with a suitcase full of explosives, a suitcase that he wheeled onto a subway car, heading down to City Hall in lower Manhattan, where, according to the diary detectives found in his apartment, Golander was planning on taking the rent control office hostage until they told him he could stay in his apartment. It wasn't any big geopolitical drama being played out here; it was just a man who was being told to move who didn't want to.

The usual range of experts were included in these reports, some providing instant psychological profiles on Mr Golander, others dispassionately recounting how 'lucky' the city had been that Golander hadn't been more proficient in his understanding and use of the demolition explosives. He could have done much more damage had he been able to carry out his intended plan, the bomb experts assured the various television audiences.

In an age when an unusual number of people who have a grudge seemed willing to take their grudges out on the whole world, hearing the explanation of why Mr Golander made himself a bomb, or learning that he could have made a worse one didn't make it any easier to watch when, on December 23rd, the local television stations broadcast the funeral mass for the eight children of St Stephen's who had died in The 16th Street Bombing.

The identification of the suspect helped close out the

story for the reporters who were covering it, but the city needed a bad guy, and Golander wasn't it. The tabloids tried to demonize him for a few days, but it didn't work. Golander had been a meek man, a recluse by most accounts, and now he was dead by his own hand. This was not a villain the city could take out its anger on. And so the feelings generated by The Bombing just floated out there amongst the city's population, unresolved. The general anxiety of urban living, now enhanced to the third power. The fear of travelling in the subway, now escalated. Suspicions heightened about anyone who looked 'different', which, in New York, could include a lot of people or no one, depending on your criteria.

Mac had to acknowledge in the week following how the experience of living through The Bombing had shaken her. Loud noises jolted her. She was exhausted, not having slept through the night once. She'd wake up in the middle of the night, startled, thinking she heard glass breaking.

Christmas was low-keyed, of course. It was the first time in her life she hadn't slept at her parents' house on Christmas Eve, but she told Peter she needed to be in her own bed. He'd agreed, and he had begged off from even attending his family's usual Christmas Eve gathering to stay with her. They drove up to Mac's family home early the next morning, and returned mid-afternoon while it was still light.

After they got home Christmas afternoon, there was a report on television of midnight Mass the previous night at St Stephen's. Mac hadn't been able to watch the funeral for the children, but she'd read the coverage in the paper. It was touching, but she'd kept the same distance she had in reading or watching any of the reports on the explosion and its aftermath. She hadn't allowed herself any emotion about this at all, except that brief tearing up when she'd first come home to Peter. This had been a big event in the life and history of New York City, she acknowledged, and one she'd been a witness to, but one that had no permanent effect on her life. Or so she thought.

Somehow seeing this brief report of the families, gathering in the midst of the friends and neighbours of their parish community, broke through the shell that Mac had placed around the experience, and the discipline she'd imposed on herself gave way. That's when she finally broke down.

Maybe it was because she knew she didn't have to see anyone for the next week, except Peter, who would be there with her, and who held her while she cried. She'd made it through Christmas, she'd made it through seeing her parents and her brother and sister and she'd assured them she was all right. Now she could finally let go.

While she had lived through The Bombing physically unscathed except for some scratches on her knees, she now had to acknowledge that she'd been transformed by the experience. Because in those first few seconds when the physical force of the explosion pushed her to her knees, somewhere deep in Mackenzie Griffin's soul, she acknowledged for the first time the absolute fact of her own mortality. She knew she was going to die.

When Mac finished her account of The Bombing, she was startled – and a little embarrassed – to look up and see that Sylvie had tears in her eyes. None flowing down her cheeks, thank God. They were just sitting there, inside the rim of her eyes.

'Mackenzie, I had no idea you were that close. My God. My God.' Sylvie moved her plate away. She'd long ago taken the last bite of pasta she was going to have tonight. 'I'm a wreck just listening to you tell about it.'

The two of them were silent while the busboy cleared their table, then Sylvie returned to the subject. 'And the group that you're doing, did you tell me that they're all survivors of this bombing?'

'Survivors in a way. They weren't actually in the subway station or on the train when it happened, but they're the emergency personnel – police, firefighters, EMS – that got there. My group is all police. But they were there and they're survivors, yes.'

Sylvie reached for her wine glass with a hint of a smile. 'The next time I complain about what a rough life I have, will you remind me of this conversation?'

They said goodbye in front of the restaurant that night, since Sylvie was going to take a cab over to her apartment on West 22nd Street. They weren't sure if they would get to see one another before Sylvie's opening, so Mac left her with the traditional theatre greeting of 'Break a leg', promising herself, as she did every time she used it, that she'd look up the derivation of that odd phrase.

Mac had time during that walk home to examine the twinges she'd felt over dinner when Sylvie was rhapsodizing about her work in *Reunion*. And even though it made her uncomfortable, she could now call those twinges what they were: pangs of jealousy. It was a feeling she'd only recently become acquainted with, and now it was a little easier to recognize.

The first twinges of jealousy had demonstrated themselves in the last few months in her relationship with Peter – not the usual are-you-seeing-another-woman jealousy, but this kind of jealousy. Professional jealousy. Not that she suddenly wanted to go into show biz. No, it wasn't that simple – or as easy to dismiss.

Both Peter and Sylvie were at or still near the beginnings of wonderful careers, and they had that kind of excitement and energy and newness to their work that let a person think he or she could climb Mount Everest twice a day and feel nothing but exhilaration.

Mackenzie wanted that kind of excitement, she wanted that kind of energy in her work and she didn't have it. She used to. She still had certain things in her work life – professionalism, dedication, habit. But no longer did she think that she had the greatest job in the world. And she missed that feeling.

She realized last September, during registration for the fall semester, that she'd been at John Jay long enough that she was now seeing returning students. People she'd first met as eager young professionals, now coming back for refresher courses or other career advancement requirements, who were returning as hardened and sometimes embittered not-so-young professionals. And what was scaring her was that she was beginning to recognize herself as one of them.

CHAPTER FOUR

Mac approached the same door of the theatre that she'd used a week ago, but found it locked. She spotted a uniformed cop at the corner of 14th and Broadway and walked toward him. He looked ready to tell her to move on, but when she told him that Lieutenant Buratti had called for her, he directed her to the stage door entrance on Broadway, and then, with a quizzical look on his face, watched her walk away.

The rain was starting to pick up again, and Mac pulled the hood up on her slicker. She was still holding it in place with one hand when she pulled open the heavy metal door with the other. As soon as she crossed the threshold, she was stopped by another uniformed cop. 'Sorry, miss, you can't come in here,' he said brusquely.

Mac looked up as she brushed the hood off her head. 'Eddie?' she said to the cop who now blocked her path.

'Doctor Griffin, is that you?' Officer Eddie Lopes said. 'What are you doing here?'

Eddie was one of the officers in Mac's survivors' group, and he would have been uncomfortable with the opinion Mac had held of him since she first saw him, which was that he had an incredibly sweet face. Warm brown eyes and full cheeks, coupled with a ready smile. He was not as tall as most of the officers, maybe five foot eight, but he had a stocky build and a barrel chest that gave him a more imposing physical presence than another man of his height might have had. He was also, Mac had learned the first time he finally spoke in their group meeting, the cop that she had seen running across Union Square the day of The Bombing.

'Hi, Eddie,' Mac replied. As she let her eyes adjust to the lighting, she took a good look around. The backstage area had a small entry way, where Lopes was posted, that gave way to a larger open area. To the left of that, occupying the whole left wall, was a control room with large glass windows; inside it seemed to be an array of electrical panels and consoles. Directly in front of her was the stage, visible through the breaks in the curtains that formed the farthest 'wall' of this backstage area. To the far right were stairs that, according to the sign, led to the dressing rooms E, F, and Men's and Women's. To the right where Buratti stood was a hallway of sorts, formed by the dressing rooms A through D on the right and the curtains that surrounded the rear of the stage on the left.

'Didn't expect to see you showing up at a crime scene, Doctor,' Lopes said. 'What are you doing here?'

'Lieutenant Buratti called me.'

As if hearing his name from twenty-five feet away, Buratti looked up and beckoned Mac toward him. As Mac told Lopes that she'd see him at the next group session, she saw that a number of the people Sylvie had 'introduced' her to were standing around, some in obvious distress, others looking as though they were in varying degrees of shock. The harsh glare of the bright work light overhead, combined with the unusual shadows formed by the light coming off the stage, gave a distorted, unreal quality to their features. Ben Wheeler and Lenny Yarnevich stood near the set of curtains closest to the front of the stage, Wheeler talking animatedly to Yarnevich and Yarnevich subtly shaking his head. A red light was evident just beyond Yarnevich's head, and made him look like a cartoon image of a devil. Curtis Leland stood in front of a break in the curtains, trying to comfort Rhonda Deveraux, who looked distraught; with them was the man Mackenzie could only recall at the moment as Jack Sprat. The sharp shadows and harsh glow from the work light made Rhonda's make up look garish. Simon Wexler, Bruce Quigley, Manny Erickson, Jonathan Humphries and Max the press agent were huddled in the corridor just in front of where Buratti was standing, and Mac had to squeeze by them as she walked toward the lieutenant. As she got close to Wexler, she was alarmed at his flushed tone and the pitch of his voice as he loudly whispered through gritted teeth, 'Well, we've got to figure it out fast!'

'Good to see you, Mac,' Buratti said as she approached. 'Sorry it has to be this way.'

She nodded in acknowledgment. That's one of the things that Mackenzie admired about Buratti. He was a good cop – one of the best she'd worked with, in Mackenzie's estimation – but he never forgot the human context. Or maybe it was *because* he never forgot the human context.

Buratti had been in one of the first seminars she'd done for police professionals back almost nine years ago, when, as a newly degreed doctor of psychology, she was convinced that her studies and academic theories could remake the world. Despite the fact that she was obviously a bit younger than the youngest participant in that seminar, Buratti had treated her with respect, leading the other participants to do the same. He had won her respect in return, and they had worked well together on a number of cases, some of which she worked on officially and some off the record. Or, more specifically, off the payroll. In fact, it was on one of Buratti's 'freebie' cases that Mackenzie had met Peter Rossellini, and Buratti never failed to remind her of that when she brought up the issue of her regular per diems.

Despite the fact that their professional relationship went way back, Mac knew that Buratti had called her tonight because Sylvie Morgan was a friend of hers, and Sylvie was presently in a situation nobody wanted their friend to be in.

'Mario, what's going on? Where's Sylvie? And who's dead?'

'The director. Gil Richardson,' Buratti said. 'Your friend is in the last dressing room. And as to what's going on, I wish I knew.'

'Can I go see Sylvie?'

'Yeah, I gotta check with the crime scene unit, see how much longer they're going to be here. And I have to check that Lopes has numbers on all these people. I'll let you know when I find out how long before we'll be leaving.'

'So you're definitely taking her in?'

'Looks that way.'

'What happened?' Mac asked, bewilderment evident in her voice.

'Beckman finished up with her a while ago. Why don't you go ask her?'

Mac walked down the hall, and Buratti called to the detective just leaving the last dressing room to let Dr Griffin in. Mac recognized him as Stu Beckman, who had also worked on the case that involved Peter Rossellini. It had been, in fact, his first case as a detective.

'Doctor Griffin. Good to see you. The lieutenant said you might be coming by,' he said.

Beckman's medium brown hair and ruddy looks were distinguished by striking grey eyes, and skin that, although it was evident that he wasn't spending as much time outdoors as he used to, was still prematurely weathered. Mac's memory of him was of a conscientious, straight-arrow cop, and she was glad to see him working the case. 'Detective, how are you?' she said in reply.

'Fine, doctor. And it's sergeant now.'

'Then congratulations are in order.' Mac looked over his shoulder to the door of the dressing room. 'Can I go in now?'

'Sure,' Beckman said, and stepped aside.

When she opened the door, Sylvie looked up, startled. She was sitting in the one folding chair in the room, in front of the lighted counter that stretched across the room's width.

'Mackenzie, thank God you're here!' Sylvie squeaked out, and started to tear up.

Mac was absolutely alarmed at seeing Sylvie. The usually brash, self-confident woman looked ghostly pale, and from the red rims of her eyes, it was evident that she'd been crying for a while. Mac hadn't seen Sylvie cry in years, maybe since Sylvie's father died some thirteen years ago, just a month before they graduated from college.

Mac put her hand on Sylvie's shoulder. 'Are you okay?'

Sylvie shook her head. 'I'm scared, Mac. I didn't do anything, I swear it. But things just went crazy here!'

'You can tell me all about it in a minute, but first, Mario tells me they'll be taking you down to police headquarters—'

When Sylvie made a noise that sounded like the

whimpering of a puppy, Mac paused. In a flash, she realized she'd never seen Sylvie really afraid before.

'—and you're probably going to need a lawyer,' Mackenzie finished up. 'Do you have one?'

Sylvie shook her head again, her chest starting to quiver with a tremor about to come upon her.

'Do you want me to call your mother and see if she still has a lawyer in New York?'

'NO!' Sylvie grabbed her arm. 'You can't call my mother, Mackenzie. You can't!'

'Okay,' Mac said, carefully removing the tensed fingers from her arm. There was amazing strength in Sylvie's hands. 'Let me see what I can do about finding a lawyer to meet us there, and then I'll be right back to stay with you, and you can tell me all about what happened.' She stepped toward the door and turned back to check. 'Okay?'

Sylvie nodded, and then teared up again.

Mac stepped outside the door and asked the officer if there was a phone nearby that she could use. There was, just inside the door that Eddie Lopes was still guarding. As Mac headed for it, searching her shoulder bag for a coin purse, she wondered who she was going to call.

She had a lawyer, but he was up in Registon, Connecticut, and more experienced at matters of wills and trusts than of possible homicides. For all that she'd worked in and around the field of criminal justice for almost ten years now, the group in which she'd developed almost no contacts was the city's defence attorneys.

While she thought about it, she decided she'd call Peter to let him know what was going on. She tried her apartment, and was surprised when her own voice came on with her usual message. By now, Peter was late. She checked her messages, and there was one from Peter, delivered just before she'd gotten the call from Buratti, saying that he was still at the studio and would be until eight o'clock. She looked at her watch. It was only seven-fifteen. God, it seemed closer to midnight.

She called Peter at the studio and filled him in on the bare bones of what had transpired.

'Sylvie?' he said, shocked. 'Your friend Sylvie Morgan? Gil Richardson's dead and they're questioning her in his murder?' Peter paused, still trying to make sense of this, but it didn't help. 'Mac, that's unbelievable!'

'Yes, it is,' Mac said. She'd had some time to try to digest the news and it still hadn't sunk in. 'Listen, I'm going to head downtown. Buratti told me this is going to go through police headquarters, and I told Sylvie I'd stay with her. But she's going to need a lawyer, and I don't know who to recommend. Do you have any suggestions?'

'Do you want me to call Irwin?' Peter offered immediately.

Irwin Steinberg, Esq. had been Peter's lawyer for going on five years now, and was one of New York's most prominent attorneys in the entertainment field. He was not, however, a lawyer whose name immediately leapt to mind when discussing a homicide.

'Irwin?' Mac said with considerable hesitation.

'To get his recommendations, I mean. He's probably still at the office.'

That seemed perfectly sensible. Certainly a lawyer would be in a better position to seek out another lawyer. 'Would you mind?'

'No, I'll take care of it. Whoever it is should meet you downtown, right?'

'Right.'

The tone of his voice changed. 'Mac, are you okay? Do you want me to meet you there?'

Mac was grateful for his concern, but instantly recognized that the presence of Peter Rossellini anywhere around the case of Gil Richardson's death would provide another ring to the media circus that was going to erupt as soon as news leaked out.

'No, I think you shouldn't be there. It would only confuse things. I'm going to talk to Buratti now, see how much time we have before we go downtown, and then to talk to Sylvie. I'll give you a call as soon as I know when I'll be headed home.'

'Okay. But you call me if you need anything else. Promise me, Mackenzie?'

'Promise.' Mac found herself, as she had any number of times over the last few months, grateful at Peter's obvious demonstration of concern.

'I'll call Irwin, then I'll be through here in about an hour, and then I'll wait for you at your place, okay?'

'Okay. And thanks, Peter,' she set down the phone with fingers crossed that Irwin would be able to come up with a candidate.

Walking past dressing room A, she passed Buratti, who was talking to the head of the crime scene unit team. When she caught his eye, he nodded his permission for her to enter. Mac stepped inside, her eyes riveted first on the body of Gil Richardson, the man who had so recently charmed her. His body was awkwardly sprawled on the floor in front of the make-up counter that ran the width of the room; next to his body was a chair that lay on its side, almost touching his right leg. Looking at him from above, he seemed to be in a dancer's position, mid-jump; his left leg straight, his right bent at the knee, with the foot near the left leg. The arms were less graceful in position: his right arm was stretched out, palm up, but the left arm seemed to be caught under his body.

Mac was surprised at her reaction. While she didn't have the experience that a police veteran had in dealing with dead bodies, she had seen a few victims over the last ten years, and she'd seen many, many pictures of crime scenes. But this one shook her. This was a man she knew, even if they'd met only briefly. This was a man she'd admired for a long time, a vibrant, talented individual who now looked markedly less graceful than he had in life. And since anyone who knew anything about Gil Richardson knew that gracefulness was important to him, that alone wafted a certain sadness over the room.

It was a room generous in size for a dressing room, but, given the people inside, and the equipment bags opened on the floor, Mac still had to edge her way over to the man whose bag identified him as being from the Medical Examiner's office. As she did, she noticed that you could still smell the odour of fresh paint in the room. The clutter along the counter – a folded copy of the Life section of *USA Today*, this morning's *Daily News*, a half-used box of Kleenex, bottles of vitamins and cough syrup, antihistamines, cough drops, an inhaler, sinus tablets, a tin of aspirin, packets of powdered cold and flu medicine, and a small hot water pot. Sylvie wasn't kidding when she said that a cold had been roaring through the company. This place appeared to be the central pharmacy for the show.

The Medical Examiner's deputy finally paused in what he was doing, and Mac felt free to interrupt. She crouched next to his equipment case. 'Do you have a cause of death?'

The technician looked at her puzzled, but glanced over at Buratti, and shrugged when he got no reaction. If the lieutenant wasn't making a fuss over her being there, she must be okay.

'Nope. But I can almost promise you this ain't gonna play out the way it looked.'

'And what was the way it looked?' Mac asked.

'Let's just say that with what I seen so far, this guy didn't die of no knife wound.'

Knife wound? Gil Richardson had been *stabbed?* 'Were you able to i.d. the knife?'

The man nodded. 'It's more of a tool knife. I heard from somebody that there are tool kits all over the place – electric, scenic, carpenters. Coulda come from any one of them.'

She stood up and Buratti waved his hand for her to come near. 'I'd say we got another ten minutes here, fifteen at the outside.' She nodded.

Mackenzie went back to dressing room D. Sylvie was almost as startled the second time she opened the door. 'Peter's going to arrange to have someone – a lawyer – meet us downtown.'

Sylvie nodded, working the tissue that she had in her hand.

Mac sat on the edge of the dressing room's counter. 'Can you tell me what happened, Sylvie?'

Sylvie closed her eyes, trying to concentrate, and told her tale in fits and starts. 'We'd been rehearsing the new number for act two. The one Ben Wheeler just put in, remember they were talking about it? The one Gil didn't want to change?'

'That night I met you. Yes, I remember.'

'Well, we'd worked it out with Duran, but we'd been rehearsing in the other space for the last week, and today was the first day we were back in here. So today was the first time we put it on the stage, and it was late when we did, maybe four. Then Gil says he wants us to do the old number, so they can have a comparison. Then Ben complains that that's unfair, because we know the old number better, and we can do it more enthusiastically, so he asked us to do the new one again. With all the bitching and moaning, we'd gone past our break, and I interrupted Gil and asked about the break. He snaps out and says we'll break when he tells us to.' Sylvie's voice was taking on a tone of annoyance, which Mac took to be a good sign.

'Then he says he wants us to do the old number again, and by this time, I figure it's a pissing contest between Ben and Gil, and pretty much went over to him and said that. I didn't say it in front of everybody – I wouldn't do that – just Ben and I think Larry the stage manager were around.'

Sylvie took a deep breath before continuing. 'Gil loses it, and starts ripping me up one side and down the other, how I'm unprofessional, how I'm unprepared, how I can't dance, can't sing, and maybe it would be better if I mastered my own business before I start interfering in other's and going on like a crazy man.' Her eyes were intense when she looked directly at Mackenzie. 'I've *never* seen Gil this way. I mean, he's a tough director, and hard to please, but he's professional, and never personalizes. And this was a personal attack, Mackenzie, believe me. My jaw was hanging.'

Sylvie looked into the mirror, but she wasn't focusing on the image that reflected back. She was seeing the events of the rehearsal instead. 'I decided to shut up, so I sucked in my gut, and we went back up on stage, and we did the old version of the number again. When we were through, Gil excused himself and said we were finished for the day, so the chorus kids left. But Ben asked Rhonda and Curtis and me to work out the vocal parts we have and smooth out this one section, so we did, and that took maybe another fifteen minutes, so it's just before six and we're getting ready to wrap up and I head backstage to see Gil.' She turned back to Mackenzie. 'I figure we have to work this out before tomorrow, because this is the kind of thing that if you let it fester overnight could ruin a working relationship.'

Another deep breath, as if trying to gird herself for the next part of the story. 'So Gil's been using dressing room A down the hall and I go to the door, and knock. I get no answer. I knock again, no answer. I knock and walk in and I see Gil slumped on the counter, head down, but sort of in a weird way. It wasn't like he could be resting in that position, believe me. So I called to him. And I go over and shake his shoulder and then he starts falling toward me – on me, actually. And I yelled out for somebody to come help, and I'm grabbing him as he falls, and then I see that in his back, left side, under the angel wings' – she turned her back toward Mackenzie, and demonstrated the position she meant by twisting her left arm around her back and up – 'there's a knife sticking out of his back. I yell again, and then grabbed it, thinking I should pull it out, I guess, but it's tough to pull out – and all of this is happening in a couple of seconds, you understand, and then Gil falls to the floor, and I'm still holding the knife, and now I'm standing over him with this knife in my hand and the body on the floor.' Her hand was held mid-air, as though she were still holding the knife, and she looked down at the floor, as though the body should be there.

'Then I hear another yell, but it's not me this time, and I look up and see Rhonda at the door and Jack Sprat is right there behind her, and then Duran is in back of him, and Ben, I think, but it's just a bunch of faces.' Sylvie's face

62

pinched up, as though she were trying to distinguish the faces in the doorway.

'And then somebody came in and grabbed me – I think it was Larry – and people were shouting and saying "how could I" and it got crazy. Somebody yelled out to call 911, and the police got here, and—'

Sylvie was interrupted by Buratti's appearance at the door. 'They're taking the body out, Mac. I'm gonna have Beckman take her down in one of the squad cars. You gonna get a taxi?'

Mackenzie moved to the doorway to speak with him. 'Yes,' she said with a nod. 'I'll follow in a cab. It sounds like you're not going directly to headquarters, am I right?'

'Yeah. I'm gonna make a stop at the medical examiners', and take this Thomas Kinsolving guy with me since he's gonna make the official i.d. But I also have to make sure the ME's office knows that this is a *very* high-profile case. The captain tells me we already got the mayor's office calling in, and I got a message to meet with the Deputy Commissioner as soon as I get downtown so she can come up with something for the press.'

Buratti shook his head at the last item. Having to deal with the press was an aspect of high-profile cases that he didn't relish. They could be a big enough pain in the ass on the routine type of cases. Somebody as famous as Gil Richardson gets killed right in the damn theatre, forget it. The tabloid guys were gonna have a field day.

The lieutenant looked over Mackenzie's shoulder and indicated Sylvie with his head. 'How she doin'? She holding up?'

'Considering,' was Mac's only reply.

'Here they come with the body. I'll see you downtown, Mac, soon as I can make it,' Buratti finished and headed to talk to the technician from the Medical Examiner's office.

The scene that followed was a weird tableau. As the body was wheeled out from the dressing room on a gurney, the members of the company formed a spontaneous guard of honour, lining the way to the door where Lopes stood.

As the gurney approached the door, Curtis Leland stepped from the line of people. 'Farewell, Gil Richardson, man of the theatre. Flights of angels sing thee to thy rest!' His benediction brought forth a sob from Thomas, Richardson's assistant, who was being helped from the stage area by Rhonda and Lenny Yarnevich. The young man seemed utterly disconsolate, his repeated sobs now coming in great huge gulps. As the trio neared the exit, Buratti offered assistance to Thomas, and helped the young man out the door.

Next, Sergeant Beckman led Sylvie through the row, and the expressions on the faces of the company seemed to encompass an astonishing range: from disbelief to sympathy, from understanding to horror, and from smiles of encouragement to sneers of revulsion. Mac found herself last in this grotesque parade, and the expressions turned questioning when they saw her bringing up the tail end of this procession in her yellow slicker. She smiled at Lopes as she walked by him, and he nodded in return.

The coroner's van was already loaded by the time Mac made it onto the sidewalk, the first car with Buratti and Thomas was pulling away, and Sylvie was just getting into the back seat of the police car while Beckman held the door. The bright television lights of the local news crews lent a surreal quality to the scene, even though the police had managed to confine them to the opposite side of Broadway, limiting their view of the activities occurring right outside the stage door.

FINALES AND OVERTURES

Mac looked up to notice that at least the drizzle had let up again, although the streets were still shiny with moisture. She stepped to the curb to hail a cab.

CHAPTER FIVE

Simon Wexler stood on the curb on the Broadway side of the building. First he watched them load Gil Richardson's body into the coroner's wagon; then he watched as the cops escorted Sylvie Morgan to the back seat of a squad car. He turned back to the sidewalk. Christ, this was *unbelievable*!

His press guy, Max What-ever-his-name, was hovering near the stage door, and Wexler beckoned him over. 'I want you to get down to police headquarters and stay on top of this thing. It's gonna be all over the papers tomorrow, and I want whatever information the cops have before I see it on the front pages or hear it on the eleven o'clock news. You got that?' Max nodded. 'Good. We'll talk later about the press release we're gonna do, depending on what the cops say. So you'll call me, right?' Max nodded again. 'I'll be at the office.'

Simon spotted his young co-producer Jonathan Humphries standing just inside the door. 'Where will you be later, Jonathan, so we can go over this release with you?' The kid had become more important in the last few days, and this kind of stroking was necessary now.

'I'll be at home,' Jonathan Humphries replied. 'I'll definitely be at home.'

'Good. Talk to you later.' Wexler turned and made his

way to the corner of 14th, and started walking to his building over on Fifth Avenue. He needed to think things through, and he needed to do it where he knew it would be quiet, and right now that meant getting away from the theatre. Thank God the chorus and most of the crew were gone by the time this happened. It would have been even more craziness if more people had been around.

Simon stopped and waited for the light to change at Fifth Avenue, but his mind kept racing. Gil Richardson dead! Who could believe it? And Sylvie Morgan with the knife in her hand? This made no sense. Although he'd heard Richardson was going after her good at this afternoon's rehearsal. He hadn't been around, but Larry had called him right after Gil's body was found – Christ, it seemed freakish even to be using that term, Gil's body – anyway, Larry had called him immediately and Simon had arrived at the theatre at the same time the first cops walked in the door.

His office was a beautiful old townhouse on Fifth, one of the last left on this part of the Avenue, but he'd be moving into the theatre as soon as the fourth floor was finished. As much as he admired this elegant old building, he loved the idea of having his office in the theatre even more. Just the way the old-time producers did. He would have appreciated having his office in the theatre tonight, because that would have put him a little closer to his bottle of bourbon and that's just what he needed now. He walked up the five stairs that led to the imposing front door, and as he unlocked it, he noticed that Jaime, the maintenance man, had polished the bronze plaque reading 'Wexler and Company' to the right of the door.

Once in the building, he double-locked the front door behind him, walked through the reception area, and up the curving staircase directly to his office. The building was

68

quiet. Of course it was well past office hours now; what made him edgy was that the building had been too damn quiet during office hours in the last year. Wexler and Company used to have twenty-two professionals on staff, plus a few support people. Now he was down to five employees, including Janet, his secretary of the last twenty-four years, and even the five were straining his budget. The three other developments he'd been working on in the last year and a half had, one by one, dropped off the radar screen. First by desire and then by circumstance, he'd concentrated only on the Century development; it had become his passion and now it was all he had left.

He flipped on the light switch and the lamps placed around the office came on. Soft pink bulbs of sizeable wattage glowed out from lamps on his desk, on the tables that sat on either end of his long leather couch, and from the recessed lighting above his bookcases and bar area. He walked over to the bar and poured himself a good sized tumbler of Wild Turkey. Straight.

He took his glass and walked toward the window, a bay window that offered a view of lower Fifth Avenue, straight to Washington Square and the arch. Ideas tumbled through his mind, all revolving around the astonishing fact that Gil Richardson was dead.

He really wasn't sure how this was going to affect him, but he was pretty certain it wasn't going to be good. A dead director on a high-profile production that was a risk to begin with might get you a lot of free publicity, but, David Merrick forgive him, he said to himself with a raise of his glass, free publicity wasn't everything.

Damn! He couldn't let this one get away from him. This new theatre was a dream of his, and had been for twenty years or more. And with *Reunion*, he'd finally found the

show he wanted to inaugurate his theatre. Working with Gil
Richardson had been the icing on the cake; Richardson was
one of the people in this world – one of the few, given his
last couple of years – that he truly admired. He'd found,
surprisingly, that he hadn't liked Richardson a whole lot. To
be frank, there wasn't a whole lot about the man to like.
Richardson was his work and that was all. While working
with him had been a dream, he wasn't a guy you wanted to
have dinner with. Unless, of course, it was a working
dinner.

But Richardson had given him some respect. Begrudg-
ing at first, but still respect. A lot of people still thought of
him as some wise-ass real estate developer who was
dabbling in the theatre. And that's what he started out as,
twenty-five years ago. Hell, he'd been married for two years
and was already twenty-five years old before he saw his first
Broadway show, *How to Succeed in Business Without Really
Trying*. That first show had hooked him, and after that he
saw anything and everything he could. His main business
at the time, then as now, was real estate development, but
then it was office parks and mini malls in New Jersey and
up the Hudson Valley that he and his father-in-law were
concentrating on back then.

And they made a very nice living at it. He'd made his first
million by the age of thirty-two. And that's when he started
diversifying his investments to include the theatre, much to
his accountant's horror. The first few things he invested in
were flops. Some adaptation of Henry James that the cast
practically slept through, and some cockamamie musical
about a guy in the South that tried to be an updated *Gone
With The Wind* and missed by a mile. Both experiences had
been valuable lessons, though, just like his old man had told
him: sometimes you learn more from losing than from

70

winning. And those first few plays had helped him learn the ropes. He figured out how to read through the bullshit of the promo materials, and he learned what to listen for at the angel auditions. He studied how the investment packages were put together. He began to understand the economics of the business.

His father-in-law's real estate empire had come crashing down in the late Seventies, like everyone's did in the East, and money was tight for a few years. Especially when his wife – now his ex-wife – decided to take whatever he had left in their divorce settlement. But Simon had kept his hand in the theatre, with small investments in off-Broadway productions, and he did well enough with a couple of small shows that ran and ran, so that by the time his real estate fortunes turned again, his interest in the theatre was still bubbling.

When the building boom of the Eighties hit New York, Simon, on his own now, finally moved into the big time of real estate development with two office towers going up in Manhattan. In 1983 he co-produced a show that only ran a year in New York, but the touring companies and especially the company in Las Vegas continued for years. That show – *La Revue* – was an odd combination of *Sugar Babies* and the Folies Bergère; it had made him a lot of money, but Simon had developed some taste over the years, and frankly the show embarrassed him. Almost as amends, he started taking the money he made from *La Revue* and investing it in straight theatre which was, investment wise, like using money for toilet paper, according to his accountant.

That same accountant told him after one opening night, 'Sure, it's a great play. It's just that straight theatre doesn't make economic sense anymore, not in New York anyway. Not unless you got some big star.'

71

But Simon was sure *Reunion* would shine, even without a star, and it was going to bring in some badly-needed money. Once it opened. If it opened. But if he won – make that *when* he won – he'd win big. He was in it on both sides of this deal, in the theatre and in the production. But there was a little voice inside that reminded him that if he lost, he was through. Given the way he'd leveraged himself on this theatre, on the production, and on the whole Century Redevelopment, he would be washed up. On that happy thought, he walked back to the bar to pour himself another hefty splash of bourbon.

God, there had been enough problems with this show already, even without Richardson getting killed. This union thing had dragged on way too long. And he knew he was out on a limb by himself on this one.

He had no problem dealing with the creative unions. Well, a little bit of a problem sometimes, because unions were a pain in the ass. It was part of their function to be. But generally he had no problem giving people a good wage – a damn good wage, in most cases, for their work. It was the other unions he had problems with. The ones that wanted to tell him how many people he would have working a show in his theatre, regardless of what the show was, regardless of what he, the director, the designer, or the composer had to say. He wouldn't sign those contracts. If his plan worked, and he got the unions to come to terms with him, he'd be hailed as a savior of the theatre by some, as a ruthless exploiter of talent by others. If it didn't work, and he jeopardized not only a new musical but a new theatre, certain people would look forward to using his body for ballast when they dropped that ball in Times Square next New Year's Eve.

Swirling the ice cubes around in his glass, Simon walked

over to the model of the Century Theatre that had sat on his side credenza for over a year now; next to it was the smaller scale model of the whole Century Redevelopment, his larger dream. Along with educating himself in the financial side of theatre investing, and trying to develop some taste in good theatre, Simon had also read quite a bit of the history of the theatre, particularly theatre in New York, and he'd been happy to learn that the connection between real estate and theatre had a long and distinguished history. After all, many producers had started out as building owners.

Building the Century had been his dream for years now. He even liked the name, and he thought of it as his own private joke. With everybody concentrating on the upcoming turn of the century and turn of the millennium, it amused him to realize he was looking back a hundred years to the turn of the last century when Union Square was the heart of the city's entertainment district. He also loved that it wasn't a new name for a theatre in New York. In fact, there had been two theatres in Manhattan called the Century. One was up just south of Central Park on Seventh Avenue, owned by the Schuberts, who had built it for Al Jolson. That Century had been home to *Kiss Me Kate*, which ran for over a thousand performances; may the name bring such luck to *Reunion*, he thought with a raise of his glass. The earlier Century was over on Central Park West, one of New York's 'spectacle' theatres – not quite theatre, not quite opera house, not quite Madison Square Garden – built in the early 1900s. It pleased Simon that his theatre's name had some relationship to New York's luminous theatre history. Somehow that fact connected him to those other producers, those other builders of theatres.

And God, he loved the look of the theatre. Quigley had

done a great job. The guy hadn't been his first choice for architect; hell, he'd maybe been his fourth or fifth choice, but he'd done a helluva job on the design. He hoped to God that everything wasn't lost in the incredible circumstances of tonight. Oh, shit, he thought, he'd better call Quigley before he learned the news some other way. He should be the one to tell him that Gil Richardson was dead.

CHAPTER SIX

Bruce Quigley replaced the phone in its cradle, clicked off the light he'd left burning above his drafting table, and noticed that his hand was still trembling as he did. He slumped onto his swivel chair and let out a long, slow whistle. Gil Richardson was *dead*? No, none of this could be happening.

He turned his chair and stood, and headed toward the south window of his West Village office. It was a view that went all the way down to the World Trade Towers, and one he never tired of. There was something about the lights that helped him concentrate.

Gil Richardson. He'd liked working with the man at first. Their work didn't exactly overlap, of course, but there was an acknowledgment between them, of artist to artist or craftsman to craftsman, however you wanted to express it. What had impressed him in those first meetings with Richardson was how the director had immediately clicked into what he was trying to accomplish with the design of the Century Theatre.

'Camden Yards,' Richardson had said the first time he'd looked over the model and the drawings. The construction of the theatre was well underway by that time, but a person could only see the total picture of the exteriors and interiors in Quigley's office with his models and his renderings.

'You're right,' Quigley had replied, astonished at how quickly Richardson, a guy who'd grown up in England and who presumably didn't know a whole hell of a lot of baseball, had articulated the connection he had made subconsciously at first, and only recently come to recognize. The Baltimore Oriole's baseball field at Camden Yards had been an architectural triumph a few years ago – a new baseball stadium, with all the modern conveniences, but one which captured the ambiance of an old park and the attendant emotions that fans so willingly expressed about the baseball temples of the good old days. In a way, Camden Yards was such a success because it was a physical recreation of people's fond memories about the old parks, memories which almost always enhanced the originals beyond what they were in reality.

The Century was like that in a way: warm tones, gas lights out front and in the lobby, an intimate feeling inside, but state of the art air conditioning and heating, and the best in curtain, lighting, and scenery technology. A 21st century theatre in a 19th century shell. It was the building that was going to make Bruce Quigley's name.

This was the kind of work he wanted to do; he was sure of that. It had historical meaning – bringing some of New York's theatre heritage back to Union Square. It was urban renewal in the best sense; some of the structures they'd cleared from this lot could have been used as poster illustrations of derelict properties. The neighbourhood had gone into decline in the Seventies after the original bargain-hunter's department store Klein's on the Square closed. In the last ten years, a number of buildings had revived their individual blocks in the area, but undoubtedly the Century was going to be the jewel in the crown, the centrepiece that would serve as the new core of the community.

The buzz in the press about the theatre building was already good. He knew that the *Times'* architecture critic would be running a piece on the Century's design the week the theatre opened, and a few of the trade publications had already done interviews with him. One even promised a cover story.

That he was looking forward to. And it was going to take every ounce of restraint he possessed not to have all the favourable press coverage on the Century blown up to billboard size and positioned outside the offices of Louden and Partners, his former firm. The firm of his ex-wife Christine; more particularly, the firm owned by his former father-in-law Charles Louden.

Bruce had never believed in the concept of love at first sight, but that was the way he'd fallen for Christine, hard and fast, at his one-time college roommate's engagement party. Later, when things started going sour, he wondered if he would have pursued her quite so energetically if he'd known from the beginning that she was not only an architect herself, but the daughter of New England's most prominent (and most successful) architect. It probably wouldn't have mattered, even if he had known, because he was that much in love with her.

Those first years were wonderful, and if there were whispers about him, he didn't hear them. Charles Louden had invited him to join the firm in the months before their wedding, and Bruce jumped at the chance. He was thrilled at the level of work he got to do over the next few years, and he didn't think anything of it when Charles Louden got most of the attention, the acclaim, and the credit.

It wasn't until there was trouble brewing in their marriage, trouble that started about four years ago now, that he began hearing those dreadful whispers. Whispers that Bruce wasn't carrying his own weight, whispers that Bruce had never contributed significantly to any of their projects, whispers that Bruce Quigley was resting on Charles Louden's laurels. When he found out it was Christine herself behind the rumour mill, he felt utterly betrayed, and humiliated beyond reckoning.

The marriage had ended quickly after that, and he'd been glad to leave the small town in the Berkshires where Louden maintained his offices. But Bruce had been admittedly nervous about changing his life so totally and abruptly at thirty-seven; it seemed like he was starting out fresh again, since their cruel ending meant that the six and a half years he'd spent with Louden had been greatly diminished in value. Those first months in New York had been a struggle, but he knew now he was within spitting distance of the end of the lean years. And the rave reviews in the architectural press were only going to be the icing on the cake.

The coverage in the general press was another matter, though. There was a lot of press that tied in the opening of the show with the opening of the theatre, and he'd noticed over the last few weeks that both Simon Wexler and Gil Richardson seemed to be taking credit for some of the ideas included in the theatre design. Maybe it was intentional, maybe not. He'd been interviewed enough times to know how words could be taken out of context, their meaning twisted away from what you had said – or intended to say.

But this was his breakthrough, the project that would bring him to the forefront of New York architects, and he had to make the most of it. He'd wasted enough years up in Massachusetts. It was time. He was almost forty years old, and he had to make his name. Now. He couldn't afford to let the Century project get away from him, and nobody – not Gil Richardson alive or dead, not Simon Wexler, nobody – was going to take it away from him, nor take away the credit he deserved.

Biting the inside of his lip, he stepped closer to the window. He hoped that nobody – press especially – got word of that last fight he'd had with Richardson. He looked at the twin towers of the World Trade Center, and watched the lights blink out one after another.

CHAPTER SEVEN

Ben Wheeler walked back into the theatre, with Lenny Yarnevich trailing behind him, concerned. Ben had left his notes and briefcase near the pit, and he needed them before he left. He scooped them up and headed for the stage door again. He was getting out of here – now.

Lenny walked him out onto Broadway, and they headed toward the corner of 14th Street, where Lenny hailed a cab for him, asking 'Are you okay?' every thirty seconds at least. Ben tried to answer him with a nod of his head. He didn't trust himself to talk.

A cab was stopped at the light on the far side of Broadway, but the driver seemed to have acknowledged Lenny's athletic arm-wave. The two men stood in silence for a few moments, until Lenny asked him again if he was okay. Ben nodded again.

At least the rain seemed to have let up for a while, and the air felt like it was clearing. He tried to take deep breaths of cool air, but didn't trust what his stomach would do if he took *really* deep breaths.

The cab pulled up and Lenny helped him into the back seat. 'Sure you don't want me to come with you?' his collaborator asked.

Finally Ben found some words. 'No, I'm okay now.' He

looked up at the older man. 'Thanks, Lenny. I'll talk to you in the morning.' He gave the cab driver his address on West 58th and sat back, as the cab pulled around the corner and headed up Park Avenue South, past the orange and white barriers that lined this side of Union Square.

He tried to rest his head along the seatback, but when he closed his eyes the motion of the cab seemed to make him even woozier. He sat up and stared out the window at the procession of headlights and rear lights going up and down Park Avenue South. His eyes might be seeing car lights, but his mind flashed with images of the last four years going up in smoke, and he snapped his head around, too fast. That did it. He knew he was going to be sick.

'Pull over!' he said to the driver. 'Pull over here now!'

'What, mon, you no want to go Fifty-Eight Street now?' asked the cabby, a Haitian in his late twenties.

'Yeah,' he tried to reply, but when the cab came to a halt at the corner of 25th Street, Ben opened the door, leaned out the back seat and spat into the gutter.

'Oh, mon, you not gon' be sick in my car, are you mon? I been on since four o'clock and made only ten dollar tonight. If I have to go clean cab, oh, mon . . .' the cabby's voice faded into despair.

Ben knew he didn't have anything left in his stomach. He'd been sick at the theatre twice already. 'No, I'm okay. I won't throw up in the car, I promise.' He hoped that was true. 'Fifty-Eighth and Seventh, please.'

The cab driver looked at him intently, brown eyes blazing, and turned to pull away from the curb. He wanted to floor it, but decided that a gentle ride would be better for this passenger and for the rear seat covers as well.

Four years! Four years Ben Wheeler had been working

toward getting his first musical on the stage in New York. Now it was only days away, and his big chance was disappearing before his eyes.

Ben had come late to music, later than a lot of his friends anyway. He was in high school before he discovered the piano; he'd never gone for the guitar the way so many of his contemporaries had. But on a piano he could do anything, and his natural talent had blossomed when his mother and step-father made sure he got lessons from the time he was fourteen until he finished high school.

His music teacher, Mr Balutin, had immediately recognized the boy's natural talent, and he also recognized that his relationship to the classics would be very limited. Ben Wheeler didn't have the discipline to sustain interest in a piece long enough to master a concerto. But the shorter works, ones that captured his interest, he mastered in an amazingly brief period of time. Thinking it might hold Ben's attention and serve as an incentive for mastering the technique that he insisted on, Mr Balutin started Ben on a special program, learning some of the American standards – songs that made up the traditional pop and jazz repertoire. A number of Broadway hits were included in that select group, and they were Ben's first introduction to theatre music.

It was Mr Balutin who told him about his hometown's place in theatre history; how New Haven had been a try-out town for many of the great musicals, including *South Pacific* and *My Fair Lady*, which had played New Haven when Ben was just a toddler. It was Mr Balutin, too, who got him his first gigs as a fill-in at one of the local clubs when he was in college. Eventually, he attracted some attention for his arrangements, and as word got around, he started getting more and more work, some of it as far away as New York. By the time Ben was in his mid-twenties, he was still two credits shy of graduation, but he was making a good living as an arranger.

That's when he met Kenny Deeler, coming up at the time as a producer of pop records. Kenny hired him to do the arrangements for a new singer he was producing, Alanna Gallani, a young woman with a fabulous throaty voice. After their first few meetings, Kenny decided the songs weren't good enough, and he talked Ben in to sitting down with him to write some new material. They came up with three for the album, and while two of them wouldn't make Ben's first cut today, the third was a pretty good pop song. When Alanna's first album went gold, Ben and Kenny started getting more offers for a combination of arrangement/production/songwriting services, and formed (naturally) Wheeler-Deeler Productions.

The next eight years were a ride on a magic carpet. Hit songs seemed to beget hit songs, and successful new artists attracted other new artists who became even more successful. He and Kenny worked with artists who sold millions upon millions of records, with only a few duds sprinkled in to keep them humble, and it was a great life.

The end started when Kenny walked into his office at Wheeler-Deeler one morning almost seven years ago, closed the door, and told Ben that he was HIV positive. At first Ben didn't believe it, because his partner looked so good, the way he always did. It was painful to remember now, but he actually stood up and accused Kenny of trying to pull some really tasteless joke. It was when he saw the tears in Kenny's eyes that he realized it was true.

It was hard to believe because he didn't want to believe

it, and doubly hard to believe because Kenny looked so damned good. He looked less good within nine months, and was dead another eight months after that.

Ben closed down the production side of Wheeler-Deeler in the weeks after Kenny died, and the business details were taken care of through his lawyer's office now. For months, he sat around his apartment, noodling at the piano until Beverly, the woman he'd been describing as his girlfriend for nine years now, threatened to call in a shrink unless he did something. He started taking long walks in the park just to appease Beverly, and one day as he was leaving the park, he passed a radio that was playing "Bali-Hai" from *South Pacific*. The tune stuck in his head, and when he returned to his apartment, he sat down and played it straight through. Then he played the other songs he remembered from the score, and was astonished at how well they'd stuck up in the attic of his brain for so long and how fresh and alive they were when he brought them out again.

He decided he'd seek out Mr Balutin, and was surprised to discover that the man he'd thought of as old twenty-five years ago was now only sixty-two. Mr Balutin was delighted to hear from his most successful student and delighted as well to encourage Ben's renewed interest in theatre music. While he bolstered Ben's desire to write theatre music, he gently suggested that, despite Ben's success in the pop arena, he might need formal tutoring in composition to tackle the various forms of theatre music.

Keeping as low a profile as possible, Ben studied for three months with Norton Reinhardt, a composer based out of Tanglewood. Reinhardt, delighted to find an accomplished student who shared his interest in musical theatre, instructed Ben in the form and structure of theatre songs, using examples from Kern to Sondheim as his textbooks. In the course of those three months, Ben realized that, for as much as he loved the melody and wit of Rodgers and Hart, the melody and drama of Rodgers and Hammerstein, the sweetness and humour of Lerner and Loewe, he was totally enamoured of the works of Glenn Leonard, a composer/lyricist who had put a show on Broadway every five years from 1949 to 1964, when he died at the too-early age of fifty-seven.

A month after he left Tanglewood, he got a call from Mabel Leonard, the composer's widow. 'I understand you're a fan of my husband's,' she said in a raspy voice. 'Norton tells me you've got a lot of promise. I'd love to meet with you when you get a chance.' Ben had been tongue-tied on the phone, but immediately accepted her invitation.

That phone call started a wonderful chapter in Ben's life; even Beverly said she'd never seen him so happy. He was working on practising his craft, coming up with new songs by trying to find lyrics that had been thrown out of former Broadway productions and seeing if he could compose for them on the spot. He started visiting Mabel Leonard for tea once a week. When he realized how much she knew about that era of musical theatre – the Golden Years as the scholars referred to them – he asked if he could start taping their conversations.

That was it. Little did he know that that innocent suggestion would be his downfall, his Achilles' heel. But even with everything that had happened, he couldn't regret those afternoons with Mabel, or the tapes he'd made of their conversations. He only regretted that Gil Richardson had heard one of those tapes by accident.

The cab pulled up in front of his building on 58th and Ben Wheeler paid his fare. Maybe if the elevator was in the lobby he could make it up to his apartment before he threw up again.

CHAPTER EIGHT

Lenny Yarnevich watched as Ben Wheeler's cab pulled away. He knew that Wheeler was shaken – badly shaken by the news. Hell, who wasn't? But Ben was shaken more than most. By the time Lenny had found him in the men's room, Ben had thrown up once already, and he still looked green. Lenny was concerned about the kid, he thought as he hailed the next cab that came along and eased himself into the back seat.

Kid. He had to stop calling him that. Wheeler was only eleven or twelve years younger than his own fifty-three, but somehow it felt as though he was from another generation. Lenny felt almost fatherly toward him, like he should be giving the kid advice.

Not that he could give him a whole lot of advice on the show. Not only was this Ben Wheeler's first, *Reunion* was Lenny Yarnevich's first musical as well. And it was the first writing he'd done for the stage in over twenty-five years.

Just after college, Lenny had written some skits for a comedy revue that had played down in the Village for a few years. It was one of those revues where they kept on adding new material, changing the show every couple of months to keep it fresh. He'd been there about a few years, when he was approached by a network executive in from LA about

89

working on a sitcom. He'd figured what the hell, it was February, he'd be glad to get out of New York. It probably wouldn't work out, but at least he'd be in the warm weather for the next two months.

He went to Los Angeles planning to stay for eight weeks and ended up staying twenty-six years. That first show had been a disaster, and limped along for thirteen weeks until it was mercifully put out of its misery. This was in the good old days when even turkeys got thirteen weeks or maybe a whole season before they were yanked off the air.

The next show wasn't that much better, nor the next show. But he was learning, and getting paid good money. Finally, in 1978, he hit as the head writer, along with his partner, Carl Shuster, of a top-twenty comedy, replacing the man who'd created the show. They stayed with that for three years, and then he and Carl were offered their own shot at developing a series. They worked on the idea, refining, polishing, and finally casting it brilliantly and when *Night School* debuted it withstood even *The Cosby Show* storm of the Eighties. *Night School* ran for eight years, for six of which Carl and Lenny continued as head writers, and when it sold into syndication, they knew they were set for the rest of their lives. They now had sufficient 'fuck you' money, as Carl put it so aptly, to do – or not do – whatever they wanted for the rest of their lives.

Lenny had had the good sense to marry his first sweetheart, Margaret Donaldson, and Mags had insisted that they take a year off once the *Night School* sale was completed. They'd travelled, got their youngest settled in college, travelled some more, and finally ended up back in Beverly Hills after only four months. Lenny knew he was not a man of leisure. He tried to figure out what next to do. He really didn't want to do another TV show, and with all this talk of new media this and interactive that, he had no idea what the hell people were talking about.

It was Mags who got him thinking about his dreams again.

'Tell me again about when you were a kid and you knew you wanted to be a writer,' she coaxed one night after dinner as they were sitting by the pool.

'You mean when I was twelve and my Dad took me to see *No Time for Sergeants*?'

'That's the one.'

'I looked around and saw all those people laughing, having a great time, with the stage lights glowing off of their faces. I figured it was magic, and I knew that's what I wanted to do.'

'You know what's always amazed me about that story? What about that made you think of being a writer?' Mags said. 'Most kids – our kids – would have associated the magic of the thing with the people on stage.'

'I was lucky, I guess,' Lenny had replied with a smile and a shrug of his shoulders. 'I knew that the actors weren't making up those words as they went along. I wanted to be the guy giving them the words to say, because I knew it was the words that were making people laugh.'

'So why don't you do that?'

'Do what?'

'Give the actors the words and make people laugh – in the theatre.'

It took him a couple of weeks to get around to it, but Lenny asked his agent to start nosing around, and find out if anybody was interested in him for the stage. To his surprise, nobody was. But word came back that they'd read something he came up with. And word was that if you came up with a strong book for a musical, people would be lining up.

By the time Lenny sat down at his typewriter, he remembered hearing one of the great book writers from years ago, in an interview on *Good Morning America.* Start with a good play, the old gentleman had said, something funny and touching, something that would work well without music. Then the music will make it better.

He thought he'd toss it off in a couple of weeks. After all, he was used to writing a half hour show every week for twenty-five weeks a year on deadline. Of course, then he'd been writing with Carl, and it always seemed faster because Carl always made him laugh. In fact, he'd tried to get Carl to work on it with him, but Carl insisted that he was perfecting his napping-in-the-hammock-routine, which he was proposing be made into an Olympic event. Besides, Carl said, if the show they wrote turned out to be any good, he might have to go to New York with it, and everybody knew that Carl, once a son of Brooklyn, now couldn't stand to be anyplace where the temperature went below fifty degrees.

So Lenny started on his own. At first he didn't know what the hell he was going to write about, and he remembered a trick they'd used in the writer's room when they were stuck. Write about what's in front of you. Mags at the time was going crazy trying to lose fifteen pounds in a minute and a half so she'd look great at her twenty-fifth reunion from a small college in Maine, and he started writing about that. Then he decided to accept her pleading invitation to accompany her, a social engagement he would normally have swum through a bay of sharks to avoid. But he watched and listened and observed the whole weekend, and by the time they were flying home he knew that what had started as a writing exercise for him had turned into the seeds of his play. It took him a hell of a lot longer than he thought it would, a year and a half. It was a bitch, but he knew *Reunion* was good.

It wasn't until he was done that he showed it to his agent, and they put him in touch with Ben. Those first meetings with Ben were over two years ago. What scared him about the future of the musical theatre was that the process on *Reunion* was considered speedy. Over three years he'd been working on this damn thing, and people were talking about how fast it had come together.

Of course, it *had* been fast ever since Wexler got involved. That was only last December, out in California. The first producer they had had crapped out on them, and they were stuck out there, maybe not able to bring the show into New York. But Gil Richardson had come through with Simon Wexler and here they were, less than two weeks from a genuine New York Opening Night.

At least they had been less than two weeks away. God knew what was going to happen now with Gil dead. He stopped himself as the thought ran through his mind. *Unbelievable! Gil Richardson was dead!*

The cab driver started up Central Park West, and Lenny reached for his wallet to get the fare ready, trying to organize in his mind what he'd have to do when he got up to the apartment. He was going to have to have some comment ready for the press, because he was sure they'd be on the phone within the next few hours.

He'd have to break the news to Mags first, and then he would call Carl out in Los Angeles. Carl would be offended if he heard this kind of news on CNN before he heard it from his partner.

Lenny could almost bet what Carl's comment on Gil Richardson's death would be. He could almost guarantee it. 'Lenny,' Carl would say, 'I knew those theatre types were a bunch of back-stabbers. But do they have to be so *literal* about it?'

As the cab pulled up in front of his building, he got out and paid the fare. One thing had been nagging at his brain, and now he remembered what it was. In one of the several arguments that Ben Wheeler and Gil Richardson had had over the production number this afternoon, he remembered Gil dramatically walking away from Ben and turning around with a parting shot. 'You'll replace that number over my dead body,' he'd said to Ben.

Nobody would take that seriously. Would they?

CHAPTER NINE

Manfred Erickson watched the coroner's wagon take Gil Richardson's body away, and loathed himself that the first thing he thought – well, second thing actually – was that he wondered what this was going to mean for their schedule. He assumed Gil's death would postpone things a bit, but having been around Wexler only a few weeks, he wasn't sure.

He walked back into the theatre and headed for the back row of seats. He sat staring at the stage for a few minutes, shaking his head at the events of the last hour.

Gil Richardson was dead? How is that possible? Gil was the reason he was on this show. In fact he was the only one in the company, to his knowledge, that had ever worked with Gil before.

That wasn't unusual. As wonderful a reputation as Gil Richardson had in the theatre pages of the New York papers, he had a strange reputation inside the business. People got along with him very well, but he had the odd characteristic of not wanting to work with people a second time, unlike other directors who developed a company of people they worked with repeatedly. It was almost as if Gil didn't want to get to know anyone really well. Or maybe it was that he didn't want anyone to know him.

That impression had been confirmed a few years ago, when Manny went to Gil's apartment, helping him with the exact lighting specifications for the interior decorator who was then finishing up Richardson's apartment. It was a great space, with an imposing view of Central Park, and the interior design was very well executed, if a little cold. He'd complimented Gil on it, mentioning that his theatre friends must have loved the way he'd framed the one-sheets for his shows. Those one-sheets, in fact, would be the prominent pieces in the apartment, once the lighting design that Manny had just reviewed with the decorator was installed. 'No,' Gil shook his head distractedly, 'none of them have seen it.'

That had been the last conversation they'd had until Gil called in late February. Manny knew about Gil's involvement with *Reunion* of course, he'd read about the run out in California, but he had just filed away the information for the next time he ran into Gil. He was up to his eyebrows at the time with a dance company that was debuting a new work as well as presenting 'freshened' versions of some repertory staples in its month-long New York run starting April 1st. But in late February Manny was reading the *New York Times* with his morning coffee as usual, and discovered that the funding for the company had been pulled virtually overnight, and even though the next ten days were spent running around trying to get new municipal, corporate or federal funding, the season was cancelled, the new productions along with it, and he was out of a job.

Within a day of that announcement, Gil had been on the phone, expressing his condolences, but asking if Manny could get on the next plane and get out to California. He could. That was life in the theatre, after all.

When he saw the first performance of *Reunion*, he knew it was a strong show. The design, however, was just not up to the quality of the work, and certainly not up to the standards that New York audiences expect. He got to work fast.

The only limitations he'd had were financial. Simon Wexler was desperately trying to hold this show within a certain budget, and since the amount budgeted for scenery and lighting had already been depleted, there wasn't too much wiggle room. Simon's answer, as always, was to simply simplify. It was a challenge that Manny enjoyed; most people don't understand the work it takes – the thinking it takes – to bring something down to its essence. Manny's designs started taking shape in the form of sketches first, then simple models; Gil was apparently thrilled with them, if his enthusiastic reaction was to be trusted. Simon, of course, started bitching about how long it was taking Manny.

Manny had to smile at that memory. Well, that was what producers did. They bitched. If not about money, about time. In the theatre – hell, in life – they were frequently the same thing.

Looking back now, he remembered how markedly more pleasant Gil had been when they were in California. By the time they got into New York, of course, the show had taken shape. The New York work was a matter of refining it, getting it to run on time, smoothing the edges. It was nuts and bolts work, and it was the point where, Manny had noticed before, Gil usually got impatient or bored. Maybe it was because most of the creative work had been done up to this point, and now was where the polishing-the-craft part took over. He'd seen the same thing in Gil when they'd worked together before.

But this time Richardson had really been getting weird, genuinely unpleasant to be around. Maybe it was because he'd been fighting off the creeping crud that had been working its way through the company for the last few weeks. But whatever it was, he'd nailed the architect, Quigley, in front of a bunch of people, and he'd gone toe-to-toe with Wheeler a couple of times over that new number Ben wanted to put in. And what was that crack to the choreographer just before he'd walked off the stage this afternoon? What had he said? 'Well, Duran, I finally realized your secret. So don't think I don't know who you are.' What the hell was that all about?

Manny stood up and walked down the aisle toward the stage. Maybe he'd have some time in the next few days to get together with the master electrician and figure out that problem with the bank of lights over the left side of the stage.

CHAPTER TEN

She could still hear Gil's voice when he turned and glared at her. 'And another thing, Duran, don't think I don't know who you are.'

The only thing that surprised Duran about Gil Richardson getting killed was that it had taken so long for somebody to get to him. If it had been up to her, Gil Richardson would have been dead many times over in the last ten years.

Duran Nadeem – née Dorothy Ann Wallace – had lived out the life story told in that clever song from *A Chorus Line,* 'Dance 10, Looks 3': a talented dancer who couldn't land the parts she needed because of her looks. At least that was her experience that first year and a half she spent in New York, auditioning every chance she got, making it through to the second-to-the last cut, and then when the producers or the choreographers or whoever was doing the hiring got a close look at her, she was out on the street again.

A sympathetic dancer, a woman a few years older than she, finally told her the reason: she was on the ugly side of plain, and she didn't do much to help herself out. Her teeth had never received the orthodonture they needed, and a bad case of adolescent acne made her skin flare up again no matter what kind of make up she tried, and her hair was a web of colours ranging from dishwater blonde to mousy brown, none of which seemed to go with her sallow skin tone.

She didn't have the money then to do anything about the teeth, but she'd at least gotten her hair to a better colour and cut when she tried out – and was hired! – for a Gil Richardson production. She was sure that this was finally the start of her fabulous New York stage career.

That fantasy had lasted through the first week of rehearsals. Gil Richardson had fired her in front of the whole dancing company, and it had been humiliating. She'd overheard him talking to the choreographer as the dancers were filing back into the rehearsal studio after a break, referring to her as 'the homely blonde on the left'. That hurt, because she thought she was looking better these days. What astonished and infuriated her was when he said, a few minutes later, and in front of the whole company, that she couldn't dance. Well, the way he put it was, 'I'm afraid your dancing isn't up to the level we require, Miss Wallace.'

Well, fuck him! A bit of a scene followed when Dorothy Ann told him what she thought of him and his opinions, to the astonishment of the rest of the company. She'd barely made it out of the studio before the tears started down her cheeks. Damn him all to hell, he could say what he wanted about her looks. Nobody, but nobody had ever faulted her on her dancing!

That afternoon proved the turning point in Dorothy Ann Wallace's first New York experience, and she was back in her hometown of Royal Oak, Michigan by the end of the month. Within a year she'd married a nice Lebanese boy from the Detroit area, Gabe Nadeem, and he was the one who'd started calling her Dorann.

Dorann talked Gabe into moving to Los Angeles before their first anniversary, and she started getting some work as a dance teacher and choreographer's assistant, particularly in music videos. She also started taking advantage of the Los Angeles medical establishment, one that paid more than the usual attention to the cosmetic aspect of life, and before she was through, she'd had it all done: her teeth straightened and bleached, her skin sanded, her tits implanted, her butt lifted, her cheekbones augmented, and her hair dyed a deep golden brown. It took over six years, and along the way she lost Gabe to an old girlfriend back in Michigan, but by the time she was twenty-seven, not even Duran (as she now spelled it) Nadeem could see Dorothy Ann Wallace when she looked in the mirror.

By the time her transformation was complete, Duran was in demand for her video work, and she had progressed to full-fledged choreographer in her own right. That's one of the things that amused her when Gil Richardson came knocking on her door –figuratively – last fall, when he was putting *Reunion* together out in California. *Reunion* called for a lot of dances contemporary to the late Sixties and the Seventies, and most classically trained dancers and choreographers looked stupid trying to design with or dance to pop music. Duran's strength was that she was not only classically trained; she'd been choreographing to pop music for years now.

Gil Richardson had seemed pleased with her background and with her work, but there was a nasty buzz when her hiring was announced. The theatre purists were alarmed. Those are the people who believe that if you've done work with a camera in front of you, it's the equivalent of spitting on Mother Teresa or something. And music videos! MTV! Horrors! What was the theatre world coming to!

As much of a bastard as Gil Richardson had been to her that day almost ten years ago, she had to admit she'd learned a lot working with him. Damn, the guy was good. The best she'd ever been around.

For weeks now, she'd been planning how she was going to tell him who she was. And then somebody had to go and spoil it by telling him. She had no doubt that's how it happened. Somebody told him. He'd never have recognized her. She had wondered if he'd even remember her, except that she was sure not many nineteen-year-old dancers told off Tony-winning directors.

What surprised her was how pissed off he was when she went to see him after he tossed those words out to her. 'Don't think I don't know who you are.' No, he hadn't been just pissed off in his dressing room. Gil Richardson had been acting crazy.

CHAPTER ELEVEN

Jonathan Humphries stood in the stage door, and turned his head first one way, to watch the coroner's wagon that held Gil Richardson's body as it disappeared south on Broadway, and then the other way to watch Simon Wexler cross Broadway, heading west on 14th Street. As he watched, a sense of unreality overwhelmed him. He felt as though he'd been hit over the head with a croquet mallet.

Gil Richardson was dead. *Reunion* might be in jeopardy. Dear God, what was he going to do!?

Reunion was his big step as a producer, the one that was going to make his name. The show that would announce that Jonathan Humphries was in the game to stay. The show that Simon Wexler had just convinced him to pump an extra two hundred and fifty thousand dollars into. Two hundred and fifty thousand that came out of his brother Paul's trust. Oh, God.

It had been risky when he took the money out to begin with. Nothing was a sure-fire investment in the theatre, although he felt as good about *Reunion* as he'd ever felt about anything. But even if *Reunion* opened and wasn't a huge hit, he'd have a while to replace the money in the trust fund. The next review of the family's finances wouldn't be until next January 15th, as it was every year, which gave him almost eight months to replace the money. But if *Reunion* folded, his mother would insist on reviewing the finances of it immediately – as she always did when there was a chance to rub Jonathan's nose in anything, and his father would go along with his wife the way he always went along with everything she asked, or said, or did. And then it would come out that not only had Jonathan lost his money, he'd lost two hundred and fifty thousand out of the sacred Paul Humphries Trust.

Actually, it was now the Paul and Jonathan Humphries Trust, it had been since Paul died twelve years ago, and Jonathan had every right to the money that was in there. But his mother had made it clear over and over again when she referred to it always as Paul's Trust, that she considered it Jonathan's only secondarily.

Jonathan had come in second in everything in life, according to Genevieve Barstow Humphries, and not just in birth order. He had wondered from the time he was old enough to think about such things, if she'd even wanted to have a second child after the sainted Paul was born. It was, after all, four years before he came along.

Four years was a dreadful span of time to occur between the brothers. It was far enough apart that they were never really pals, but close enough that Jonathan was always just starting out on experiences that Paul had just finished. He'd first noticed it at camp. They'd both gone to a private school in New York until they were thirteen, so camp was their first experience of travelling without their parents.

The first camp Jonathan went to, Paul had gone to three years previous while little Jonathan was in day camp in Manhattan. The camp counsellors all referred to him as Paul's little brother. His mother's words to him on seeing him off were, 'Maybe if you try hard you'll do as well as Paul did in the water sports, Jon.'

When it was time to go to boarding school, he went to the same one Paul had just graduated from, where he was also known as Humphries' little brother. His mother and then his teachers had sternly reminded him of the family honour he had to uphold, since Paul had won honours in history and medals in debating, and had been designated a National Merit Scholar.

He was sure it would have been the same in college, except he refused to go to Dartmouth and elected to go to Yale instead, much to his mother's horror. It was one of the few times, if not the only time, he could remember his father standing up for him.

Paul had backed him up, too, on the choice of college. Jonathan and Paul had actually gotten along pretty well, and might have had a genuinely good relationship if they'd lived about a thousand miles from their mother.

But then Paul had the bad taste to get himself killed in a car wreck at the age of twenty-three, just before his last year of law school. It was a tragedy – all the more so because Paul was driving drunk and had wrapped himself and his sports car around a tree on the Saw Mill River Parkway. The only good news was that the crash had occurred at two-thirty one Labor Day morning when the road was virtually empty, and Paul hadn't killed anybody else.

The fact that Paul was drunk had never been mentioned in his parents' home after the initial visit from the police. Jonathan had tried to mention it once, and gotten his face slapped by his mother. It was the first time she'd touched him since his confirmation day when he was twelve.

Paul was idealized in death way beyond what he was in life, and the word 'remember' had turned into one of the tyrannies of Jonathan's life. 'Remember how well Paul used to dive?' his mother had said at dinner the night Jonathan came home from Yale in his senior year, having led the Yale swim team to an inter-mural championship. Jonathan was a champion swimmer, but had never really learned to dive. Paul, of course, had done both.

'Remember Paul's valedictory address?' his mother had said when they were posing for snapshots at his graduation. Jonathan had graduated with honours, but Paul had been valedictorian at Dartmouth.

When he'd finished his MBA at Wharton, and been recruited by one of New York's most prestigious investment banking firms, he thought certainly the ghost of Paul would be put behind him. Until a night not quite three years ago, when he and his colleagues were celebrating the coup of bringing two rival computer firms together that had created a new hardware and software giant in the industry. It was a bold and insightful move, one that had made Jonathan a millionaire in his own right at the age of twenty-eight. The night after the deal was announced, at the hastily arranged celebration at The Plaza that he and his colleagues had arranged for friends and family, he was bringing another bottle of champagne to his parents' table to refresh their glasses when he heard his mother say to his father, 'Just imagine if Paul had had these opportunities.'

Jonathan felt the air being sucked out of his lungs, but at least he had managed to set down the full bottle of champagne instead of dropping it.

He'd realized after that night that it was pointless to try to compete in any endeavour that Paul might have possibly been interested in, which pretty much eliminated most ways a young man of his background and education could make a living in New York. He decided he'd stay in investment banking, where he had done very well, and on the side, he'd just go ahead and do what interested him.

That was how he'd gotten into theatrical investments. He'd loved the theatre since he was a kid. It was one of the few things he got to do on his own with his father, because Paul, like his mother, didn't care for the theatre that much. He'd been lucky with his first few investments; small shares in modest shows. His fourth show tanked completely, but even that experience he considered a worthwhile lesson; the guy producing it was a flake, and Jonathan had sensed that from the beginning but hadn't acted on it. After that fiasco, he was as careful about assessing the producer as he was about assessing the project, which is how he got involved with *Reunion* when Simon Wexler did.

Wexler had taken him under his wing, promising him a virtual apprenticeship in producing. 'I tell you kid,' Simon had said to him. 'It's not because you're a Park Avenue type I want you in on this; in fact, it's in spite of that. But you remind me of myself when I was your age and I only wish I'd taken the plunge like you're taking. You come in with me and I'll make a producer out of you.'

He thought he'd finally buried the ghost of his brother Paul after the Plaza fiasco, but last week, after one of Simon's pep talks about how wonderful things were going to be once *Reunion* opened, Jonathan was surprised to recognize the thought that raced through his mind: after *Reunion* opened, he finally wouldn't have to hear about how much better Paul would have done it, because Paul would never have attempted any such thing. Jonathan wouldn't be 'the second of the Humphries boys' any more.

Now if he could just be sure they'd get the show open. He hadn't been able to read the expression on Simon's face when he'd asked him what Gil Richardson's death would mean. Simon had just . . .

Damn! he promised Simon he'd call Joan Byers. He glanced at his watch. He should still be able to catch her before her dinner party got underway.

CHAPTER TWELVE

Joan Henley Byers set the phone back down in its cradle and stared at it. Gil Richardson was dead. Murdered, it sounded like. What was the world coming to?

She heard the front door bell ring, but she knew Andrew would take care of her first guests while she collected her thoughts. And that was going to take a few minutes, because this was very big news.

Not just because of her investment, although that would be something to think about later. No, because Gil Richardson had been a cornerstone of the theatre in New York for over twenty years, and now, in the course of a few minutes, he was gone. That was a tragedy for the theatre.

And it would be sad if *Reunion* didn't make it because of this. Richardson had worked his magic with this show, and it was going to be a big one. She was certain of that. She knew that most people, even some of the producers she had invested with, regarded her as a dilettante; a 'rich, fat broad with too much time on her hands' to quote the description one had given of her when he didn't know she was eavesdropping. But she'd developed her instincts over the years. She started out thinking of herself as a patron of the arts; now she thought of herself as a business woman. When it came to judging a show, she knew what to look for.

She knew what to look for in a few other situations, too. For example, the situation in which she presently found herself, with her husband *shtupping* the lead actress, that Rhonda whatever-her-name was. Until Jonathan's phone call, she thought this was going to be her biggest problem with *Reunion*. The damn fool hadn't even been smart about covering his tracks.

She hadn't been lucky in marriage – any of them. When she'd graduated from Wellesley twenty-three years ago, she wished she'd been like the more independent thinkers of her classmates and stayed single for a long time. Instead, her parents had shepherded her into a marriage within two years, to one Timothy Cronin, deemed by her parents and the society pages to be A Prize Catch. Actually that hadn't been a bad marriage; she and Timmy gave one another lots of room, to use one of the popular phrases of that time, although he made different use of his than she did of hers. The marriage had lasted seven years, until a few months after she'd turned thirty. She would still be married to Timmy if he hadn't been caught by his best friend Ed Gruber *in flagrante delicto* with Gruber's wife Elizabeth in the master bedroom of the Gruber's summer place out at Quogue. Circumstances – and her parents – really required that Joan file for divorce.

The trauma of that divorce was that it was the first recorded in her family's history, if one was to believe her mother. The good news was that she got quite a settlement from Timmy. The bad news was that most of that settlement went to pay off her second husband, Fernando, the fitness instructor she met at the spa where she went to try and get rid of the thirty pounds she'd put on while living through the embarrassment of what the gossip columns called 'the Park Avenue Double Divorce Scandal'.

Fernando had been a sweetheart, and it wasn't until they had whittled the thirty-plus pounds off her body that Joan realized they had absolutely nothing else to talk about. Although Fernando's command of English wasn't too great once the conversation diverged from physical fitness topics, he was bright enough to get himself a good lawyer, and that was how Joan ended up paying most of Timmy's settlement out to Fernando, much to her mother's horror.

After the Fernando fiasco, Joan had sworn off marriage, and concentrated on her fund-raising work for the various charities and public causes her family had always supported. She also decided to personally supervise her own investments.

Investments were how she met Gregory Byers, who was assigned to her account at the brokerage house when the old gentleman who had handled the Henley family's account for years up and died unexpectedly. The firm had assigned a senior officer and two younger staff members to learn the holdings and to supervise the account. Gregory was one of those younger staffers, and he and Joan ended up spending a lot of time together.

Joan found Gregory charming. He seemed to find her witty and smart, and she was a sucker for anybody who thought highly of her. Joan didn't bring a lot of passion to the marriage. She had never been a particularly passionate woman, except for those early days with Fernando, down at the spa.

She wasn't quite forty when she married Gregory four years ago, but she'd smartened up considerably. There was a detailed pre-nuptial agreement this time. Not that it would do her any good. The first divorce was bad enough. The second was less traumatic, perhaps, but still a major embarrassment, despite her best efforts to keep both the marriage and the divorce out of the papers. She'd realized weeks ago, when she first got the drift that Gregory was screwing around on her, that a third divorce was simply not an option.

With a slow smile she thought of the other possibility that had occurred to her. After all, there were various solutions to this particular problem. And she wouldn't mind being a widow. Now *there* was a role she could play.

CHAPTER THIRTEEN

Gregory Byers tried to peel Rhonda Deveraux off his body, but damn! the woman was like a cat. Her mouth and hands and legs and hips seemed to have suction cups built into them. It wasn't until after he'd gotten to know Rhonda – and after that, gotten to 'know' her in the biblical sense – that he understood how certain women came to be called sex kittens. She certainly could cling like one.

He tried to come up for air once more but he only got a quick gasp in before her mouth covered his again. The woman was insatiable.

'Please, baby, please,' she moaned in a low whisper, as she reached for the knot in his tie, 'don't leave me like this.'

Eyes wide open, Gregory stole a glance at his watch when he could get his wrist into sight. Seven forty-five! Great. He had exactly fifteen minutes to get out of here, catch a cab uptown, and change before Joan's dinner party. He wasn't going to make it.

'Rhonda, please, Rhonda,' he said, pulling his lips away from hers and arching his neck so she couldn't get to them anymore. She started kissing his neck instead. 'I've got to go, Rhonda.'

As though a switch had been turned off, Rhonda stopped. She stood back from him with a fire in her eye.

'You're not kidding, are you?' He shook his head. 'You're really going to leave me like this?'

Gregory wasn't sure what the 'like this' meant. Having to answer questions from the police? Because she'd looked at him to help her answer the simplest of questions when the detectives had first come around. Scared? Because she was afraid someone had overheard their showdown with Richardson? Horny? Because even for a woman with a voracious appetite, he'd never seen Rhonda quite this eager.

Of course, his history with Rhonda wasn't extensive, but it had been three weeks now. And what a three weeks it had been. He had never been around a woman like Rhonda. He didn't think they existed, except maybe in the pages of *Penthouse* magazine with those letters that everybody thought were made up. But this woman was a sexual athlete of world-class standing. In the Olympics, she'd be a gold medalist. A multiple gold medalist.

She wanted him any place, any time. In the last three weeks, they'd done it not only in her dressing room (on the floor, on the counter, and, his least favourite, on the sticky leatherette couch) but also in the back of a taxi, and the kitchen of the small apartment she'd sublet on East 20th Street. By the time they actually had sex in her bed it seemed almost too easy or too dull for her. A little bit of the thrill was gone for Rhonda when the situation was ordinary. The only way she could make up the difference was in volume, and that first time, he thought she'd kill him. She'd even tried to get him going once in a restaurant, but that was a little too adventurous even for him.

Gregory finally extricated himself from her embrace by promising that he'd see her in the morning. This was the way his schedule had been lately: he'd leave the apartment, telling Joan he had a breakfast meeting with clients, or early meetings at the office, and he'd stop at Rhonda's for a quickie. Then he'd try to concentrate on work for the day, but that was becoming a challenge. He'd leave just in time to make it to the theatre by six when rehearsals broke, coming up with some business excuse – papers to sign, to set an appointment with Jonathan – and after the company had dispersed, he'd sneak in to meet Rhonda in her dressing room. He couldn't believe this craziness – and he didn't know how much longer he'd be able to keep it up. Literally or figuratively.

Thank God Joan hadn't found out. He'd never given her cause to question him before, and he was grateful now at all the temptations he'd passed up in the last few years. It's amazing how many women throw themselves at wealthy men. Or men they think are wealthy. He'd had a few chances even with some of Joan's 'friends', but he'd never tell her that.

He genuinely liked Joan. She was a good woman, and the marriage was everything he'd thought it would be, everything his father had prepared him for. Going back twenty years, when he was just starting college, his father had reminded him of two things: first, he was going to be the first Byers to graduate from college; second, he should keep his fly zipped and not make any stupid mistakes. His father had started coaching him from the time he was sixteen that it was just as easy to marry a rich woman as it was to marry a poor one, and that philosophy had directed much of young Gregory's life.

It had determined his major in college: business administration. It had determined his career path: he made sure to impress the recruiter from a large national consulting firm that offered to pay for employees' graduate work. And it had determined the job that he moved into once he'd finished his graduate work: the old money investment counselling firm that handled the Henley family's fortunes.

He'd been there only two years, and had made a good name for himself when he was selected as one of two younger associates to handle the Henley account. The day Joan walked into the office, he knew his dream (and his father's) was about to come true.

It had been a campaign he'd waged, a subtle campaign, but within a year he was married into the Henley family, and living on Park Avenue, where his father always wanted him to live. And the marriage to Joan was okay, nothing less than he'd thought it would be. Sure, she'd let herself go a bit in the last few years, but that didn't really make any difference to him. He'd always had to give himself a pep talk before climbing into bed with Joan, even the first time.

He'd always been a man of controlled urges, because his father taught him that that was the way to get what you want in life. That's why this thing with Rhonda had taken him by surprise. He was thinking through his zipper for the first time in his life, and he was almost forty years old now.

He'd tried to explain it away. This thing with Rhonda was just a physical thing, he'd tell himself, an aberration, like a quick, high fever – and it would be over soon. That's what he'd promised himself And that's what he told Gil Richardson – or tried to tell him – the day before yesterday, when Richardson had found Rhonda riding him on the floor of her dressing room.

Less than twenty-four hours later, when he arrived at the theatre yesterday afternoon, Richardson called him into his dressing room to let him know that the details of that scene would be reported back to Joan – discreetly, of course, and with a great sense of shock and sadness, but reported back to his wife nevertheless – unless Gregory did exactly what the director told him to. The sonofabitch was blackmailing him.

He had to get out of here – now. Joan was expecting him. But first he had to go through a few things with Rhonda, so they wouldn't look quite so suspicious the next time the police came around to question them.

CHAPTER FOURTEEN

Rhonda was steaming as she threw her things into her black and white striped patent tote bag. She took a quick glance around her dressing room to make sure she had everything, and saw in the mirror that she still had a high colour to her face. The colour was from getting pissed off, not from passion. Those last few minutes Gregory had spent coaching her on what to say to the police, how she shouldn't look at him when they asked her a question, how she shouldn't talk about any of this to anybody – what was that all about? And couldn't he have told her all this stretched out on the couch?

She couldn't *believe* Gregory left her to go to his wife's damn dinner party. Didn't he know – couldn't he tell – that she needed him – *bad*? Well, it wasn't so much Gregory that she needed. But a man. She definitely needed a man. Any man. Sex was acknowledged by most people as one of the basic human needs, but for Rhonda it was a little higher up the scale than for most. Way ahead of food, for example.

Rhonda Deveraux first slept her way into a role in her sophomore year at Menomonee High back in Menomonee, Wisconsin. Of course, she was Ruth Dugan then. She'd started sleeping around – or, in the current term, 'became sexually active' – when she was fourteen, and she discovered that she enjoyed it a lot. And she didn't have to go through too many boys before she found out she could use it to her advantage.

The Menomonee High Combined Drama and Glee Clubs were putting on their yearly spring production. That year it was going to be *Bye Bye Birdie*, and Ruth really wanted the role of Kim. It wasn't the lead, but it was the ingenue role, and there were a couple of songs she knew she could put across. So she decided to put out.

It was the custom at Menomonee High that the lead roles would go to seniors, if possible, so Ruth knew it was going to be a hard sell. So she managed to convince Mr Schultz, the new English teacher who was doubling as the drama coach and play director, that she would need some guidance to prepare for the auditions. She met Mr Schultz in his office very late afternoon of the Thursday before auditions, and set a record by seducing the twenty-five-year-old Mr Schultz within twenty minutes. The part was hers when the casting was announced on Tuesday.

That afternoon was the first time Ruth had ever done it on a desk, and that was still one of her favourite locations. In fact, the whole episode was still a fond memory for her. Too bad it had been a long time since she'd been involved with anybody who had a desk, at least a desk in a private location.

As it turned out, Ruth was wonderful in the role of Kim. She was head and shoulders above the rest of the cast, and Ruth's mother heard murmurs at intermission about how 'that girl was a star'. Certainly no one found fault with Mr Schultz's casting decision.

Mr Schultz, however, once he had come out of his post-coital daze, could scarcely look himself in the mirror. He always expected to see the Menomonee County Sheriff behind him when he looked over his shoulder, and he was unable to make eye contact with Ruth Dugan for the rest of the semester. Mr Schultz unexpectedly resigned over the summer, still wondering what a jury's decision would have been if people knew *exactly* what had gone on in his office that afternoon.

Too bad he didn't leave a note for his successor, for Ruth used the same approach – with the same end effect – on the next two drama coaches, and ended up playing Laurie in *Oklahoma!* and The Girl in *The Fantasticks*. By the time she got to college, she decided she preferred this way of winning a role. In some odd way, she always felt more confident that a role was really 'hers' if she'd earned it that way. Of course, once she got to the university level and began running into more gay men in the decision-making capacities, her tactics weren't of too much help. But she'd left college after three years, when she was understudying the role of Aldonza in a summer tour production of *Man of La Mancha* that was very well reviewed. The tour extended into the fall, the woman playing Aldonza bowed out after Labor Day, and Ruth found herself actually starring in a first class road show, and getting her Equity card besides.

It was when she went for the Equity card that she changed her name. She'd never cared for the sound of Ruth Dugan, anyway. Two short syllables, both concentrating on the same vowel. She decided that the name of Rhonda Deveraux, one of the many stage names she'd dreamt up over the last few years, had all the elements she required: it sounded glamorous, it sort of rolled off the tongue, and it would look good on a marquee. She'd been Rhonda for five years now, and if her instincts were right, after this show opened, she'd be using that autograph she'd been practising for the last five years.

Maybe she should go back and say *if* instead of *after* the show opened. She couldn't believe this, Gil Richardson dead.

He was an odd one. A real talented man, that she could tell from the months she'd worked with him, but odd. Their conversations in the last few days had been just as businesslike and just as impersonal as the conversations they'd had after the first rehearsals back last fall. At least the conversations before he'd found her on top of Gregory.

She'd come on to Richardson like gangbusters, but he didn't give her a second glance. Her first reaction was that he was gay, of course, but then he didn't give off any gay vibrations either. One of the dancers described Richardson as being *a-sexual*, which was a concept that absolutely gave Rhonda the creeps. How could somebody live being *a-sexual?* She had trouble when she was *a-sexual* for a couple of days. And especially after any kind of emotional crisis, like they'd all been through this afternoon, she needed it bad.

Rhonda lifted the strap of the tote bag onto her shoulder and set out down the hall past the other dressing rooms, wondering if Curtis was still around. Hell, that proved how horny she was: she even gave a passing thought to fucking the old guy tonight.

CHAPTER FIFTEEN

After bidding his farewell to Gil Richardson, Curtis Leland walked back to his dressing room, the third one in the row. Once inside, he quietly reached for the large canvas bag he always carried to rehearsals, and found at the bottom the silver flask he also carried to rehearsals. Unscrewing the top, he took a good long swig of the brandy.

Aaaah. Nothing like it to take the chill off your bones of a damp evening, or to chase the chill from your heart when you've seen a good man die too young.

Once more Curtis was struck by how life's real dramas can exceed those on-stage. Who would believe that this talented young man, so vibrant, so full of ideas, would be found dead backstage in this sparkling new theatre, and that lovely Sylvie would be the suspect? Another swig of brandy helped him focus on the question.

He was hard-pressed to believe Sylvie actually killed the man. True, she was a bit brassy, and a bit full of herself. That was hardly reason to suspect her of murder; she was a New Yorker, after all. A certain brassy boldness was to be expected. And the young woman was a professional, that was certain. She was a damn good actress.

One thing was for certain: whoever killed Gil Richardson had killed the best patron Curtis Leland had ever had. He would be forever grateful to Gil, the man who 'discovered' him at the age of sixty. Curtis was doing a second lead in a new play at The Actor's Theatre in Louisville when Richardson came to the show, and he knew himself lucky to be doing that. For too much of the last twenty years, he'd suffered the usual actor's frustration of not being allowed to act. The play, it turned out, was better on paper than on the stage, but Richardson had made a point of coming to see him backstage, and promised he'd remember Curtis when the right thing came along. Curtis didn't want to remember how many times he had heard that before, but took Richardson's offered card with thanks.

When he got the call last summer to come to audition for *Reunion*, he was astounded when Richardson seemed to recall his performance in its totality. It had been over three years since they'd had that brief exchange. He was devastated when he didn't get the role of The Professor after that first round of auditions, devastated in a way he hadn't allowed himself to be in years. But he knew *Reunion* had the potential to be the most commercially successful thing he'd ever been involved with, and it was about damn time he started thinking commercially. Or so his ex-wife said. Of course, she'd said that fifteen years ago, the day she'd walked out, along with the fact that she was sick of living with someone who observed life rather than lived it. It took Curtis a while to realize that she was right: he did live his life on the stage. 'Real life' for him was a chance to scrutinize behaviour, detect nuances in character or speech or manner, all toward using those details in his creations on stage, where his real life existed. When he faced up to that realization, he decided it wasn't fair to involve anyone else in that enterprise, and he never married again. The theatre was his only love.

124

Curtis couldn't remember a show he'd loved as much as *Reunion*. From the first round of rehearsals, the stint in California, even when it got tense out there when a few people got fired after Wexler took the show on, he'd loved it. He'd even loved the touring.

But the last week, maybe the last ten days, it had been an unhealthy kind of tense. The edginess of the producers had been evident for a while and seemed to be getting worse; in fact, Curtis was keeping his fingers crossed that the show was going to make it to opening. It had been evident, too, that Gil Richardson was just not himself, or that was the only explanation that Curtis could come up with for the director's noticeable temperament over the last few weeks. Perhaps that dreaded cold that had been plaguing the company had been settling in more heavily on Richardson. So many members of the company had been battling it.

Although perhaps there were other explanations for Gil's snappish behaviour of late, Curtis mused as he took another sip. It was obvious that he and Ben Wheeler weren't getting along. That was too bad. Two talented young men. Their talents would be very complementary if they would just allow them to be. The animosity between them had become noticeable only in the last few weeks, and had grown markedly, and the tension that it generated filtered throughout the company.

And of course there was Goldman, that dreadful union man. His habit of waylaying people moving in and out and around the theatre had everyone jumping at shadows. Just this afternoon, when Curtis had tried to take advantage of their overdue break and get to the men's room, the fool had blocked his way down the hall! He admired Goldman's stick-to-it-iveness, but did the man have to be chasing people down hallways? Especially when they were on their way to the toilet? Devotion to the union cause was one thing, but obsession was another.

Of course, he could say that, since the actors' union had made peace with the producers a while ago. Or at least they had agreed to make peace. Curtis didn't know what he would have done if it was his union that was left out in the cold. This was the best role he'd ever had in his life, and there was a lot he would have forgone to keep it. And that was at the heart of the union movement, wasn't it, giving up individual gain for the good of all. One for all and all for one, wasn't that the point? And isn't that what didn't exist any more?

CHAPTER SIXTEEN

Howard Goldman was sweating as he hurried down the steps into the subway station on Seventh Avenue and 14th Street. His walk across 14th from Union Square had been at too fast a pace for a man his age; fortunately, because of the dampness of the evening, no one noticed the beads of perspiration on his brow.

His breathing was accelerated, too, and he tried to catch his breath. Before, he used to be able to take the shuttle train across 14th when he was in the Union Square neighbourhood. Now, with the station still in the confusion of reconstruction, he had to walk clear across to Seventh Avenue.

He waited only four minutes by his watch before the uptown express train came along. The first few cars were practically empty, and he took one of the double end seats to himself and settled in for his ride to 96th Street. By the time he had to walk up those stairs, his sixty-eight-year-old heart should be back to its normal rhythm. If only he could stop thinking about the scene at the theatre, since that only made his heart start pounding more.

He wanted to curse when he thought of the reaction of those people to Gil Richardson's death, pretending it was a greater tragedy when an important man died. What bullshit! Every death is a tragedy!

That was the problem with society these days. Everybody was so interested in celebrities, all the magazines and newspapers drowning people in details of celebrity lives, how they looked, what they wore, what they ate. It was all bullshit, and it corroded the brain. Nobody seemed interested in the little man any more, nobody cared about what real people in their neighbourhoods were doing, unless it showed up on the eleven o'clock news. In some ludicrous way, things only became real to people these days if they saw them on television. What kind of world was that? When people gather together to sit in a room and watch a box. Or worse, sit alone in a room and type a message to people thousands of miles away and think that's communicating.

Nobody gave a damn about the guy next door any more. All anybody wanted to know about was talk shows and cyberspace and, while they're talking about all this nonsense, nobody noticed that sweatshops were making a comeback.

It pained him to think it, but there was absolutely no sense of community any more; he was sure people didn't even know what it meant. It was a worry that ate away at him, because a sense of community was at the heart of the union movement. If things kept going the way they were, the union movement was quickly going to be a thing of the past.

That, Howard found hard to believe. Howard was a child of the union movement, literally. His mother had been a garment worker in the Twenties, and his father was one of the union organizers combing the Lower East Side for recruits. When Simon Goldman wooed Edda Rothstein, it was for more than union membership. Howard, their only child, was raised on the glorious tales of how the union movement would transform American society. Ordinary workers would be entitled to fair wages, decent working conditions, security in a job well done, and they would build an even better future for their children.

And, in a way, that's what happened. The workers that his father had gone to stand shoulder-to-shoulder with in Flint and Chicago in 1937 had finally, bloodily, won the right to unionize. Ten years later, in the booming post-war economy, Howard graduated from City College of New York, and when he announced to his classmates that he was going to work for the unions, he received their congratulations all around; that was a great job, after all. The union movement grew in the late Forties and through the Fifties beyond even his parents' dreams.

For a while it looked like the next generation of union membership was guaranteed. But as those workers of the Forties and Fifties became more prosperous and provided that better life for their children, those children didn't connect the security of their own futures with the union movement. Their futures were in better education, white-collar work, houses in the suburbs, vacations in Florida. In other words, management. In a generation and a half, the union movement had spawned its own generation of management.

That wasn't the only change, of course. The bulging union rolls of the time had meant bulging union coffers. And there were union leaders who didn't even think of resisting the temptation. Howard's own father had been one of the first to spot the coming trouble, back in 1953, when he saw newspaper pictures of union leaders playing golf with the management of two of New York's largest shipping companies. He'd thrown the newspaper in front of Howard, disgusted. 'Playing golf! At three o'clock in the afternoon! Do they know what their union members are doing at three o'clock in the afternoon? Working! That's what!'

So it had gradually unfolded. Corrupt union heads, dwindling industries, fewer jobs, a president who turned out to be a union breaker. The last twenty years had been hard ones, and Howard was glad his father hadn't lived to see them.

That was why this theatre contract was so important. The theatre unions were still alive, still vibrant, and this Century Theatre was going to attract a lot of attention when it opened. That's why he couldn't lose this one. That's why the union council had put him on the job when the relationship between Wexler and the representative from the Technicians' Union had become so acrimonious as to be unworkable.

Howard checked out the window to see what station they were pulling into. Good. 72nd Street. Only one more stop.

He thought again of the dead man. Gil Richardson was a talented man of the theatre and his talents would be missed. But Richardson himself wouldn't be – not by Howard Goldman. For in all these discussions, all the meetings, all the arguments he'd had over the Century Theatre and this new production, Richardson had professed to be neutral. As much as Howard could work up a fiery passion against an enemy like Simon Wexler, a man he considered a ruthless exploiter of people, his passion turned to an icy hatred for someone feigning impartiality. Especially someone like Gil Richardson, whose own life and career had thrived in the unions. His loathing of the man had become almost a physical repulsion.

Still, tonight he was as close to a dead body as he'd ever

been in his life, and he was shaken. Amazing how the touch, the feel, the look of human skin changed so quickly when there was no longer a pulse beating underneath it. There was no doubt that a life had passed.

The training Edda Goldman had given her son was deeply rooted, and respect for the dead was one of the things his mother had reminded him of on a regular basis. In spite of himself, in spite of what he thought and felt about Gil Richardson, in spite of what had transpired between them, respect for the dead was necessary. As the train pulled out of 72nd Street and headed into the dark tunnel, Howard Goldman started to whisper the words of the Kaddish.

CHAPTER SEVENTEEN

When Mac stepped into the street to hail a south-bound cab, the man Sylvie had pointed out to her as Max Osgood, the show's press agent, approached her and introduced himself with a firm handshake that had a considerable pump to it. 'Didn't mean to out and out eavesdrop, but did I hear the lieutenant say you were going downtown?'

Mackenzie dropped her arm when she saw a cab pulling away from the 14th Street light toward her. 'That's right.'

'Mind if we share the cab? I'll even pay the fare,' he said with a quick smile that even he knew was lame. 'It's just that I have absolutely no idea where we're going.'

'Sure,' Mackenzie said, and got into the back seat, sliding across as best she could with her slicker on. She leaned forward to speak around the protective barrier to give the cab driver their destination, and leaned back, staring out the window at the still-shiny streets.

The young press agent wasn't going to let her stare in silence, however. 'Who was it who said be careful what you wish for?' he asked as they headed down Broadway.

Mac turned to him, surprised at the question. 'I'm not sure it's an attributable quote. I think it falls under the category of folk wisdom.'

'Well, whoever came up with it, it's true,' Osgood tilted

his head knowingly. 'Just today, I was telling this friend of mine at one of the big agencies how tired I was of coming up with these asinine ghost stories just to keep something in the papers, otherwise all of the attention would be on the union trying to stick it to Simon.' He was patting his raincoat pocket, and then reaching inside for the pocket of his suit jacket. 'Ghost stories or union strife – great range of stories, hunh?' He never paused for a response; Mackenzie imagined that he rarely did.

'Anyway, I said to my friend, all these great press clips and reviews that I have on the show are all from out of town, and New Yorkers don't want to read about out of town. It just doesn't exist, I tell you. In the Big Apple, you tell people you got great reviews out of town, you might as well tell them you got great reviews on *Neptune*. They don't wanna hear about it!' In his inside jacket pocket, Osgood finally found a small plastic bottle of Rolaids, and sighed with relief. He offered Mac one as though they were candy, and when she declined, he popped a few into his mouth. Mac turned toward the window again, hoping the antacids would keep him quiet for a few minutes.

'Except London, of course,' Osgood started in again, talking around his tablets. 'New Yorkers still look to London about theatre, but that's basically it.'

Mac turned to him with a half-raise of the eyebrow, hoping that her expression wouldn't convey too much interest in his monologue. If this was his style when he had a non-responsive audience, what would this man do if he was actually encouraged to talk?

Osgood kept on. 'Foolish me, I thought things would get easier once they came into New York for the final rehearsals. I imagined great stories about the first theatre opening in New York in a dog's age, clips about the show, but then this union flap happened, and the press always goes where the controversy is, doncha know?' Mac now had a good idea of where the rhyme for Rhonda Deveraux's name had started.

'And wait till they get a load of this,' Osgood said as the cab started slowing. 'Oh, God, they're here already!' The bright lights of a few television mini-cameras were already evident in front of the police headquarters building.

Mackenzie started to get out of the taxi. Osgood paid the driver and stepped out beside her. 'Just this morning, I said I'd give my right arm – anything – not to have to field another story about the union crap. I swear to God, I didn't mean murder.' He looked over at the clutch of reporters. 'Like they say, be careful what you wish for.'

Mac headed away from the press, but as she walked around, she could see that a reporter from the local all-news channel was doing a live report and a CNN reporter seemed to be setting up to tape a report as well. It seemed that Gil Richardson was going to be making headline news again.

As she was working her way to the main door, Mackenzie blinked her eyes when she saw Irwin Steinberg himself getting out of a town car and heading toward her, briefcase in hand, and her heart sank. Her earlier assessment hadn't changed. As well known and apparently well respected (or feared) as Irwin was in the entertainment industry, he was not the first lawyer one would call if they were in trouble in a criminal matter. Irwin probably wasn't the one-thousandth and first, either.

But he was here, and from the way he was walking toward her, he was pumped with adrenaline.

'Dr Mackenzie,' he greeted her with an outstretched hand. 'I mean Mackenzie.' Irwin made that mistake all the time, thinking that Mackenzie was her last name. 'How are you?'

'Hello, Irwin. Thanks for coming down,' Mackenzie said returning the handshake and glancing as casually as she could toward the car hoping someone else had gotten out on the other side. Someone else like a criminal lawyer.

'Peter tells me a friend of yours might be in some trouble here,' Irwin said, rubbing his hands. 'So what've we got?'

'Well, Gil Richardson is dead—'

'—the director, right? The director of the show your friend is in?' Irwin interrupted.

Mackenzie nodded. 'Yes. And they're questioning Sylvie Morgan.'

'She's the friend of yours?'

'Right.'

'How long have you known her?'

'Sixteen years.' Was it that long? Mackenzie thought to herself. Yes, it was.

'Think she did it?'

'Absolutely not.'

Irwin smiled at Mac and nodded approvingly. Friends like this you wanted on your side. 'Okay. Let's get inside and see her,' he said, taking her elbow to usher her inside.

As they neared the large doors, Irwin turned to the now somewhat larger crowd of photographers and reporters. 'Hope to God they didn't bring her in past that mob.'

'There is – or at least there used to be – an entrance through the underground garage that will bring you up directly from the basement. I'm assuming they took her in there,' Mac answered.

As they headed for the main desk, Irwin said, 'Police headquarters! Jeez, this really gets the old blood pumping for a lawyer, let me tell you.' Mackenzie stole a glance at his expression, and Irwin seemed to be enjoying this a little too much.

It had been a few years since Mackenzie had had occasion to be at police headquarters, and they had to get directions that took them up elevators and down corridors before they found the interrogation room where Sylvie was being questioned. Sergeant Beckman was in the doorway, as they approached.

'Dr Griffin. The lieutenant said you'd probably be here. He called in a couple of minutes ago, and he said to tell you that he expects to be here within an hour. Any luck, forty-five minutes.'

'Thanks, Sergeant,' she said and indicated the room beyond. 'Are you heading in or out?'

'Out. I just got her some tea.'

'This is Irwin Steinberg, who'll be representing Sylvie just for tonight. Can I go in to introduce them?'

'Sure.'

Sylvie was sitting by herself at a long rectangular table, both hands surrounding a Styrofoam cup that sat on the table in front of her. She almost started to cry when she saw Mac again, but when she spotted Irwin she held off. Sylvie was not about to cry in the presence of a stranger.

Mac made the introductions and Irwin walked around the table to shake Sylvie's hand, then pulled out a chair for himself and sat down. Mac continued past the introductions with, 'Until other arrangements can be made, Irwin will be representing you at least for tonight.' Maybe if she repeated it enough, it would sink in.

'Okay,' said Sylvie in a small voice. 'Thank you for coming.'

'Okay, Miss Morgan, tell me, have you talked to anyone?'

Sylvie looked puzzled. 'What do you mean?'

'Have you talked to anyone since Mr Richardson's body was found?'

'Sure.'

'To whom?'

Sylvie looked into the distance and replied. 'I talked to Mackenzie, I talked to people in the company, I talked to the cops that came in—'

'You talked to the cops?' Irwin asked, immediately agitated.

'Sure.'

'You shouldn't have done that!'

This ticked Sylvie off. 'Well, maybe if I was a criminal, I would have known that, but I'm just a working actress, and when somebody walks in and finds Gil Richardson's body at my feet and asks me what happened, I tell them what happened!'

Mac was relieved by Sylvie's outburst. This was the Sylvie she was used to, not the teary-eyed pale imitation she'd seen when she first walked into the dressing room.

'Okay, okay, let's calm down here, a minute, Miss Morgan. May I call you Sylvie?'

Sylvie gave a quick nod of approval.

'Why don't you tell me what happened?'

'Irwin, before you start on that, I want to go and see what I can find out,' Mac interrupted. 'And do you think we need to be prepared for the possibility that a bail bond is going to be required?'

'I won't know until I hear her story and hear what the police have to say. Why?'

Mac looked at Sylvie. 'Am I right that you won't have the cash to come up with bail?'

Sylvie's eyes had widened at the mention of this subject. This was something she hadn't considered. She shook her

head and answered Mac. 'If we're talking anything over –
oh, six hundred dollars – yeah, you're right.'

'Am I also right that you don't want me calling your
mother to ask if she has the money?'

Her hands flattened out on the table, Sylvie leaned
toward her friend. 'No, Mackenzie, you absolutely can't do
that. Please,' she pleaded.

'Let me go make some calls,' Mackenzie said, 'and you
can tell Irwin what you told me.'

Out in the corridor, Mac leaned against the wall for a
moment just to think. She couldn't imagine that they would
actually arrest Sylvie, but it was better to be prepared. If her
memory served her right, only ten percent of a bond
needed to be in cash. That was the good news. Bad news
was that bail in a murder case was usually pretty high. The
good news was that Sylvie was an upstanding citizen, so
they probably wouldn't request a high bail. The bad news
was she was an actress, and theatre people still weren't
thought of as the souls of reliability. Good news, bad news.
Fifty fifty.

She headed down the corridor, and ran into Beckman
again, who pointed her toward the public phones. She
dialled her parents' home in Connecticut.

Hearing Sylvie's reply about six hundred dollars being
the extent of her savings had reminded Mac once again of
how extraordinary was the privilege in which she'd been
raised. Her parents were both academics, just as she had
become, and they both came from wealthy old Yankee
families. The Griffins – Mackenzie included – had had the
assurance of financial security since they were children, and
the freedom to pursue the careers of their hearts' and
minds' choosing as adults. Sylvie, too, had pursued the
career of her heart's choosing, but at the cost of arriving at

age thirty-four with six hundred dollars in the bank. Mac wondered if she would have had that kind of commitment.

Her father answered the phone on the third ring. 'Mackenzie! A pleasure to hear from you on this rainy night. How are you?'

'I'm well, Dad, but I'm calling on a serious matter.'

'Really?' her father replied, and she could tell he'd brought the phone closer to him, since the sound of his voice changed instantly. 'Are you sure you're all right?'

'Yes, Dad. It's my friend Sylvie. Sylvie Morgan. She's being questioned about the death of Gil Richardson, the theatre director.'

'Goodness! Your mother just told me she'd heard a news bulletin that Gil Richardson had died. Now what do you mean they're questioning your friend?'

Mackenzie decided not to go into all the details. 'They're not sure how he died.'

'But there's no evidence of foul play is there?'

'Well, it's all pretty murky, now, but I'm absolutely sure that Sylvie didn't have anything to do with his death.'

'And how is it that I can help you, dear?'

'I just wanted to let you know that I'm going to be moving some money from my trust account tomorrow. And it might be a great deal of money, maybe fifty thousand dollars,' Mac figured a worse-case scenario would get the bail up to a million dollars, 'or up to a hundred thousand, and I wanted to let you know, just in case that trust officer calls again.' A super-cautious new trust officer at the bank had gone on alert when Mac and her brother both withdrew funds from their trust accounts in January to invest in a friend's new fashion business.

'And what's the purpose of the money, Mackenzie?'

'I might have to use it to post bond for Sylvie.'

'I see,' he said and paused, but the silence was a thinking one. 'You know, I think I'll keep this just between the two of us, Mackenzie. No need to bother your mother with the details, as I see it.'

'That's probably a good idea, Dad,' Mackenzie said, smiling into the phone.

'So I'll call the bank in the morning to make sure Mr Cookson doesn't call here and get your mother on the phone by mistake,' Walker Griffin whispered softly into the phone.

'That's probably a good idea, too.'

'How is your friend?'

'Waiting right now for the decision on whether or not they're going to arrest her, so it's a bit tense.'

'Sylvie. She's that rather pert girl, isn't she? Didn't your mother and I see her in a few plays at the University?'

'Yes,' Mac said as she smiled to herself again, 'that's the one.' Not since she had stopped reading *Seventeen* magazine many years ago had she seen or heard the word 'pert' used. Only her father – and maybe her mother – could still summon up the term 'pert' to describe Sylvie.

'Why don't you give me a call tomorrow, Mackenzie, and let me know how things are working out. Will you do that for me?'

'Of course, Dad. And I'll be able to let you know, too, if I've had to move the money.'

'All right, dear. Good night, then.'

Mac stared at the phone for a few seconds before she replaced the receiver. She'd long ago realized her parents were unusual. In her early adolescent years, that fact had made her unhappy, and she wished her parents had fit in more. Into her adulthood she realized that she valued their differences. And after a conversation like this with her father, she realized she was just plain lucky. After all, she thought as she set down the receiver still smiling to herself, she not only had parents who were souls of stability, she had a 'pert' friend.

As she made her way back to the room where she'd left Sylvie and Irwin, she heard her name called out. She turned to see Mario Buratti approaching.

'Pretty good timing,' she said as she looked at her watch.

'Funny how a call from the mayor's office helps you cut to the front of the line,' he said with a knowing wink. 'This is gonna be good news for you, though for me it's a pain in the ass. We're not gonna be holding your friend. The Medical Examiner says that the preliminary examination indicates that Richardson was already dead when he was stabbed. The only evidence we got against Ms Morgan here are eyewitnesses who saw her holding a knife over Richardson's body, and her fingerprints on the knife handle, I presume, but if that knife didn't kill him, then we got nothing to hold her on,' Buratti shrugged his shoulders eloquently, and then dropped them. 'Unless we get around to enforcing some desecration of dead bodies statute or something.'

Mac looked at him, surprised by the news. 'So what did he die of, if he was already dead when he was stabbed?'

'Aw, hell, they don't know, Mac,' Buratti said, wearily, rubbing his face with the palms of his hands. 'They're just starting. And they'll have to go to the toxicological screenings which can take a good long time.'

'Any chance it was natural causes?' Mac asked.

'Let me see. A healthy dancing type, what? forty-eight, forty-nine years old, dead, found with a knife in his back. I don't think I want to try to sell this to the mayor's office as death by natural causes, aggravated by a knife in the back.'

'So what's next?'

'I'm gonna go in and tell your friend that she's free to go for tonight, and then we start in fresh tomorrow morning. I'll let you know.'

Buratti walked in, Mac following behind, and gave Sylvie the news that she was not going to be detained. She put her head on the table in relief, and Mac went to stand behind her. Irwin Steinberg introduced himself to Buratti, and was surprised (and a bit flattered) that the lieutenant remembered their brief meeting from almost two years before, during the investigation of the case that had brought Mac and Peter Rossellini together.

The briefly congenial atmosphere was changed when Buratti got into his warning that Sylvie should expect to be recalled for questioning.

'I was surprised to hear that she had been questioned this evening without benefit of counsel, Lieutenant. I'm informing Miss Morgan not to speak with any police officers again on this matter, unless she is accompanied by counsel.'

'That is her privilege,' Buratti said, and headed for the door. 'Talk to you tomorrow, Dr Griffin.'

Mackenzie acknowledged his request with a nod, and turned her attention back to Sylvie. 'Ready to leave?' she said.

'Am I ever,' Sylvie replied.

Mac moved to get Sylvie's coat for her, and looked over at Steinberg. 'Thanks for coming down, Irwin. I really appreciate it. I'm going to take Sylvie home now.'

Steinberg stepped around the table to join the two women. 'I've got the car service downstairs waiting. Peter told me that if I didn't see you home *personally,* I could count myself out of a client.'

'But I was going to get Sylvie home and settled in.'

'Mackenzie, you don't have to do that. I'm okay. Really I am,' Sylvie insisted.

'Then it won't take long, will it?' Mac replied with a firm tone. 'But I'm going to make sure you get home okay.' She looked at Irwin, thinking the matter had been solved.

'Then I'll wait,' he said. 'Why don't you let me go down first, and see if we can get the car to pull into that garage area you were talking about. I'm sure that crowd of press people has grown since we've been in here.'

'Good idea,' Mac said as they got into the hall. Buratti was still in the corridor, talking to Beckman, and they gave Irwin the information he needed.

After Beckman filled him in on a few details, Buratti was prepared to go face the cameras with the Deputy Commissioner for Press and Public Affairs. He was hoping that, once he briefed her, the Deputy Commissioner would take all the questions. The only thing Buratti was comfortable saying to the press was 'No comment.' But in a case like this – a famous director turning up dead backstage of his own production, and damn little to go on – 'No comment' wasn't going to cut it.

The traffic was light, but it had started to rain again. When they got to Sylvie's building on West 22nd Street, Mac again gave Irwin the chance to escape, but he said he'd wait for her. He had a few calls to make, anyway.

'Do you want me to stay with you?' Mac asked, once they got inside Sylvie's apartment.

'No, Mackenzie, of course not,' Sylvie said, immediately heading to the kitchen to put on water for some tea. 'I'll be fine. I'm not sick or anything like that. Just wrongfully accused, isn't that the phrase?'

'I know you don't want to hear this, but you have to call your mother,' Mac said quietly.

'No!'

'Sylvie . . .'

'What do I say, Mackenzie? "Hi, Ma, how are you? What was on the early bird special tonight? Oh by the way, I was taken in for questioning on a murder?" '

'You don't have to tell her about that,' Mackenzie said, getting a coaxing tone to her voice. 'But you do have to tell her about Gil Richardson's death. It's going to be all over the late news tonight, it's been on CNN already, and she'll wonder what's up. She knows you're in this show, that you've been in this man's company for four months now. So you better suck in your gut, call your mother, and be prepared to give a good performance on the phone.'

'Shit,' Sylvie said reluctantly. 'You're right.'

Mackenzie started for the door. 'Do you need anything else before I go?'

'No,' Sylvie said, and stopped her friend with the touch of her hand. 'And Mackenzie, I don't even know where to start, and I absolutely refuse to start crying again. So I'm just going to say a simple thank you. So – a simple thank you.'

Irwin Steinberg was talking on the cellular phone when Mackenzie emerged from Sylvie's building, and she was pretty sure he'd been on the phone the entire time she'd been upstairs. The joke around Irwin's office, according to Peter, was that when Irwin died, they'd have to have specially-trained undertakers to pry the phone out of his hand.

The brief trip to Mac's apartment made her nervous, since Irwin was telling her how he hadn't been on a criminal case since his first year out of law school eighteen years ago, and how good it felt to get the juices flowing again. Mac was horrified at the thought that Irwin might actually want to continue representing Sylvie.

Perhaps the direct approach would work best. 'Thanks, Irwin,' she said as she got out of the car. 'I really appreciate your coming down tonight. And I'll give you a call tomorrow to see what criminal lawyers you can recommend for Sylvie.'

CHAPTER EIGHTEEN

When Mackenzie unlocked the door to her apartment, she was surprised to see a light on. Then she saw the light was from her kitchen, straight ahead of her past the entrance hall, and Peter Rossellini was standing in the middle of it.

'You're here,' he said, surprised. 'That was a pretty quick trip.' When Mac reacted with a quizzical look, he finished. 'I meant from Sylvie's. Irwin was on the phone with me when you were walking out.'

Mac put her still damp but not dripping raincoat on the corner of the closet door and walked directly into Peter's embrace. He felt warm and dry, and, as she had noticed more and more over the last months, she felt safe in his arms. Not just physically safe, although there was that factor, but emotionally safe.

One of the moments that made Mac realize she had fallen in love with Peter Rossellini was the first time she cried in front of him. Last August, after returning from the wake of one of her John Jay colleagues, a woman who had died too young and too hard from breast cancer, Mac had started to cry while telling Peter about the woman. Mac, following the pattern of her family, was not comfortable with open displays of emotion. But when she started crying in front of Peter, she was surprised when she didn't try to

147

stop herself. Even more telling was the fact that Peter didn't try to stop her, which seemed to be the most typical masculine reaction to feminine tears. He simply held her, which was what he did now.

'Rough night, hunh?' he said, rubbing her back. 'How's Sylvie?'

'Okay, considering. She's really been through it in the last few hours. What's that wonderful aroma?'

'Lemon chicken from the Hong Kong Gardens and vegetable egg rolls. They just delivered it five minutes ago. I had them on standby.'

Mac looked up at him. 'That's perfect. Thank you for doing that.'

'Go sit down and I'll bring the cartons in,' he said, turning her around and heading her toward the dining table.

Over two servings of lemon chicken, and one and a half egg rolls, Mac recounted for Peter the events of the evening, ending with her little alarm signals that Irwin might actually want to represent Sylvie.

'Don't worry about it,' Peter assured her. 'He'll be onto something else by tomorrow. And I promise you we'll get someone else to represent her, if she needs it. But Irwin'll be talking about his night at police headquarters for months, I guarantee it.'

Mac started to clear her place, but Peter's hand stopped her. 'Nope, this is full service night. I'll get these while you go check out the news coverage on this Richardson thing. I know you want to see that.'

Mac smiled. He knew her so well. She headed into the living room, settled cross-legged onto the couch, and started waiting through the commercials until the next half-hourly report on CNN would begin.

Peter did know her well. That was one of the good things to come out of the difficulties of the last several months, her realization that Peter did know her very well, and that he loved her anyway. It had been difficult to relax into her relationship with Peter, having been duped a few years ago by her then-fiancé. That man, a fellow academic, had seemed to be enamoured of Mackenzie, but, in fact, he had been positively enthralled with her family's money.

That was one thing she had never had to worry about with Peter. Peter Rossellini was one of the most successful singer/songwriters to emerge onto the pop music scene in the last few years, and a lack of money was not one of the things he had to worry about in life again. But one of the things Mac loved about him was that his work was about the music, and not about the money. Just as Peter knew that, although Mackenzie came from money, it had been ingrained in her until it was encoded in her DNA that her privilege was never, ever to be flaunted, nor could she ever rest on her predecessors' laurels.

Sylvie had teased that they had become the odd couple over the last year and a half: the academic and the pop star. They had put some effort into keeping their private lives private, and, given that they were in New York, it had worked. Peter's one concession to his celebrity was moving, at his manager's insistence, from the loft he'd lived in for two years to a more secure building, a new luxury high rise along the East River. His apartment was virtually as the decorator (hired also at his manager's insistence) had left it, because his time was spent either touring, in the studio or with Mackenzie. Having experienced the dangers of celebrity relatively early in his career, in the case that brought him and Mackenzie together, Peter now took advantage of his celebrity only when he needed to, like he would this fall when his new album would be coming out, and he needed to be in the public eye to promote his music. But otherwise, he lived his life as a financially successful musician and songwriter who could afford to live very well in New York, which was the goal he'd been striving toward for fifteen years.

They may be an odd couple, Mackenzie thought, but seeing Peter in her kitchen when she walked in tonight, with cartons of good Chinese food in his hands, made oddness very appealing.

Peter brought in mugs of tea, set them down on the low table in front of the couch, and sat down next to Mac. She turned sideways so that her back was to the arm of the couch. 'Where are the fortune cookies?' she asked.

'You get those with the refills on the tea,' he said, draping her legs over his before he reached for his mug.

'Forgot them, didn't you?'

'Yep. Anything on yet about Richardson?'

Mac shook her head, reached for her tea and the remote control. 'It's about ten twenty-five,' she said looking at her watch. 'CNN should have a ten-thirty report, right? And then the regular news at eleven.'

Peter looked down at the top of her head. Mac was saying she was okay, but he was a little concerned about her. This past six or seven months had been rough on Mackenzie; first the change from teaching to this study that she was working on, a change that hadn't made her all that happy, in his opinion. Then living through The Bombing and its aftermath had taxed her more than she wanted to admit. A jolt like tonight couldn't help.

He first saw the signs that something was up last September, when Mackenzie had come home from seeing another of Sylvie's off-off Broadway plays. He was working in the studio as usual, and had begged off, even though it seemed that this one might actually be a funny play, if the review in the *Village Voice* was any indication. He'd seen a few of the more experimental pieces Sylvie had done, and this sounded more audience-friendly than most of those, some of which seemed to have been written to annoy the audience.

He was waiting for Mac at her place when she came home that night, and even though she said she'd enjoyed the comedy, she'd looked as if something was troubling her. When he asked her what it was, her answer bowled him over. 'Do you realize how lucky you are, how important your work is?' she said.

The lucky part of her question didn't surprise him; he'd known enough bad luck in his life to recognize good luck when it came along. And the last few years, for the most part, he'd been rolling in good luck. It was the important comment that surprised him. He still felt self-conscious at times about being a guy who barely graduated from college, and here he was with a woman who was a doctor of psychology. In comparison to her work and her teaching, writing and singing pop songs didn't seem very important. So he asked, 'How do you mean important?'

'You and Sylvie – maybe everybody who is a performer, I don't know – you move people, you get them to laugh, you get them to cry, you connect with them where they live their lives.' Mac's eyes were as intense as he'd ever seen them. 'Remember when we first met, and I had to read so much of that fan mail of yours?'

'Sure,' he nodded.

'Some of those letters were amazingly touching. How your songs comfort people, encourage them, cheer them up, even if they just make them dance around the room.

151

That's so human. And that's what makes it so important.'

This wasn't the definition of important that he'd expected, so maybe she wasn't thinking the same version of lucky that he was either. 'And the lucky part?'

'You're becoming what you always wanted to be.'

'Yeah,' he said in an off-handed tone, expecting her to continue. Maybe their definitions of lucky weren't all that different.

'You and Sylvie, you've both worked for a lot of years, and it's finally paying off. You're at a wonderful time in your lives.'

She seemed to leave herself out. 'Mackenzie, are you saying you're not?'

'No,' she said. 'I've been very lucky, too, I know that.' She paused, as if she didn't know how to continue. 'It's just that I've already been what I always thought I wanted to be and now I don't know what's next.'

Peter was startled when she looked up at him and he saw a pain in her eyes that he'd never seen before. Then he reached for her and held her tight, not knowing what to say.

Mackenzie's reaching for the remote brought him back to the moment. 'Oh, let me turn it up,' she said. 'Gil Richardson's the lead story.'

They watched as the anchorwoman delivered the headline, and then led into a taped summary of Richardson's career. Images of him as a young dancer appeared first, then pictures of the posters of the string of Broadway hits he'd been involved with. A more recent picture was shown as the summary concluded, Richardson wearing a black turtleneck. 'That's exactly the way he looked when I met him last week!' Mac said softly. 'Good,' she said when the tape changed to the scene at police headquarters, 'here's the report from downtown.'

The gaggle of press she had seen from the side was evident from a different angle in the videotape. The reporter introduced the excerpt from the press conference with the comment, 'NYPD officials are being very circumspect about the information they are giving out tonight.' A taped report was shown, showing the Deputy Commissioner for Press and Public Affairs at a podium, where she announced that they would not be announcing anything. 'Mr Richardson's death is under review. Some of our most experienced officers are on the case, and we expect to have some information for you shortly.' When the camera moved slightly to the left, Mac saw Mario Buratti standing in the crowd behind the Deputy Commissioner. 'Look at how thrilled Mario is to be there,' Mackenzie joked to Peter. Buratti had an absolutely doleful expression on his face.

The reporters' questions barraged the Deputy Commissioner, but she had been able to stonewall them so far. A lone voice rose from the crowd. 'Commissioner, with the homicide detectives behind you, are you giving us a hint that Gil Richardson was murdered?'

'No, I'm saying that we have some of our most experienced officers reviewing the circumstances of Mr Richardson's death, and we hope to have some information for you in the near future.'

'What about the reports that the police brought someone in for questioning?' a woman's voice yelled out.

'No comment.'

'Lord, I hope they don't find out that it was Sylvie,' Mac whispered.

The reporters tried to pin the Deputy Commissioner down on just what she meant by 'near future' but she didn't budge, and the taped report ended. The reporter in front

153

of headquarters finished his account by saying the press would be there all night, but didn't expect any news until the morning at the earliest.

Mac aimed the remote control and flicked off the set.

The next morning Sylvie called at five minutes after seven. Peter answered the phone and handed it to Mackenzie. 'Hi, Sylvie. How are you this morning?' she said, trying to make her voice sound as though she hadn't just awakened, which she had.

'Well, I didn't have as good a night as you did, Mackenzie, I can tell you that already. That's some answering service you have.'

Sylvie sounded more herself, even at this early hour. That reassured Mackenzie.

'Listen,' Sylvie continued, 'just in case you're worried, I'm through with crying. What I am now is pissed off.'

'Yeah?' Mac said, sitting up. This was sounding more and more like the real Sylvie.

'Yeah. I mean where do these people get off, not believing me? I know that we're not talking about old friends here, but gimme a break! I've been working with some of these people for going on five months now. Do they seriously think I'd kill Gil Richardson because he *insulted* me?'

'And—?'

'This is where the hard part comes in, Mackenzie, asking you this. Because you've done so much already.'

'What is it you want me to do?'

'I realized about two o'clock this morning that the police not charging me is one thing. Everybody thinking I probably did it is another. And those people in the company are gonna be givin' me the fish eye until they find out who

154

did kill Gil Richardson. I really can't go back to work until this is solved, and I'll be damned if anybody is going to screw me out of the best part I've ever had.' Sylvie took a breath, trying to calm herself and get her volume back down to seven a.m. levels. 'Mac, I know this Buratti guy is a friend of yours. Can you see what you can find out from him, see if you can find out how long before they have some answers?'

Mackenzie couldn't respond immediately, for she felt a tug of resistance and then a pang of guilt that she had felt it. She had been glad to do what she could last night, glad to be there for Sylvie, glad to arrange representation if needed. But she was really hoping that was all that she would be called on to do, particularly since the case against Sylvie would be pretty weak, and Irwin's designee – or God forbid even Irwin himself – would certainly be able to handle it. That scenario, given a moment of clear thinking, was unrealistic. Of course Sylvie would come to her. Of course. She would just have to take her reluctance and her fatigue and deal with them.

She hoped the reluctance she had felt for those few seconds would not be in her voice. 'I have my group this morning, Sylvie, and then I'll be calling Buratti. In fact, he told me last night that I should check in with him.'

'And you'll let me know?'

'Whatever I can. Where will you be?'

'I'm not sure. Check here first. Or I'll leave a message for you.'

'Okay. Talk to you later then.'

'And Mackenzie?' Sylvie paused briefly. 'If I said thank you from now until the turn of the millennium it wouldn't be enough. But thank you.'

'You're welcome. Now bye, Sylvie.'

Peter walked in with two mugs of coffee, holding a small white bag in his teeth. He dropped the bag on the bed. 'We forgot the fortune cookies last night. Want yours?'

'Of course. Aren't coffee and fortune cookies one of the new recommendations for a healthy breakfast?' Mac took her first sip of coffee and smiled approvingly, then set her mug down to open her cookie. Her eyebrows arched immediately.

'Looks interesting,' Peter said. 'What's it say?'

Mac held up the small paper and read it carefully. 'Study present difficulty carefully. Things are not what they seem.'

CHAPTER NINETEEN

At five minutes past ten, despite the threatening grey skies, Mac decided she'd walk to the 18th Street precinct house where her meetings with The Bombing rescuers took place. It wasn't the most therapeutic of environments, but it had the advantage of being easy to get to for the officers, most of whom were drawn from that precinct.

On her way over, Mac wondered again at her reluctant initial response to Sylvie's request and the reasons for it. It was not like her at all; her initial impulse was always to be of help – to family or friends, anyone she perceived as needing her. If anything, she had a bent for doing too much, according to some of her colleagues. Even a momentary reluctance to come to Sylvie's assistance was out of character for her. But her responses on a few occasions in the last several months had been out of character for her. Maybe it was part of the general disquiet that seemed to have taken over her life in the last year.

It had started gradually, and at first she thought it was about her personal life, specifically about getting older. She had been relieved that Peter understood immediately when she started talking about the anniversaries that had piled up in the last year or so and how they had unnerved her. A few years ago when she and Sylvie had gone to their 10th class

157

reunion at Riverside, it hadn't seemed like any big deal. But last year, some of the girls from her prep school class had organized a 15th reunion dinner, and she was taken aback to see so many of the classmates, faces she still carried in her memory as adolescents, show up looking like the women in their early thirties that they had become. For some reason, it was that signal about the passage of time that made her stop and take notice.

Not long after that, her sister Whitney had celebrated her 29th birthday, and was talking to Mac about the blow-out party she was planning for her 30th. Mac well remembered when Whitney was born. She remembered her parents bringing the baby home from the hospital, and laying the infant in the almost-five-year-old Mackenzie's lap and telling her that she now had a little sister to watch over in addition to her younger brother Chad.

That was almost thirty years ago, and Mackenzie's memory of it was crystal-clear. It was startling to realize that she could remember something that happened thirty years ago so distinctly.

She was also coming up on the tenth anniversary of receiving her doctorate, and ten years at John Jay. Part of the reason she had gone into this work was to make her contribution toward saving the world. Her work was supposed to be making a difference, and the difference should have been obvious by now. It wasn't. Things were supposed to be getting better, and they weren't.

So when Mac was first approached about doing the study – officially known as the Psychological Evaluation of and Study of the Effectiveness of the Personnel Involved in the Criminal Justice System or PESEPICJ, an acronym which had devolved quickly into the PEPSI study – she eagerly accepted. Perhaps her malaise would be cured by sidestepping the academic year and returning next year with a fresh eye and a fresh attitude toward her students and her courses.

She had spent the summer with Dr Harold Parsons, a former psychologist with the NYPD now with a public policy institute in Albany, and Dr Annabeth Gershon, a psychologist and statistician, as they designed the study. Mac found this part of the job enjoyable, and it tied in with her own professional development. In the last two years, her professional concentration had shifted from studying the psychology of criminal behaviour and developing tools for law enforcement that derived from those studies, to the psychological stresses and needs of those people working within the criminal justice system.

The PEPSI study would interview cops, prosecutors, public defenders, judges, prison employees and probation officers across the state, and then evaluate the effectiveness of the criminal justice system as it was perceived by those working within it. There was at the same time, a similar study being developed on the existing social welfare programmes. In both studies, extensive interviews would be conducted with the selected personnel from September to December, and the final report would be issued the following May.

Because her experience at John Jay had brought her into contact with a wide range of criminal justice professionals, Mac was designated to handle the interviews with the police and probation officers, prosecutors and judges in New York City. By the end of October, when Mackenzie was about half-way through the interviews, Peter noticed that Mackenzie's spirits were noticeably down. The reason was not a mystery to her. At least at John Jay, as routine as her classes might have become, she still had some young, idealistic students in each new semester who spilled some hope out into the classroom. She'd never appreciated the leavening effect those young students had until now. Now, day in and day out, she was in contact only with professionals, almost all of whom were discouraged, even more discouraged than she.

By the time the interviews ended in mid-December – just a week before The Bombing, in fact – Mac was numbed. Her first interviews with the prosecutors and the judges were eye-opening but not shocking. She'd heard and read enough about crowded court calendars and the percentages of cases that were plea-bargained to be prepared for those interviews. It was when the cycle moved onto the probation department that her internal alarms started signalling. She heard tale after tale of probation officers who never saw their probationers after an initial meeting, because there was simply no time. Budget cuts had doubled, sometimes tripled caseloads to the point where each officer was handling well over a hundred, sometimes two hundred, probationers. They were no longer doing the job they had been trained to do; now they were 'administering caseloads'.

Time after time the word productivity had come up. The word that sounded so wonderful when spouted by the people on the budget side of the process. 'Greatly increased productivity' simply meant, in human terms, that fewer people were doing the same amount of work, if not more. Where they had been ten probation officers, there were now six. They were handling the same number of cases, of course, usually more, but now the budgeters could say that 'productivity' was up by 60 percent.

As disheartening as the interviews with the probation officers were, Mac's interviews with the police officers were out and out depressing, especially those with the younger cops who had been on the force seven years or less.

Mac knew going in that police morale was at a very low ebb. Another of the commissions that seem to investigate the department on a fifteen- to twenty-year cycle had exposed a grotesque underbelly to the NYPD: the investigation had brought to light a degree of corruption and venality among a group of officers that shocked the city and the department alike. Even the repeated assurances that it involved only a small group of officers didn't help the standing of the police in the city, particularly in the minority communities.

That low standing in the community seemed to enhance a siege mentality that had been growing in the force. Across the country, the ratio of the number of police to the number of crimes had fallen astonishingly so that it was now the inverse of what it had been twenty years earlier, and cops everywhere were feeling beleaguered. Frequently they expressed concerns for their own personal safety, physical symptoms of stress and fatigue, a shortening average tenure, a higher rate of early retirement, an escalating divorce rate, and a high suicide rate among police were some of the symptoms of that beleaguerment.

Mac noticed, especially in her interviews with younger officers, that the unhealthy 'us vs them' mindset was in evidence and growing. There was also among these younger officers a more pronounced combat mentality, of the police being 'the thin blue line' that separates civilization from barbarism – an outgrowth of that same 'us vs them' mentality. Only for these young officers, the 'them' group seemed to grow larger and larger with each month of service, until the 'us' was comprised only of police. This was especially true of the young officers, many raised in the homogenized, predominantly white communities of the suburbs, who had had in their life virtually no interaction with members of different ethnic groups – be they Chinese, African, Russian, Hasidim, West Indian, Hispanic or African American – except in the context of criminal investigations, where they were perceived as possible suspects at best or proven criminals at worst. And if your experience of Chinatown is limited to dealing with its known or suspected criminals, soon all Chinese drift into the 'them' group.

As Mac was conducting these interviews, she paid even more than the usual attention to the newspaper reports of police activity in the city, especially the comments from political and community leaders. What she was reading began to trigger distant bells of alarm. Both the police department and the various sub-communities that made up the city seemed to be operating under the misconception that police control crime.

It is the entire community that controls crime, through its smaller institutions of families, schools, businesses, and churches; those are the elements of society that shape individuals, that deem behaviour acceptable or unacceptable, and, in extension, criminal or not criminal. The police are but a single element in that larger community and can only respond to crime, or may, at times, by their presence, prevent it. But a community that thinks the police control crime is deluding itself. And a police department under the misapprehension that it controls crime is an institution in a constant state of frustration.

Mac's interviews with the police officers also revealed a weariness that seemed to be contagious, and was evident in the older and younger officers alike. The weariness came through especially when they spoke of the inter-service rivalries that affected the public safety system in the city.

Veteran police officers were still disturbed that the transit police had been consolidated with their department, since the NYPD had always assumed a superior posture to its fellow service. Police and firefighters were in a years-old but continuing controversy over who was in charge at emergency scenes. The firefighters were constantly scrutinized by the Emergency Medical Squad, whose members were worried that firefighters were being trained to do their jobs. (It was a 'productivity' issue, a city council member said.)

After two and a half months of interviewing, and hearing preliminary reports from colleagues conducting interviews around the state, Mac was still struggling to deal with a fact she had only recently admitted to herself, but one she had not been able to articulate to anyone else as yet. That fact was that she had spent the last ten years of her life serving a criminal justice system – on the academic side, to be sure, but serving it nevertheless – and it was a system that was crumbling. What she was seeing was a system of criminal justice and public safety fashioned by a community that didn't want to deal with its problems, by politicians wanting to address those problems through election day but not beyond, and by bureaucrats whose solution for everything was to cut its costs.

And, Mac thought, as she got to the steps of the precinct house, just to prove that some years are tougher than others, she had gone from two and a half months of dealing with overwhelmed, discouraged, and sometimes bitter people, to these weekly group meetings with the survivors of The 16th Street Bombing.

In January, Dr Jerome Pernick, a former colleague of Dr Parsons' who was still with the NYPD, had approached

Mac about handling one of the groups they'd put together of officers who had been on the scene of The Bombing. It had become evident soon after the disaster that many of those who had participated in the rescue effort – civilians, firefighters, EMS workers and police alike – were going to need help in dealing with it.

Dr Pernick urged Mac to do this because she was in the unique position of having been there. If not an eyewitness to the carnage in the subway, she was at least an earwitness to the tragedy's beginning. She had a sharper sense than most that this was one of those events that became a specific demarcation in time. There was life Before. And there was life After. These men – and they were all men in her group, because the sexes had been segregated for this phase, since men and women handle the grieving process so differently – were having trouble dealing with After.

Mac made her way down the hall to Community Room B, where four of the six officers in her group were already lined up at the coffee urn. The room was painted an unfortunate institutional light green, the fluorescent light overhead had an annoying buzz, and the seven wooden chairs with extra-hard seats that were now in an oval were probably requisitioned during the LaGuardia administration, but at least the coffee was good and hot at the beginning of every session. The greeting she received from the officers was considerably warmer than it had been the first day.

When she tried to tell Peter about her first meeting with this group, she told him she didn't want to hear any more stories about tough audiences from him. People who had paid good money to hear music weren't a tough audience, compared to six cops who didn't particularly want to talk to her – and some not even to each other.

164

Three of the attendees had requested and or volunteered for the group once they heard about it. The others weren't exactly ordered to attend – Mac and the supervising psychologist wouldn't stand for that – but it was strongly suggested that they be there. The sweet-faced Eddie Lopes had been part of that contingent.

Even the men who had volunteered for the programme were surprised that it was Mac leading the group – they had been expecting a man – but that initial resistance had been overcome when they learned of her credentials. The fact that she had been close to the scene that day also helped to win them over, as Dr Pernick thought it would.

For those, like Eddie Lopes, who were reluctant, she decided to take the bull by the horns. 'This city has been through an extreme trauma,' she started that first session. 'Certainly the people who were in the Union Square Station, those who survived, have suffered a great personal trauma. St Stephen's School has suffered enormously, and the families of those children who were lost have an unimaginable burden. Those children who survived now have a memory that is very hard for a nine year old to live with. It's hard for an adult to live with, isn't it?' She got a few nods in response.

'What you may not realize is that you have been through a trauma that can be every bit as difficult to cope with. We're here to help you with that. We're here because the city, the department, and your colleagues are concerned about you.' That made a few of the men squirm in their seats, a few others sit upright in defiance of what she'd said. Nobody had to be concerned about *them*.

'There is concern for you, for your health, and concern that if we don't address these issues, it may affect your performance. So we're here not only for your benefit, but for the benefit of your partners, your fellow officers, and for the public you serve.'

Mac had been brought into this because of her background in dealing with police officers, not because of any particular expertise in dealing with survivors of disasters, so she had had to do some reading. She'd learned a few things that helped her prepare: first, it was believed that psychological effects on survivors were more severe and longer-lasting when the disaster was one of human origin, as this was, as opposed to a natural disaster. Second, it was common for people involved in such man-made disasters, especially one as grim as this had been, to develop an 'emotional anaesthesia' to distance themselves from the event. Anxiety, depression, and disorientation were also common symptoms. The suggested approach in dealing with the survivors' trauma was to get them started talking about the event and their perception of it. Telling and retelling the story, according to one of the sources she had read, was a way of gaining control over the situation they had not been in control of when it happened. It was a way, too, to finally process what they had distanced themselves from and to make some meaning out of it.

That was all well and good in theory, but she couldn't exactly tell the group that. So she started this way: 'I think it would be a good idea if we started by giving a brief summary of our stories that day. I had just come out of the grocery store on 15th Street and was heading toward the Square when the bomb went off.' There were a few interested eyebrows raised at her; obviously they weren't all aware that she had been that close to the scene. 'And the thing that amazed me the most − after the sound of the explosion, that is, and the fact that it felt like the sound waves alone were what knocked me down − is the peculiar

166

quality of the silence that followed. Did any of you notice that?'

She got a few heads nodding, and one 'Yeah.'

'After I got to my feet again and made my way down to the corner, I saw one uniformed officer sprinting across the north end of the Square like he was in the Olympics—'

'That was me,' the sweet faced officer to her right said, the officer she now knew as Eddie Lopes. 'I was on patrol up on Broadway near 18th, so I was about as far away, maybe further, than you were when everything exploded. Then I went tearing across the park when I saw the smoke coming from there.'

Mac nodded, and when Eddie didn't go any further, she continued with her narrative of her experiences.

When she finished, she turned to the man to her left. 'Officer Gerrity, why don't you tell us what happened to you that day?'

Officer Gerrity, like Officers Green, Avant, Stevens, Blakeney, and Lopes following him, told his story first in an official, reportorial style, full of police jargon. That was to be expected. This was part of the emotional anaesthesia.

The officers eventually started opening up, and some of the experiences they recounted were painful to listen to. A total of ninety-seven people had died that day, between the people on the two subway cars completely destroyed in the explosion, the people in the badly damaged subway car across the platform, which included the students from St Stephen's, and the people waiting on the platform. Another seventy-eight were seriously injured, and another fifty were treated at the scene for smoke inhalation, cuts and bruises, and other minor injuries. There were plenty of stories to go around, and they were wrenching to listen to.

Officer Gerrity, they learned over the course of the first

few weeks, was struggling with the fact that he'd been apart from the main scene of the bombing, handling what might have been an ordinary emergency on any other day but one that had gone disastrously wrong that day. His activities had been confined, in fact, to the upper part of the station, where minimal damage had occurred, a few hundred feet to the west of where the explosion had been concentrated. When he arrived in the station the token clerk had yelled for him to come over to where a woman was prostrate on the cement floor of the station just inside the turnstiles, in front of the large map of the entire subway system. The woman had been hit on the head by one of the large posters that had fallen off the wall in the moments after the bomb went off. Normally that wouldn't have been a major problem in these circumstances, but the woman had gone rapidly into the advance stages of labour. 'You think she was trying to get to the hospital on her own?' the token clerk had said to him. They looked at each other and shrugged. Who could tell?

Gerrity tried to flag down one of the EMS teams, but a pregnant woman didn't seem as urgent as the other disasters waiting on the other side of the station, and a senior EMS technician stayed with him only long enough to review a couple of points from their emergency first aid training.

The token clerk assured him that she had two kids of her own, 'Although I was out of it when they were born, thank God,' she said to him. 'But at least I know the basics from my pre-natal classes.' In the midst of all that noise and chaos, right there in front of the subway system map, they did as best they could to assist this mother through her child's birth. The woman, who had seemed groggy to Officer Gerrity from the moment he approached her, delivered her baby within fifteen minutes. Then she died.

Gerrity still shook his head when he recalled the moment. 'There I was, holding this red, sticky, squalling little thing, looks like a healthy baby boy, and when I asked the mother what his name was going to be, trying to get her to focus, she didn't answer.'

At first he thought she'd fallen asleep, but then he noticed her chest wasn't moving at all. He handed the baby to the token clerk, who still knelt by his side, and moved around to check on the mother. When he couldn't find a pulse and couldn't feel her breathing, he ran after and grabbed one of the EMS techs streaming in the west side of the station, and insisted that she come with him. The young woman checked the mother briefly, shook her head, and said, 'She's gone.' The tech rose to her feet, paused a moment, and then joined the crush of emergency workers heading to the east wide of the subway.

Gerrity still couldn't believe it. 'The baby made it, but the mother didn't? In the midst of all these ambulances, rescue teams and the like, we – I – couldn't help a mother delivering her baby? What the hell is that?' He pressed the heel of his hand across his forehead when he got to this point in the story. 'And after, I get to the hospital – over at St Vincent's, checking on the baby, to make sure he's okay. And this woman's husband shows up, thanking me for helping his son, and I don't know. I just lost it.'

Mac knew from a conversation with his commanding officer that Gerrity had appeared to handle the events of that day pretty well initially. Obviously he had not confided in his commanding officer as he had in this group. But right after New Year's there was another of those cheery reports of a cab driver delivering a baby en route to the hospital, and the smiling faces of the mom and dad and cabby seemed to have gotten to him. That's when the commander told him about the group, and Gerrity agreed to attend.

Mackenzie had suspected from Gerrity's first recounting of his experiences that he was wrestling with a particular, and so far unidentified by him, sense of failure. Gerrity had responded to a scene that was unparalleled in the city's experience, yet he was called upon to handle a predicament that fell into the ordinary category. In the midst of a city's trauma, he was involved in a situation that normally would have had a joyous ending, and instead it had turned to tragedy in front of him. While fellow officers had been lauded for their heroics, Gerrity, in his own estimation, had blown a routine call. No one blamed him, of course, but he had. But he was now noticeably freer in talking about the details of that day; his progress was observable, and Mac was pleased at that.

As the officers continued telling their stories, the detail grew with each retelling. If Mackenzie had not read the newspapers coverage of the 16th Street Bombing in detail, their accounts would have been shocking. But she had, so the accounts became distressing in a different way because they became so personal, and the toll that day had taken on the rescuers became clearer. But that was a realization that came gradually, as the officers let more of their reactions filter into their accounts. It wasn't until the sixth week that the group had heard the full version of Avant and Stevens' experiences, one of the grimmest of that day.

Officers Avant and Stevens had been on 14th Street in a patrol car, and they arrived on the scene at approximately the same time Eddie Lopes did, coming from the opposite direction. As in the previous weeks in the more detached accounts, they told their story together, because that was the way they experienced this disaster – together.

Avant and Stevens were the first to arrive on the centre downtown platform, or rather on the pile of rubble that was what was left of the centre downtown platform. They had run through the station, realized that the stairway that came up from the platform near 15th Street was where the smoke and dust was coming from, and headed directly there, leaving the screams of passengers at the opposite end of the station ringing in their ears. That was the stairway they headed down.

'I never seen anything like it,' Stevens said at that point. Charles Avant, an energetic black man in his early thirties, had been doing most of the talking so far this morning, but now he let his partner of the last three years get at least a few words in. 'I didn't know concrete and steel could dissolve into such little pieces.

'When we got down to the last stairs that were intact, it was hard to see through the smoke and all, but we could see that the whole centre platform in front of where the detonation occurred was gone, and there were two subway cars with their ends torn off and nothing in between them except a pile,' Avant continued. 'It took us a couple of minutes to figure out that that pile had been a subway car, too.'

Stevens picked up the story. 'When we heard some voices that seemed to be coming from these wrecked subway cars, that's when we figured we were gonna have to scramble over this pile of debris in front of us, to try to figure out how to get to the people, see who was injured, see who could move, get the people out of there. And that was when Avant went back to call and make sure the dispatchers knew the extent of the damage. I stayed down there and started picking my way across the rubble. I got about ten feet into it—' he stopped, unable to continue.

171

'That's where I found him, a couple of minutes later, when I came back down the stairs,' Avant picked up. 'I called out to him, started to fill him in on what the dispatcher had told me about the equipment and personnel we could expect, and then I noticed he hadn't said anything, and I started climbing over the same pile. That's when he finally said something, and he started yelling at me to get back. I couldn't figure what the hell was going on. I thought maybe he had spotted something or somebody, that there might be an armed suspect or another bomb, and like I said before, I had gone down there first thinking it was probably a gas main or something, so a suspect was not what I was looking for.'

Avant stopped, as if it were Steven's turn to continue, but Stevens didn't. 'What was it that made you stop on the pile?' Mac asked softly.

Stevens took a long breath. 'I had lost my footing, and slipped, and here I was on a pile that I thought was all concrete and debris from the stairs or the platform or the ceiling, but I look down at my hand where I had caught myself from falling, figuring out how to balance myself so I can get up, and I see a woman's purse. An old-fashioned one, navy blue with this gold-coloured clasp thing across it, and a stiff handle. My grandmother had one just like it. And then I look closer and I see the handle a little clearer and I see part of a woman's hand still holding onto it, sticking out of the debris.' He paused, needing a little of that emotional anesthesia to finish telling his story. 'And then I start looking around, and I see things here and there – a piece of fabric . . . a little blood . . . some paper . . . the top of a shopping bag from Saks . . . a Christmas ribbon . . . and it hits me. This pile I'm standing on, no, I'm crawling through . . . it's debris mixed with body parts . . . and people's personal effects.' His voice had thickened, as it had each time he got close to this point in the story. But today he'd come closer to telling it all than he ever had.

'It wasn't until I started walking across, trying to get to him, that he snapped out of it,' Officer Avant continued. 'And then he starts yelling at me, and scrambling backwards to where I was. I think he's gone crazy on me, but then he grabs me, and says "Look down" and at first I don't know what the hell I'm looking for, but then I see I'm standing next to this brown thing, 'bout the length of a good fireplace log, and when I look closer, I see that it's fabric, like a brown heavy wool. And then I look closer still, and it's somebody's sleeve, and the arm is still in it. I couldn't believe what I was lookin' at, so I turned around and then I start seein' all kinds of things I don't wanna see, and I made it back to the stairs, about half-way up, when I started gagging.'

Officer Avant stopped at that point, and Stevens didn't pick up the narrative. Finally Mac turned to him to prompt him on. 'And where were you when he made it back to the stairs?'

'I was on the stairs, too, but not up as far as him. I stopped on the bottom step and looked around. We could still hear these voices, this moaning, you know, it had gotten louder in the five or ten minutes or whatever it was since we first got there, and I took a good look around and realized there was no way to get to those people in the car except to climb over that pile.'

'And did you?' Mac asked. She knew, of course, that there had been people waiting on the platform who were killed. Final identification of all the victims took more than two weeks, because the debris that was removed from the platforms had to be literally sifted through in an attempt to identify the last of the victims. There had been twenty-three people about to get on the train. They were all killed instantly. The final list of those killed in The Bombing hadn't been released until New Year's Eve.

'We had to,' Avant finally said, only a hint of defensiveness left in his voice. That was a sign of progress, Mac thought. All these men had been defensive in the first re-telling of their stories, as if they hadn't done enough. As if it had been their fault. 'No other way to get down there and figure out the situation. We ended up going back and forth three, four times. I was scared we were going to have to start carrying stretchers over that pile, but by the time the EMS people got down there, they figured it was easier getting people out that 16th Street entrance.'

'Anything else?' Mac asked softly.

'Yeah,' said Stevens, who had been quiet for a few minutes now, as he sat forward in his chair. 'It came out later that one of the bodies in that pile – or some of the body parts in the pile should I say – might have belonged to this son of a bitch Golander, since the explosion mixed up what was on the platform and everything – or everyone – who was in that car where the bomb went off. The thing I regret from that day is that I didn't know which parts were his so I could have spat on them.' He sat back muttering, 'Goddam son of a bitch.'

Murmurs of agreement with his opinion of the bomber passed through the other officers. One of the difficulties in dealing with the psychological aftermath of this bombing was that people needed more of a villain to blame. It would have been easier to vent their rage if the object of their fury had been a terrorist, or a blatant criminal type or someone the newspaper could have demonized more successfully. Golander had been, to all accounts, a rather meek man, an unlikely candidate to wreak this much horror. This group of officers was having a particularly difficult time dealing with the idea of Golander, and so he had become their definition for 'a Goddam son of a bitch'.

'I haven't had dreams that bother me in a long, long time,' said Officer Avant. 'Since I was a boy. But after that day, I have dreams about walking across that pile, and voices crying out with each step. Wakes me up shaking every time I have that dream.'

After Officers Stevens and Avant had finished recounting their story, she turned to Eddie Lopes, who had still not opened up beyond his brief comments in their first meeting. He always deferred to one of the other officers, or waited until he knew the session was about to end before indicating a willingness to speak. Since they were midway through the sessions that had been planned, it was late for him to begin.

'Officer Lopes, we haven't gotten to your account of the day yet. Why don't you start with when I saw you. I still remember the sight of you running across Union Square Park.'

CHAPTER TWENTY

The first thing he remembered about that day was the running. He'd been on foot patrol on Broadway, just in front of the sporting goods store between 17th and 18th Streets, when he heard – and felt – the explosion. And then he was running. Running so fast he thought his heart was gonna bust out of his chest. Running and having no idea what the hell was going on.

As soon as he got to the north-west corner, he saw that the explosion, or whatever it was, had occurred on the east side of the park. He ran across the curving north side of the Square, and when he remembered that day, he could still smell the scent of pine that surrounded him as he rounded the north-east side of the Square. Union Square had a thriving farmer's market on Wednesdays and weekends; while there wasn't too much fresh produce around in December, Christmas trees were plentiful in the few weeks right before the holiday. One of the regular vendors, Lopes was pretty sure his name was Eric, had apparently been unloading a small flatbed full of trees when the explosion hit. At least twenty wrapped trees had fallen in a heap around the man, and the scent that was released in their fall was pungent and pervasive, even in the cold air. 'What the hell happened?' Eric yelled as he ran by. 'Don't know,'

177

Eddie replied over his shoulder. 'Watch yourself.'

When he got to Park Avenue South, the street that formed the east boundary of the square, Eddie came to a jarring halt. He couldn't believe what he was seeing: a hole in the street, toward its west side, a hole maybe eight to ten feet around, smoke and dust billowing out of it. Big chunks of concrete were lying around the hole, as if sprayed out in a pattern. What the hell could have caused that? A gas main? Nah, there wouldn't be a gas main here, would there? This close to a subway station?

As he saw a cabby creeping down the avenue, he stepped into the street and halted the vehicle. The guy's eyes were the size of those chocolate mint patties his grandmother used to love. He saw the taxi's roof light was on, which meant the guy didn't have a fare. 'Pull over here a minute,' Eddie said.

'That could have been me,' said the taxi driver, a Jamaican from his accent, probably in his early fifties. God, he was right, thought Eddie. If the timing on the traffic lights had been off by a few seconds, they could have had cars blowing up over Park Avenue South in addition to whatever the hell had gone on down below.

Eddie heard sirens approaching from a distance. 'I want you to stay here for me, for a couple of minutes. The emergency vehicles are on their way already, but I want you to tell them that I'm going down this entrance.' He turned and pointed to the subway entrance that was opposite 16th Street. 'You got that?'

The taxi driver nodded. 'Got it. Bless you, mister,' he added with a shake of his head. No way anybody'd get him to go down those stairs.

As he neared the stairs to the subway, Eddie heard voices across the street. They were from some kids from the

178

private school a couple of blocks east, kids who were crouched on the sidewalk on 16th Street, about a half-block away, some of them crying from the looks of it. Good. That meant there wouldn't be many of them down in the subway yet.

He got to the stairs of the subway entrance, and prayed as he was heading down that the gate would be unlocked. The entrance, the northernmost to the Union Square station, was usually unlocked by 3:00 pm so the school kids could use it, and it was about that time now. This was one of those unattended entrances, the kind that had a full-body turnstile to get in, and it left you at the far end of the platform in between the express and local tracks. You had to have a token on you to use this entrance, though, because there was no token booth. He started reaching for his right pocket, hoping he had a token in the change. Otherwise he wouldn't be able to get onto the platform.

He ran down the stairs, and the gate was unlocked. Good! He turned to run down the second flight of stairs, and was lucky to catch himself on the handrail, because the lower part of the staircase was in shambles. As he waited for some of the dust to clear so that he could see what was going on, he felt his sinuses and chest reacting to the smoke and dust already. As he worked his way down the stairs, he realized he wasn't going to have any trouble getting through the turnstile. What was left of it was hanging by a hinge.

He eased his way past the hanging turnstile and down what was left of the stairs that led to the platform. The stairs were at an angle here because the tunnels and the tracks started a long graceful curve at the north end of the station, heading east toward Lexington Avenue. Securing himself next to a sturdy part of the banister Eddie stopped to see what he was walking into. There was some light coming from the uptown platform, and he had his flashlight on him, too – the damn thing had been slapping into his thigh when he was running here. He unhooked it, and turned it on the scene ahead of him, but that lone beam barely made sense out of the hell that was in front of him.

There was a hole in the ceiling of the subway tunnel. Of course. He was looking at the other side of the hole he'd seen in the street. He'd never thought of subways having ceilings, until now. But there, above where the express track would be, he could see the bright light of the afternoon sun. That made sense.

But as the dust cleared, very little else of what he saw made sense. The last two cars of a local train, off to his right, were tilted up on their side, like some grotesque oversized toy train, and the third car forward, what was left of it, was at an even odder angle, so you could tell it wasn't even resting on the tracks.

Eddie strained to see through the smoke and dust, and from what he could tell, the damage seemed to be centred on the downtown express track, to his left. There was a huge amount of debris – a pile still smoking and shifting. And it wasn't until Eddie looked at the subway car forward of that pile, its ragged edges looking like a tin can opened with a hand crank can opener, that Eddie realized the pile of debris had also been a subway car. The hole with daylight showing through it was directly above the pile. Sweet Jesus, a subway car had exploded. How in God's name had that happened?

He looked across to the uptown platform; the north end of that platform ended almost seventy-five feet before the downtown side, which seemed like a stroke of good luck today. Some of the metal support beams that created a barrier between the uptown and downtown tracks were bent and twisted, lots of debris had fallen on the north end of the platform, but it appeared totally empty of people. If any uptown express train had been in the station, it would have been severely damaged in the explosion as well, if those metal beams were any indication. Lucky as it was, Lopes was surprised that there weren't any people waiting on the platform. Unless a train had just left. That was a possibility. He prayed that's what happened.

As the dust cleared a little more, the sound started to come through. It was almost as though his vision and hearing were in synch. The more he could see, the more he could hear. There were voices. Voices crying out, voices moaning. He could hear them now.

He edged his way down the stairs, relieved to find that they were still solid, just covered with more of the debris that must have flown with the force of the explosion. Already the dust was starting to get to him, and he started to cough. A short, shallow cough. He kept coughing as he edged his way onto the platform. Further ahead, toward the stairs that came down from the main part of the station, the whole platform was rubble, but here the platform seemed to be still intact, but full of debris. He edged along, testing his footing with each step.

The last car of the local train was the first one he came to. He flashed his beam inside, and saw that there were people – there were bodies anyway, God knew whether they were alive or not. But he had no idea how to get the doors open, and the windows were too small to try to get in. He stopped, put his ear near one of the broken windows and listened hard. Moaning. Good. At least they were alive.

He paused where his footing was surest and tried to raise the dispatcher on his radio. He couldn't get through the logjam of calls he heard going in. At least it sounded like help was on its way. He could only hope that word was getting out upstairs that they needed every kind of emergency service there was here today. Police, fire, EMS, bomb squad, the emergency unit from the Metropolitan Transit Authority – everybody.

He inched down the platform to the next car, and as he got nearer he saw that the end of this car had been torn away, too, like the one on the opposite track, when the car in front of it had, from appearances, risen up and been ripped apart, its side and top sheared off. In the beam of his flashlight he could see three of the long benches of moulded seats on the platform. There were two bodies visible, and his guess, from the angle at which they were lying, was that they were dead.

He turned back to the second car from the end, the one that had had its front sheared off. It was tilted back toward the curved wall of the subway tunnel. Eddie shined the beam of his light through the opening that had been a window at the torn front end of the train, and his heart almost stopped. Little kids, lots of them, thrown around like puppets, and he could hear soft crying. He saw some movement near the separation in the seats where the next door was, and he beamed his light in that direction. A nun! At least she was dressed like a nun. She had on a blue coat, and one of those short veils that came to her shoulders. She squinted and then shielded her eyes from the beam of light with her left hand, and said, to whoever was at the other end of the light, 'The children. I've got to get the children out of here. Can you help?'

'You okay, Sister?'

'I think so. We must get the children out of here.'

'Help is on the way, Sister,' Eddie assured her. He looked toward the stairs he had come down and saw people edging down the stairway. 'In fact, I hear some activity now. It shouldn't be too long. Are any of the kids seriously injured? How many did you have with you?'

'Twenty-five.'

Twenty-five children! His heart leapt into his throat.

'But there were a few of us with them. Mrs Gutierrez and Mrs Wadczyk. And Sister Bernadette. Sister Bernadette,' she said in a louder voice. 'Sister Bernadette! Can you hear me?'

A faint voice toward the end of the car said, 'I think she got hit in the head. She's bleeding, Sister.'

'Is that you, Mrs Gutierrez?'

'Yes, Sister.'

'Are you all right?'

'Yes, Sister.'

'Do you have any of the children with you?'

'The six I was watching, yes.'

'Are they all right?'

'I think they are alive,' the woman replied in a trembling voice. 'I do not know if they are all right.'

The sound of the voices had brought more sounds: the whimpering of the children as they came out of their daze.

'Sister,' Eddie said. 'I'm just going to check the last car and get the rescue team here, okay? I'll be right back.'

'Very well, officer. Thank you.'

Eddie checked the last car, and a few of the 'bodies' he had spotted before were starting to move. Better news than he expected. He raced to the bottom of the stairs when he saw the first firefighters and police in disaster attire arrive. They each carried bright emergency beacons.

The police contingent was led by a lieutenant, a man Eddie didn't recognize. 'What's the situation here, Officer?' the lieutenant asked.

'Got a couple of people in that car,' he said, pointing to the last local car. 'They're moving around, looks like they made it through so far. Next car I got twenty-five school kids, maybe eight, nine years old, I don't know. Two nuns and two mothers with them. We're gonna need plenty of stretchers to get them out of here. Next car, a couple bodies on the platform. That's all that I've identified so far. Can't get any further down the platform. Can't see anything across the way.'

The senior firefighter turned to his next in command and sent word to the street about the number of stretchers and ambulances that would be required for this exit alone. Eddie walked with the lieutenant to the opening at the front of the second car, where he'd been talking to the nun, and, with the lieutenant's emergency beacon they were able to see more of the car. It looked like somebody had taken it and turned it on its side, which was pretty much what had happened.

The brighter light seemed to provoke more of a response from the children, and now muffled sobs were audible as well as moans. 'Sister, it's me, Eddie again. Got the lieutenant here, got stretchers and ambulances on the way, we're gonna start getting you out of here real soon.'

'Sister, this is Lieutenant Catrow. Have you been able to assess the children's condition?'

'For those right around me, I think it's mainly scrapes and possibly a broken bone or two.'

'That's good, that's good.'

'I'm concerned, though, Lieutenant, that I can't seem to get a response out of Mrs Wadczyk. She was sitting close to the end of the car where you're standing.'

As the lieutenant moved his light around, both he and Eddie could see that the door of the operator's cab was lying diagonally across the tilted car. Eddie was able to hoist himself up and look at the other side. Shit! Some badly bloodied little bodies were in that end section of the car, along with the body of a woman with shoulder-length light brown hair. It looked like the door had hit her full-force.

'She's down here, Sister. Looks like she's unconscious, but I bet she's going to be fine.' Eddie looked at the lieutenant, and the older man nodded, obviously approving of his white lie.

'Sister, this is the lieutenant again. It will probably take us a while to try to get these doors opened, but we could start passing the children through this opening here, if you're able. Do you think you can do that?'

'I'd love to be able to do that, lieutenant, but I'm afraid my arm is broken. And I'm not sure of my leg.'

Both men were startled by the stoicism in her voice, and they looked at one another, eyebrows raised. 'Guess we go to plan B, hunh, lieutenant?' Eddie said.

'What's that?'

'I'm a pretty compact guy. I can squeeze in there and start handing kids out until we can get the doors cut open.'

The lieutenant looked at the car, and furrowed his brow. 'I guess for those kids who are in good shape, yeah, we can do that. Let's see where those ambulances are.'

As the lieutenant beckoned the stretchers forward, Eddie took off his coat, unstrapped his equipment belt, and hoisted himself up and through the opening. Clinging to the side, standing on the edge of a seat row, from what he could tell, he adjusted the emergency beacon to give him the maximum light. When he turned around, the light had illuminated at least ten pairs of eyes, now staring at him, little dark stars in a sea of whimpers.

185

He had to figure out the best way to manoeuver down the car, get the kids and bring them back to the entrance. It was going to be tricky, because of the angle of the car.

He managed to make his way toward the nun – whose name was Sister Margaret, he learned on the first trip – and bring back the first child, a boy who miraculously appeared unharmed except for a dripping cut above his eyebrow. He took the children who were apparently uninjured first, hoping that by the time those with broken bones or a few who were still unconscious needed to be evacuated, the doors could be opened. Eddie had carried out five kids by the time the MTA emergency crews got down and opened the doors at the end of the car, and they were then able to get the injured children, Mrs Gutierrez and Sister Bernadette out and loaded into ambulances.

Sister Margaret insisted on being the last one taken from that end of the car. It turned out she did have a broken leg as well as a fractured arm. 'Eddie,' she called to him before she would let them carry her stretcher down the platform. 'Eddie,' she said again, reaching for his hand. They had become fast friends in the last hour it had taken to clear the car. 'Bless you for all you've done.'

'No, Sister—' he started, but she wouldn't let him finish.

'Eddie, Mrs Wadczyk is dead, isn't she?'

He swallowed hard. 'It looks that way, Sister.'

'And the children who were sitting with her?'

He just shook his head.

The nun closed her eyes and for the first time, Eddie saw pain wash across her face. She wasn't aware that her hand still held his, or that her clasp had now turned into a death grip.

186

'We gotta go, Sister,' said the EMS attendant.

'You'll get them out of there, won't you, Eddie?' she said.

'You know we will, Sister.'

He watched her being carried down the platform toward the stairs, and stepped back into the car for a moment, looking around in wonder that so many had lived through that scene he'd first witnessed when he came down here. It was then that he heard her.

Maybe she'd been awake for a while, but there had been enough noise that no one had heard her yet. Eddie edged down to the end of the car where Mrs Wadczyk's body lay, and peeked over, holding the lantern up for better light. There, looking up at his were the snappiest brown eyes he'd ever seen. They were teary eyes, but they were definitely alive.

'Can you talk, honey?' he said to her.

'Yes,' she replied, and he almost got light-headed. This kid had been here for over an hour, maybe closer to two by now, and nobody had spotted her. They, of course, had decided to clear all the survivors before removing the bodies, and, given what they'd spotted when they first looked in, this area of the car hadn't even been looked at since.

He saw that she was pinned by the bodies of her classmates, so he didn't even ask if she could move. 'What's your name?'

'Franny.'

'Franny, hey that's my little cousin's name, too. Francesca, but we call her Franny.'

'Me, too.'

'You mean it? You're Francesca but they call you Franny? Now, isn't that somethin'.' He almost got nauseous when he took in the details of the carnage that surrounded the little

187

girl. 'Franny? I'm just going to go get some more help, and I'll be right back, okay, honey?'

'Okay.'

Eddie edged back to the door that had been opened, got onto the platform and ran to the lieutenant who was directing all the activity from near the stairs. The man paled when Eddie told him what he'd found.

'We need equipment down here now, sir, to get that door up and get those bodies out so we can get to her.'

'Okay, Lopes, you go back and stay with her, I'll get somebody upstairs to tell them we need the equipment team down here.'

Eddie returned to the car, and this time, in examining the end that had been blown off, he saw there was a small opening closer to where the little girl lay. Calling another cop over, he had the man help him move some of the wreckage out of the way, and once he got his balance, he was able to crawl into the opening, which was on the little girl's left side.

'Franny?' he said, keeping his attention rigidly focused on her. Her head was fairly pinned, so she couldn't see that she was surrounded by the bodies of her classmates. 'It's me, Eddie. I'm back.'

'I'm scared.'

'Yeah, it's been a pretty scary afternoon.'

'Can you hold my hand?'

'Sure,' he said. 'I think I can get my hand in there. Can you put your hand out?'

He saw a couple of fingers wiggling, and reached for them. 'There,' he said as he grasped her hand. 'That's better. Just let me get settled here.' He shifted his weight as carefully as he could, fearful of anything upsetting the delicate balance that had kept her protected through this chaos. He finally got into a position that had him slightly above and behind her left shoulder. But at least he could hold her hand.

'So Francesca – Franny – what's your last name?'

'Ferraro'

'No kidding? Like that politician lady?'

'Un-hunh.' She was quiet for a moment, then asked, 'What's your name?'

'Lopes. Eddie Lopes.'

'Lopez? My girlfriend's name is Lopez.'

'No, this is sort of like Lopez, but my father's grandfather came from Portugal, and they spell it a little different, and they say it different too.' Through the broken window, he saw the equipment team assembling on the platform, and he knew he had to start distracting her. 'So, Franny, tell me about where you were today . . .'

Eddie held her hand through the next hour, talking with her, getting her to talk about the Christmas show she'd seen, about the ice skaters in Rockefeller Center, about the Christmas tree there, about anything he could think of to keep her occupied while they worked to cut away the door that was jammed diagonally across the car, still resting on top of Mrs Wadczyk's body.

The equipment they were using to cut away the wreckage seemed to spew something in the air, something that triggered his coughing spasms again, but Eddie held onto her hand and listened as best he could over the noise.

Once they cleared the door, he had to distract her while they moved the woman's body, so he told Franny stories about when he was in the third grade, stories about the people in his neighbourhood, and about what he got for Christmas when he was a kid. He asked Franny what she wanted for Christmas, and promised if she picked out the one thing she wanted the very most, he'd make sure Santa would get that for her. She didn't react noticeably to that, but he couldn't tell if that was because she was too old to believe in Santa, or if she just didn't believe him. For the last half-hour he'd been having a harder time getting her to talk. Franny seemed to be drifting off to sleep and Eddie had had to shake her hand a few times to wake her up.

After they'd cleared the door and Mrs Wadczyk's body, it became evident they were going to need the jaws of life to free Franny from the twisted metal that imprisoned her. When the guy who would operate the jaws of life arrived, Eddie didn't want to move from Franny's side, but he finally realized he had to. He squeezed her hand again, and told her he'd be waiting for her when they brought her out on the platform. 'Remember, we got a date to try that pizza down in your neighbourhood. You, me and my cousin Francesca. And remember you promised it's gonna be better than the ones in my neighbourhood.' He didn't get a reply out of her, but he thought he felt a return squeeze on his hand.

When he got back on the platform the lieutenant ordered him upstairs to get some fresh air. He coughed his brains out once he got up there, but, God, the air smelled fresh and it felt wonderful. He didn't realize until he left that scene down below, but the smell of death was already seeping through the subway cars and the platform.

It seemed a long time that he was waiting up top for her to come out; it was dark now, had been dark for a while. Eddie didn't even know what time it was until somebody told him it was seven o'clock. Four hours. Funny: it seemed like minutes and somehow it also seemed like years.

He saw the equipment team come up the stairs, and he looked for the stretcher behind them. That was odd. Normally, they'd get the stretcher out first thing, and then

190

bring the equipment out. He walked toward the stairs, and saw the face of the man who operated the jaws of life. The guy just shook his head.

He headed to the top of the stairs, still watching for the stretcher. It never came up. Lieutenant Catrow plodded up the steps wearily, and caught Eddie's eye as soon as he looked toward the street. 'Sorry, Lopes. By the time they freed her, she was dead.'

That was the story Eddie should have told the group, the story that he wanted to tell the group, but every time he even thought about the girl in the privacy of his own apartment, he started to choke up. And he was gonna be damned before he'd cry in front of other cops or even in front of this doctor, nice as she was.

So he gave a clinical, detached summary of his official actions that day, and while he included Francesca's story, he capsulized it to mentioning that there was one little girl he'd had to stay with for about an hour, but 'She didn't make it,' he said, with a shake of his head. 'That was a tough one.' He paused. 'Her name was Francesca, but they called her Franny.'

Mac waited a few moments, but it became obvious Eddie wasn't going to proceed beyond this distant retelling of some excruciating events. Even the other cops had been shaking their heads when Eddie described finding the car with all the schoolchildren trapped. She looked around the group and back, and asked Eddie one of the clichéd shrink questions she tried so hard not to use. 'How do you feel about what you've just told us, Officer Lopes?'

Eddie stared at her, his eyes blazing. 'I didn't become a cop to watch little kids die within three feet of me and me not be able to . . .' his voice cut off, and he shook his head.

Mac knew he wasn't going to continue. But he did add one last thing. 'Did I tell you her name was Francesca?'

Mac usually returned to her apartment after the sessions, and since Eddie Lopes was usually headed to his Union Square patrol, they had started walking to 15th Street together after the meetings, as they did today.

From the first, Mac had noticed the way people reacted to Eddie, and his response to their usually friendly greetings. Eddie Lopes was the kind of cop commanders dreamed about – bright, vigilant, aware, responsible, and accepted by the community. He was very good at what he did, and Mac made a point of telling him so.

She had also gradually coaxed more details out of him about his four hours down in that darkened subway station, and about how he felt toward the painful assignment fate had dealt him that day. Mac wondered at times if Eddie realized that these five-block walks were substituting for the more customary shrink's couch. Unusual therapy or not, she thought she got a bit more of a sense of what was troubling him.

Today they had taken the route that brought them straight down Park Avenue South, and Lopes studied the orange and white barriers that still surrounded the 16th Street entrance to the subway, where so much of the drama that he'd played a part in almost five months ago had taken place.

'You know you're a hero, don't you?' Mac asked.

He looked at her startled. ''Fraid not, doctor. No heroes here.'

'Why? Because Francesca died?'

He stared at her, eyes flaring a bit. 'Isn't that a good enough reason?'

'You aren't counting the seventeen children you brought out from that subway, are you?'

Lopes shook his head.

'Tell me if I'm wrong, Eddie, but I think somewhere, deep inside, you're still thinking that if you'd stayed with her, she would have made it.'

Eddie's head snapped around and he looked at her, his eyes widening in surprise. Mac couldn't tell if the surprise was from anger at the accusation that could be implied in what she'd said, or recognition, that she'd finally given words to what he'd been feeling.

'You don't have to say anything, Eddie. Just think about it. And know that you did everything humanly possible for Francesca, but not everything is within human power.'

Lopes was quiet, and his eyes looked unusually bright, even in the grey noon time light. Mac patted his sleeve. 'I know you're a hero, Eddie. We just have to work on you believing it.'

When Dr Pernick had first approached her about leading this group, Mackenzie never hesitated. Later, she wondered if she should have. By the time they were into their second month of meetings, Mac had reminded herself any number of times why she had gone into the academic side of psychology and not the clinical side. It wasn't just the usual predictable answer, the one that said her parents were academics, so she became one, too. A good part of the reason was that academic life, despite its aggravations, was profoundly less painful. Dealing with these men and their pain was challenging and eminently worthwhile, but it was using up the last stores of her reserves, and Mackenzie realized she was very close to being tapped out.

CHAPTER TWENTY-ONE

When Mac got back to her apartment, she tried to call Sylvie at her apartment, as she had promised. After getting only busy signals over a fifteen minute period, she decided she'd check in with Buratti and try to reach Sylvie later.

Buratti answered his phone at the precinct with his usual bark, and seemed glad to hear from her. 'Good, Mac, glad you caught me. I'm just heading out the door, down to the theatre.'

'Any news yet?'

'Nope. But I'll trade you. There's a couple of things you might be able to help me with. How about I keep you posted on this case, and you trade with a little unofficial help on the side?'

Mackenzie had to smile. Buratti had become a master at getting freebies out of her a long time ago. 'You got it, Lieutenant.'

'I'll meet you at the theatre in – what? a half hour?'

Mac checked her watch; that would just give her time to get something to eat, to call her father as she had promised, and walk over to the theatre. 'I'll be there.'

Buratti decided to head across to the East Side and take Park Avenue downtown, but cross-town traffic was impossible, as usual. The stop-and-go gave Buratti plenty of time to try to figure out what he'd do if his next two stops didn't offer any more clues about Gil Richardson and who did him in. Some odd things had already come up about Mr Richardson, and he was eager to talk to Mac about them.

Buratti was glad that Mackenzie Griffin would be joining him. Sorry that it was her friend's involvement that got her in on this case, but still glad to have her on it. Ever since he met her – and that was going back nine, maybe ten years now – Buratti had appreciated Dr Griffin's sharp mind, her ready grasp of a case. Say what you want about training, Buratti was still convinced that there was a characteristic to good detective work, something beyond deductive reasoning, an intuition that was born into you. Whatever it was, Mac had it. God knows where she got it or why, especially given the family she came from. But she had it. He'd always appreciated her help in the past and he was looking forward to having it again.

He was a little concerned about her, though. He'd inherited his mother's opinion that most blondes looked a little sickly, as pale as they were. He'd had to adjust after he started working with Mackenzie. His eyes had gradually gotten accustomed to Mac's fair colouring, but even with that factored in, she didn't look great.

And there was one other thing that had been bothering him, and he had finally figured it out this morning. He couldn't remember the last time they had talked more than three minutes – he didn't think there was one in the last eight years, anyway – when Mac hadn't inquired about Gloria and the kids. Gloria she'd met only once, and the kids she'd seen only in a succession of their school pictures, but she always asked after them, always, even in quick 'I got a question' conversations.

He hadn't seen much of her in the last eight or nine months. While he might have run into her if she were up at John Jay on her usual schedule, she was off working on this PEPSI study that everybody was talking about. Some cops were bitching about it already, before it was even done, but Buratti knew that he trusted this one more because Mackenzie Griffin was involved with it. God knew something had to be done after that last scandal that ripped the department apart. And if the study really did what they said it was gonna do, it was important work, and a tough job for Mac.

He'd called after he'd heard she was on the scene at that 16th Street Bombing, but he'd only spoken to her briefly. He'd heard through the grapevine that Mac was involved with a group of some of the cops who'd worked that scene. What a nightmare that was. Maybe that's what still had her down. And maybe getting her involved in this case would give him a chance to find out for sure.

Mac's lunch consisted of a carton of fruit yogurt, eaten while standing in front of the television, watching to see if CNN was still covering the story of Gil Richardson's death. They were, but after a brief summary of the obituaries being published about the deceased, the announcement was made that the New York police still were investigating the circumstances of Richardson's death. Mac noticed that the reporter was now stationed in front of one of the Times Square theatres where one of Richardson's earlier shows was playing. Apparently that colourful marquee made for a better television picture than the canvas-wrapped Century Theatre.

After a brief conversation with her father, Mac set out for the theatre carrying her rolled up umbrella; the skies were heavily overcast, and the rain promised for that evening looked like it would arrive earlier. Buratti had just walked in ahead of her, and was heading toward the dressing rooms.

'Hey, Mac, I'll be with you in a minute,' he said. Mackenzie replied with a nod. He headed down the hall, and turned back again. 'I hear your friend Sylvie's out in the audience, by the way.'

Sylvie was *here*? Mackenzie found that very surprising. She would have assumed that this was the last place Sylvie would be today. She found her way out to the auditorium from backstage, and spotted Sylvie sitting in an end-of-the-row seat about half way up the left side aisle.

Sylvie's eyes flashed when she saw her friend. 'Mackenzie. Welcome to my nightmare.'

'What are you doing here?' Mackenzie asked. 'I tried to phone a few times.'

'You and everybody else I've met in the last ten years who watches television news or reads a newspaper and who knew I was in this show. When I got the tenth call by I think it was eight-thirty this morning, I just took the phone off the hook.'

'But why come here?'

'One of the ten who got through to me was Duran,' she beckoned with her head to the stage where the choreographer she had pointed out to Mackenzie a week before was rehearsing with a young woman who moved awkwardly about the stage, an opened loose-leaf notebook in her hand. 'They're rehearsing my understudy and Duran told me I needed to be here in case they hadn't gotten all the notes on Miss Goodwin into Duran's script, in which case I'd have to help them out.' She looked at Mackenzie with a doleful expression. 'It's also called rubbing salt in the wound.'

Sylvie looked back at the stage. 'The good news is, she's awful.'

Mac watched the activity on the stage for a few moments and had to agree with Sylvie. The awkwardness of the woman's movements was matched by the inadequacy of her voice; it was most uncomfortable to witness.

Sylvie leaned toward Mac. 'I guess we can eliminate any *All About Eve* plot here. I think if she framed me for murder so that she could take over my role, she'd be a little better prepared, don't you?' Sylvie's raised eyebrow told Mac that at least her friend's unusual sense of humour was still intact. 'So how 'bout it?' Sylvie continued. 'Any word from your friend yet?'

'Not yet, but there should be this—'

'Is that him waving for you now?' Sylvie interrupted with a nod of her head.

Buratti was hailing Mac from the side exit. 'Gotta go. Talk to you later.'

Buratti waited until they got out to the sidewalk. 'Beckman's still doing the interviews of everybody who was here yesterday. I'm going to head up to Richardson's apartment now – up on Sixty-seventh, Sixty-eighth, around there, and I plan on getting back here mid afternoon, to talk with a few more of these people. Why don't you come along with me now if you can, and I can start on the questions I have.'

'Let's go,' Mac replied, and headed for the passenger side of the unmarked car Buratti had parked in the tow-away zone.

Buratti waited until the southbound Broadway traffic cleared, and cut diagonally across the avenue to make the turn onto 13th Street and head cross-town. 'So you stay more current with this stuff than I do, Mac. Tell me what you know about this Richardson guy.'

'Well, I'm not an expert, but there was a good article about him in the *Times'* Arts & Leisure section a few Sundays ago. It was one of the stories that tied into the *Reunion* opening, of course, but it was pretty much a profile on Richardson.'

'Complimentary or not?' Buratti asked.

'The writer doing the piece was pretty complimentary about Richardson, but he did mention the trouble that Richardson's had with the press, or some members of the press and the critical establishment.'

'How so?'

Mac attempted to summarize the article for him, but that was a challenge. It wasn't the usual puff piece that generally was a staple in pre-opening publicity. The writer's thesis was that Richardson's problem was that he couldn't be categorized. The more definite pigeon-holed was the term used, however. Was he a dancer, yes, that's the way he started. Was he an actor – yes, he'd done that, too, and done well at it. But Richardson said that nowadays he mainly thought of himself as a director, but even there he ran into trouble. Was he a musical director? Obviously. He'd won Tony Awards in that category. But was he also a *serious* director? Richardson had directed a straight play early that season in Chicago, and was talking about bringing the play to New York next season. The profile's writer said that would only stir up the whole controversy again.

She tried her best, and Buratti seemed to get the main point of the article – that Gil Richardson was a man of many gifts, and not a talent to be trifled with.

Buratti nodded as the information settled in. 'Did you tell me you met him?'

'Last week. We were really just introduced, but I was thrilled.'

'A fan of the guy's were ya?' the lieutenant teased with a smile. 'So, tell me about his accent. Where do you think he came from?'

Mac looked at him quizzically. That was pretty common information about the director. 'Well, he was from England, but he'd emigrated here with his parents in his late teens or early twenties, according to the things I've read. So his accent was – well, I'll tell you what that profile on him said. It said that he'd so perfected the mid-Atlantic accent, he sounded like he came from a point directly south of Greenland.' She leaned forward to see if she could catch a bit more of the expression on his face, but he was studying intently the swarm of cars ahead of them on Eighth Avenue. 'Why are you asking about that?'

'We started doing some checking on the computers this morning, to see if we could notify a next of kin.'

'And—?'

'They told us at the theatre last night that he didn't have any next of kin here, but we were trying to get some information, see if maybe there's somebody in England we should notify. I mean, there's usually somebody. But there's no record of him with INS.'

'With Immigration? How about if he's still a British subject? Maybe he never became a naturalized citizen.'

'Either way, INS should have some kind record of him – if he was naturalized, when, or if he's a resident alien, his status and green card and that kind of thing. But the woman who does our computer searches – and she's good, believe me – she says she can't find anything on him in terms of place of birth, date of birth, next of kin, nothing. The theatre company here gave us a social security number, but the only thing we can tell is that it was issued in New York maybe twenty-four, twenty-five years ago.'

'That's odd, isn't it.'

Buratti nodded, but stared at the traffic ahead of them, which looked to be clearing once they got past the usual construction mess around 42nd Street. 'I just got an intuition about this case that it's not gonna shake out the way we think.'

Buratti parked around the comer from the front entrance to Richardson's building on Central Park West. The doorman directed them to the building management office, and the manager on duty, a prematurely balding man in his 30s named Mr Pressman, escorted them up to Richardson's apartment, murmuring his regrets over the news of the director's death in a succession of clichéd phrases for the entire time it took the elevator to rise fourteen floors.

Mr Pressman unlocked the door to Richardson's apartment, and ushered them in in the manner of a maitre d'. Before the man could enter, however, Buratti told him they'd check with him when they were through, and the building manager understood that he was being dismissed.

Even with today's grey skies, light poured into the apartment from the large wall of windows on the opposite side of the living room. The entrance foyer where Mac and Buratti stood was a few steps above the living room, as was the dining area which was a large open area to the right of the sunken living room. Buratti reached for the switch panel to the left of the door, and recessed ceiling lights spotlighted large posters – the size they use to advertise shows in the subways – from Gil Richardson's shows that dominated the long left wall of the living room and the shorter wall expanses on either side of the entrance.

Except for the posters, Mac noticed, there was almost no colour in the room, which made the already large room – it appeared to be about eighteen by thirty – look even larger. The walls, carpet, upholstery on the large L-shaped sofa and the two large overstuffed armless chairs were in varying hues of a peachy-sand. The few hard surfaces that there were in the room – a big coffee table at least four feet in diameter, tables that stood at both ends of the sofa's 'L', and the impressive piece of exotic wood that had been shaped into a dining table – were absolutely bare.

There was a large plant – almost a tree, really – at least six feet high standing to the right of the group of windows on the raised platform that formed the opposite end of the living room.

Buratti looked at the view over Central Park West, and then down at the large expanse of pastel carpet. 'I tell you one thing. This guy never had any kids in here.'

'Actually,' Mac said, stepping down, 'it doesn't look as though there was ever much living in this living room.' She'd seen department store furniture displays that had more warmth than this place. 'Except for the posters, there's barely a hint that Richardson lived here. Or anybody.'

'Well, let's see what we can find,' Buratti said, leading the way across the living room and up the steps. He paused briefly in front of the windows. Mac stopped next to him. 'If the view makes you stop on a cloudy day,' she said, looking across the park that was struggling to come into green, to the cityscape of Fifth Avenue and the East Side, 'imagine what the view on a pretty day would look like.'

'Hell, you'd never get anything done,' Buratti replied, then headed to his right, walked through an archway and made a U-turn. 'Okay, that's the kitchen, don't need to check it at this point.' He pointed to past Mac, to a hallway in the opposite direction. 'We try that way next.'

The short hallway led to the master bedroom/bathroom to the right, a room that also had a view of the park albeit one that looked south, and to a combination guest bedroom/office across the hall, where the only view was of an air shaft to the side of the building. This bedroom/office was lined with bookcases at one end, with a small desk built into the middle of them. While the bookcases and desk were painstakingly neat, they did not seem devoid of life, as the living room had.

'Why don't you start taking a look at the bookcases, Doc, see what you can see, while I check out his bedroom?'

Mackenzie started reading through the shelves, and by the second bookcase she was astonished at the selection. She had no idea there were so many variations and permutations of subjects pertaining to theatre – theatre design and architecture, costume design, stage lighting, scenery. There was even more of a selection when you got to Richardson's specialties – books on the history of the musical theatre, English music hall traditions, voice production, exercises for the singer, the evolution of choreography, theories of musical composition, and many, many song books. This was the library of a theatre professional, and it left Mackenzie awestruck.

'Nothin' in the bedroom,' Buratti said as he stepped into the room, 'but a boatload of prescription bottles in the medicine cabinet. I'm gonna call the guys down at the ME's office and read some of the names off to them, see if it helps. You find anything?'

'Not what you're looking for, not in the books anyway,' Mac said as she stepped around the desk. She looked down and there, set to the side, was a flat grey box. 'But his laptop computer is here. Want to take a look at that?'

'You know how to get it goin'?' Buratti asked. 'Don't you need a password or somethin'?'

'Not necessarily,' Mac said, opening the cover and adjusting the screen to the proper angle. She flipped on the power button. 'Not if we're lucky. And if we're *real* lucky, the programs that he used most frequently will be on automatic start-up.'

'Yeah?' Buratti said with a raise of his eyebrows. 'You know all about this computer stuff, Mac? I'm impressed.'

'Not all about it, but enough to get around.' She waited for the machine to boot up. 'There,' Mac said. 'We're in luck. It opened onto his personal organizer. It's a calendar, address book, that kind of thing.' She moved the small trackball at the bottom of the keyboard. 'The other programs that started up are word processing and one on personal finances.'

'We might have to take this thing with us, Mac,' Buratti said. 'But while we're here, see what you can find out in that personal organizer thing.'

Mac started leafing through the pages of the calendar in the last week, and then the last month. 'It seems he had a number of appointments with a Dr Christopoulos. An appointment about three weeks ago with someone at Chase Manhattan, and the day before that with one of the big brokerage firms. He's got appointments with Wexler listed, and one with the other producers. A few miscellaneous names with addresses indicated. But most of his calendar is filled in with rehearsal times.'

'Can you see if there's a number for this Dr Christopoulos?'

Mac moved to that address section of the program.

'Here's Christopoulos's number,' she said and read it off to Buratti as he copied it in his note-pad. 'Do you want the numbers on the other guys?'

'If you can, yeah.'

'If they're here, you got 'em.' They were, and he copied those down as well.

'How about the finances one,' Buratti asked. 'Can we take a look at that?'

'We'll see,' said Mac. 'I've only worked with one of those, and I think there's more variation in the programs.' She was able to find her way into the listing of Richardson's expenditures, but the listings they reviewed since the beginning of the calendar year seemed routine. At least nothing jumped off the screen.

'Why don't you close this up, and we'll take it with us,' Buratti said. 'Beckman mentioned that one of our new guys is some kind of computer whiz, so I'll have him check it out. Meantime, I'm going to call this Dr Christopoulos and then check in with the ME's office.'

Mac shut down the computer, and continued her perusal of Richardson's book shelves. She could hear Buratti on the phone in the bedroom, struggling with the names of medications as he spoke to his contact in the Medical Examiner's office.

'Well,' Buratti said as he crossed the hall, 'according to Dr Christopoulos' office, he's due back in town tonight, and should be checking with them tomorrow morning. So we'll try to catch up with him then.' He picked up the computer and extended his arm for Mac to precede him into the hallway. 'As for our friends at the ME's office, they tell me that Richardson apparently had this reputation of being a really healthy guy – dancer, in good shape, all of that. Not one of those health nuts, but close. Well, according to what they've seen so far, red meat was about the only thing that wasn't in Gil Richardson's body.'

That news brought Mac to a halt as they got to the steps in the living room. 'Drugs? You're saying Gil Richardson was on drugs? That makes no sense.'

'They're not saying he was on street drugs, or anything illegal, even. Just that they'd already picked up traces of uppers, downers, every kind of thing.'

'Maybe this doctor will be able to tell you what was prescribed for him and why.'

Buratti stopped just before they got to the front door. 'You know, I should just take those prescriptions with me, and ask Christopoulos about them. Richardson's sure not going to be needing them any more.' He handed the computer over to her. 'Can you hold this a minute, Mac?'

Mac waited by herself in the living room. As she looked around, she remembered how thrilled she'd been to meet Gil Richardson just last week. And how unlikely it seemed then that she'd ever be standing in his living room. There was an elegance about this room, she realized, as there had been about its occupant. But it was the most coldly impersonal room she'd ever seen in a private home, and strangely sad because of that.

While Buratti finished up with the building manager, Mac was struggling to hold onto the computer while trying to open her umbrella. The rain had started while they were upstairs, and while it wasn't heavy yet, it was enough to make the ride downtown messy.

Buratti pulled the car around the front of the building to pick her up, and he was complaining about the windshield wipers when she got into the passenger side. 'These guys never remember to check the window cleaning fluid. Look at this!' he said in a tone of disgust. 'Streaks all over the place!'

Mac settled in, placing the computer securely at her feet. 'So with the drug information from the Medical Examiner's office, do you think you're closer to solving this thing?'

Buratti came to a stop at a red light, and looked at her. 'Do you think your friend's going to suddenly confess to stabbing a dead body?'

'No,' she said with a gentle snort.

'Then I don't think we're real close to solving this thing.' He waited for the light to change and started down Columbus again.

'Well, we could always start looking into those stories they were pumping out about the ghost of Century Theatre,' she said with a grin.

'Yeah, that's just what I need. My stock in the commissioner's office and the mayor's office isn't real high these days.' He moved over to the right lane. 'I'm gonna head down Ninth Avenue, like I should've done this morning.' Once he passed Lincoln Center, he took up where he left off. 'I got a sneaky feeling I'm gonna have to come up with some story of how a drug overdose – accidental or intentional, we don't know – but how a drug overdose ends up with a knife in his back. With what I got to go on so far, I'm gonna look like enough of a jabeep, so I'll be damned if I'm gonna start asking anybody questions about ghosts.'

Mac enjoyed Buratti's discomfort. 'I think that's probably a wise move,' she said solemnly.

The travelling wasn't as bad as Buratti had expected it to be. But it was still just past two. Rush hour was gonna be sloppy if this rain kept up. He turned to Dr Griffin again.

'So I heard you're working with some of the cops from

the 16th Street Bombing. Tell me how're those guys doin'?'

'Some better than others,' Mac said with a weary smile. 'Is that enough of a shrink answer for you?'

'You're allowed. How about that study you're working on?'

'I wrapped up on the interview side about four months ago, so now we're working on the report itself. That's the more tedious part of it for me.'

'Think it will be worth the effort?'

'Hard to tell.' They had stopped at a red light again, and Mackenzie listened as the windshield wipers slapped back and forth in the drizzling rain. 'Actually, it was a lot rougher assignment than I thought it would be.'

'How so?'

Mac didn't want to go through the whole story with him, so she just went for what was closest to home. 'A lot of the young cops out there are burning out fast, Mario. It wasn't a walk in the park talking to them.'

'It's that noticeable, hunh?'

Just as they passed Port Authority, Mac turned in her seat so that she was facing him more directly. 'I was reading a draft of the social welfare report the other day, and one of the interviewers had inserted a handwritten note. One social work supervisor said that the "kids" she had working for her – I think in her definition that's anybody under thirty – but she said these kids were as burnt out as she'd been after ten or twelve years on the job. Only for them it was eighteen months or two years.'

Buratti took in her comment, but waited until he got to the next stop light to respond. 'You know, now that I think about it, I've noticed that with some of the young ones in the precinct. There's something there that you don't see in guys my age. Not that there are that many guys my age around. I'm comin' up on my twenty-fifth year, and I see some of these young guys quitting after five, six, eight years on the job.'

'Did you ever feel you were about to burn out?'

He turned east on Twentieth Street, heading toward the theatre. 'We didn't call it that then, but there was a time early on when I came pretty close to quitting.'

'What happened? Do you remember?'

'I'll never forget. I was working out of the East Village precinct, and my partner and I were the first to respond to a domestic disturbance call. Those have always been wild ones, you never know what the hell you're walking in on. Anyway, we get to this run-down building, half-vacant, and the neighbours send us up to the third floor. We find the apartment easy enough, because this guy is bellowing like an animal. This totally terrorized woman – she's maybe twenty-two, twenty-three, lets us into the apartment. The guy is one of the first really wild drug collars I can remember. He was absolutely out of it, and I swear he had the strength of ten men. Once we got him cuffed, and that took some doing, the woman – and she's buzzed too, but a regular buzz – well she's crying and pulls me into the bedroom. And there's this spot on the wall, and then she points down to the floor, and there's a baby, looking just like a broken baby doll.'

Mackenzie squinted her eyes shut, not wanting to imagine the scene.

'The baby was five months old, and he'd thrown her against the wall because she was crying,' Buratti continued. 'It was a big case, headlines for days in the papers. It was so . . . beyond the run-of-the-mill depravity of the city.'

'You said you almost quit?'

'I went home that first night, and Michael was about

three, and Angela was just a baby, a couple months younger than the baby who died. I just stood next to their cribs and stared at them half the night. I went to my sergeant the next day and told him I couldn't do this job anymore. He told me not to worry, that he'd been on the force twenty years, and he'd never seen worse than that.' He smiled and shook his head at the memory. 'Nowadays, a story like that doesn't raise a ripple – unless it's a slow news day.'

He pulled up next to the theatre in the same tow-away spot he'd occupied before. 'Young guys today, young women, too, they see stuff like that over and over again in their first three, four years on the force.' He looked right at Mackenzie. 'And Doc, let me tell you, you can get brutalized by that kinda shit.'

They used the same stage entrance, and as soon as they got inside, they heard loud voices. Lots of loud, angry voices. Coming from the stage area. 'What the hell is going on?' said Buratti, to no one in particular, and headed toward the stage to investigate what the commotion was.

Mackenzie saw Beckman approach from the hallway and he intercepted Buratti with 'Lieutenant, glad you're back.'

Buratti turned and beckoned Beckman close. 'Can you tell me what's going on here?'

'All hell broke loose about ten minutes ago.'

CHAPTER TWENTY-TWO

Buratti walked closer to the lighted stage area and pulled the curtains to one side to see who the participants in this high-decibel conversation were. Most of them he recognized from yesterday: Wexler the producer was there, looking pretty red faced; Jonathan Humphries and the architect Quigley stood a pace or two behind him. Thomas, that assistant of Richardson's, seemed to be going toe-to-toe with Wexler, and the designer, Manny Erickson, had just stepped in between the two of them. Those five, standing near the centre of the stage, seemed to be the only ones directly involved in this discussion. The others on stage, including Mac's friend Sylvie Morgan, the older actor Leland, and the choreographer, were spectators and listeners.

He pulled the curtain aside to give Mac and Beckman a chance to see, and they stepped forward on either side of him. Sylvie spotted Mac almost instantly and started edging her way around the stage as the argument continued.

'—there's not a chance the theatre could be ready in time, anyway, Thomas,' the designer was finishing.

'That's not why he said no,' replied Richardson's assistant, indicating the producer.

'Why? You want to know why?! It's goddam creepy that's

213

why!' Wexler yelled right into Thomas's face.

The young man, who had seemed so reserved in Mac's two previous encounters with him, now seemed fiery. 'No, it's because it won't earn you any money, *that's* why!'

'You little shit . . .' Wexler started.

'Maybe if we printed tickets and you could charge admission, *then* you'd let us have Gil's memorial service here.' The designer had to put out a hand to Wexler's chest to keep him away from the young man after that comment, and looked to Bruce Quigley and Jonathan for some help in restraining the older man. Quigley stepped forward and put a hand on Wexler's bicep to pull him back.

'C'mon, Thomas, it's just not going to happen,' Manny said calmly.

The grieving young man responded in a quieter voice than he'd used before, but it was obvious that his passion had not abated. 'Gil Richardson gave his life to the theatre, he died in the theatre, and he should be memorialized in one.'

Wexler seemed to have gotten some control over himself. He sounded calmer when he replied, 'And I say a funeral isn't going to be the first thing that people ever attend in this theatre.'

'But if it's—' Thomas tried to start again.

'Might I suggest something?' Curtis Leland interrupted.

The men involved in the discussion turned to him. '*What?*' Wexler finally said.

'I agree with Thomas that Gil should have a memorial service in a theatre,' he began, and Wexler's eyes blazed in his direction. 'But I think that memorial service should wait a few months until his friends in the theatre can collaborate, and prepare a memorial tribute fitting to the man.' Curtis stepped forward until he was in the midst of the five men.

'It seems to me that the ceremony that is upon us Monday is his funeral, and that should be at a church, or wherever his family wishes.'

'He didn't have any family,' Thomas said sullenly.

Curtis patted the young man's arm. 'Then, as the members of his last company, we'll be his family, Thomas.' He looked pointedly at Wexler and then around to the other people standing on stage. 'Won't we?'

There were barely audible murmurs of consent from those gathered.

'That's a great idea, Curtis, and you're right,' Manny said, grateful that somebody had come up with a solution. 'The memorial service should be in June, maybe.' He turned to the young assistant. 'And Thomas, I promise you this. Wherever it is, here or some other theatre, I'll do a beautiful setting for it. Designs from all of Gil's shows. Beautifully lit. Elegant. Theatrical. Just like the man. I promise you.'

'Now Mr Quigley,' the older actor said, looking over toward the architect, still keeping his hand on Thomas's arm, 'you may remember this as well. I seem to recall Gil expressing some admiration for that church over on Fifth Avenue. The one that was renovated not long ago.'

Bruce Quigley smiled at the way Leland had defused the situation. 'That's right, he did. We talked about what a great job they'd done on the building.'

'Thomas,' Curtis continued as he started to lead the young man toward the stage exit, right past where Buratti and the others were standing, 'why don't you and I walk over to that church and see if we can talk to the rector about having Gil's funeral service there?'

Everyone in the theatre, on stage and backstage, seemed to let out a sigh of relief as the two men got nearer the door.

'Don't know if he's interested in running for office,' Buratti said, 'but the guy gets my vote.' He turned to Beckman and motioned him toward the hallway. 'Come tell me what news you have for me. And make it good, please.'

As Beckman moved to follow him, Larry squeezed by and walked into the stage area, where Wexler, Quigley, Humphries and Manny were still conferring. 'Mr Wexler,' he said. 'Janet just called from your office. She said you should get over there as soon as you can.'

Wexler looked surprised and puzzled at the message, but said his goodbyes quickly and headed for the door.

'Mac,' Buratti called. 'You gonna join us?'

'Be right there,' she replied, and turned to Sylvie. 'How are you holding up?'

'Okay, but it's been weird, having to be here. People giving me the fish-eye all day, whispering over in corners. I realized that if this isn't cleared up, and people still suspect me of having whacked my director, any performing career I have will be limited to product demonstrations at the local supermarkets or original productions for local cable access channels. Not a pretty thought.' She looked at Mackenzie with a hopeful expression. 'How about you? Any *good* news?'

'Hate to say it, but we don't know much more than we knew last night. Some interesting possibilities, but not much real information.' She looked over to where Buratti and Beckman were waiting for her. 'I better get with them. I'll catch up with you later.'

Buratti and Beckman headed for the last dressing room, where Mac had first talked to Sylvie yesterday.

'So when did all of that start?' Buratti said, pointing his thumb over his shoulder, indicating the stage area, as he headed for the far side of the counter that ran the width of the room. He perched on the edge of the counter, waiting for Beckman and Mac to find their own places.

Beckman sat on the opposite end of the counter. 'This Thomas guy showed up not too long ago, tried to get into the dressing room that Richardson had been using, and seemed pretty annoyed when I told him he couldn't go in, that it was still a taped-off crime scene. He was pissed off at that, and then when he started talking to Wexler, things blew up fast.'

'Tried to get in there, hunh?' Buratti asked.

Beckman nodded. 'The composer, this guy Wheeler, he also wanted to get into Richardson's dressing room earlier, too, and he seemed real perturbed when he couldn't. Said Richardson had something of his that he needed, that it might be in the room. I told him we'd let him know when we release it.' Beckman looked at his notes and paused. 'I think we should talk to Wheeler again, and you should be in on that next session. We'd do it now, but he's gone home sick, I hear. That guy was real squirrely when he couldn't get into the dressing room.' Beckman paused. 'This Lenny Yarnevich was real distressed telling me about the bad blood between Richardson and this Wheeler guy.'

Buratti seemed interested in Wheeler's desire to get into the dressing room. 'Have we taken a look at what's in there?'

'Yeah. Nothing that's gonna be of obvious use to us, just a few things I think we should hang on to. Like Richardson's notebook, rehearsal calendar, his briefcase—'

'It'll be interesting to see what these guys who want to get into the dressing room go after,' Buratti interrupted. 'Let's keep an eye on that. How did the rest of the interviews go?' Buratti asked.

217

'Basically, more detail on what we got last night. People witnessing Richardson and Sylvie Morgan fighting, he leaves the stage, later she leaves the stage, there's a commotion, the witnesses see her standing over his body with a knife.' He finished with an apologetic shrug toward Mackenzie. 'But from what you've told me we're getting out of the ME's office, this is all barking up the wrong tree. Right?'

'Right,' nodded Buratti with a sigh. 'I passed along some information on the drugs that Richardson was taking, and that may help them sort it out enough that we know what it was that killed him. But we still don't know how. I don't think we're talking suicide here. An accidental drug overdose is hard to explain with the knife sticking out of his back. But we don't have any signs of struggle where he was killed, so it's not likely that anybody forced him to take something and then knifed him.' Buratti ran his hand over his face, yawning. 'I don't know what to make of it.' He looked back to Beckman. 'Who else do you have to talk to?'

'I'm waiting to talk to this Duran Nadeem, the choreographer. She's been rehearsing the whole time I've been here, but she told me they're wrapping up pretty soon. And I've been trying to follow up on who else was seen in the backstage area here just before Richardson's body was found.'

'People not in the company?' Mackenzie asked.

'Yeah, this guy Gregory Byers, husband of one of the producers. And Howard Goldman, a guy from the union council.'

'Why don't we find out how long this choreographer woman is going to be,' Buratti said, 'and then you can make those calls you need to, and then maybe we can finish up here. At least for today.'

★ ★ ★

Beckman started the interview with Duran Nadeem. 'Miss Nadeem – or is it Mrs?' he started.

'It's Duran,' she said, twisting off the top of a large bottle of sparkling water. She took a long drink of it before setting in on the counter next to where she sat.

'Duran,' he started again, less comfortable using her first name, 'we've had reports from a couple of people that there was some trouble between you and Gil Richardson recently.'

'You mean the "Duran, don't think I don't know who you are" thing the day before yesterday.'

Buratti picked up the questioning. '*Was* there a problem between you and Gil Richardson?'

'You might say that,' she said with a weary smile. She gave them the capsule version of her earlier encounter with the director, and of her evolution from Dorothy Ann Wallace to Duran Nadeem. When she finished she took another long sip of water, and then rattled off both the questions she expected and the answers she'd prepared. 'Do I think he recognized me? No. Do I think somebody told him who I was? Yes. Was he pissed off? Yes. Do I know who told him? No, and it doesn't make any difference to me who did.'

She stretched out her legs and flexed her feet, every movement revealing her life as a dancer. 'But the real question you want to ask is did I kill him? Am I right?'

The two cops nodded their heads almost imperceptibly. It was unusual to have somebody conduct their own interview, as this woman was doing.

'No, I didn't kill him. But there were plenty of times over the last ten years when I thought about it.' She slid off the counter and picked up her water bottle again. 'Just for the record, I don't think Sylvie did either,' she said, looking at the cops first and then at Mac. 'She's too much of a pro. Richardson was on her case bad, but Sylvie was giving as good as she was getting. She was pissed off when she left the stage yesterday, but she wasn't homicidal.' She took another long drink of her water. 'Gil was the one who had gone wacko. I went to talk to him after that "Duran, I know who you are" thing and the guy went batshit on me. Absolutely crazy! Like my changing my name was a personal insult to him.'

'Mind if I ask you a few questions maybe you haven't thought of?' Beckman said with a tight smile. This woman was getting ready to leave, and by his count she had only answered one question they had put to her.

'Sure,' she said, leaning back against the counter again.

'Can you tell us who you saw in the backstage area yesterday?'

'Besides the actors and the crew?'

'Besides the actors and the crew.'

'Let's see. Manny and the architect were around with Larry, still talking about the problem in the stage left lighting. Gregory Byers was here, trying to pretend he wasn't sniffing after Rhonda. Does he think we're all blind—' she looked at her audience of three with an expression of disgusted impatience '—and deaf, if you know what I mean?' she finished with a telling raise of her eyebrows. 'Lenny and Ben were around, as usual, talking in whispers in the corners. Same for Wexler and Jonathan, except they don't whisper as much. The union guy, Golden or Goldman, whatever his name is, was trying to talk to people until Larry ushered him outside again. I remember seeing some delivery guys coming in just as we were finishing a break, but somebody else will have to tell you more about that.' She thought for a moment, fingering the mouth of her bottle. 'And that's about it.'

Both Buratti and Beckman nodded that they were done, and Duran excused herself in a flash, with a brief smile toward Mac.

'That was quick,' said Buratti. ' 'Course it helps when you got both the questions and answers prepared.' He turned to Beckman. 'Why don't you make those calls? I'm going to see if I can get anything to drink around here.'

Gregory Byers stayed at his desk later than usual for a Friday. He didn't know if he should stop at the theatre on the way home, since that was the normal schedule he'd been following, or if he should stay as far away as possible. Or would that look suspicious?

Not looking suspicious had been the focus of his attention in the last few days. He'd arrived fifteen minutes late for Joan's dinner party last night, despite a cab ride of near miraculous speed, and the expression in her eyes when he'd bent over her chair to kiss her had seemed more than the usual peeved-that-he-was-late look.

Joan had not announced the news of Gil Richardson's death until after coffee was served, and after that, it was, of course, the only topic of conversation. When Joan began one of her anecdotes with 'I talked to Gil just last night,' Gregory at first felt light-headed and then he thought he'd lost sensation in his legs. *She talked to Richardson! Last night! Oh Christ!* He thought he'd gotten to the man soon enough, but maybe not. The sonofabitch had said he'd give him forty-eight hours!

He closed one fund prospectus he hadn't been reading for the last hour and a half and opened another to keep in front of him. He was still trying to decide whether or not to stop at the Century.

If he did go to the theatre, it was a sure thing that Rhonda would be all over him the minute he walked in the door, and he didn't know if he could chance that. The voice mail message she'd left for him this morning had been sizzling. First she let him know how pissed off she was that he'd left her 'needy' last night; then she decided to forgive him if he showed up today and she'd promised what they'd do and where. Her descriptions were vivid enough that he decided to change his access code to his voice mail to be sure that no one else could hear his messages.

His phone rang and he reached for it automatically. Damn! he thought as the phone was half-way to his ear. He should have let the receptionist get it. That opinion was reinforced when he heard the first words from his caller. 'Gregory Byers? This is Detective Stuart Beckman.'

Ben Wheeler was throwing up again, this time in the small bathroom right off of his studio. If he kept heaving his guts out, he was gonna lose ten pounds by Sunday. He hadn't kept anything down in days.

He still couldn't believe that he hadn't been able to get into Richardson's dressing room to see if he could find the goddam tape. In fact, he couldn't believe the whole series of events that had led to him heaving his guts out every few hours.

More than two weeks ago, when they'd been having problems with the love song for the second act, Richardson had come here to Ben's studio to hear a couple of possibilities he'd worked on.

When Ben had worked on the songs over the weekend, he'd kept his tape recorder running as he usually did during his work sessions, just in case inspiration struck. That evening when Gil Richardson joined him in the studio, he hadn't needed to refer to the tape for the first new melody he'd come up with, but the second one wasn't as clear in his mind or his notes. He popped the reference tape in the player, not noticing that he was playing the wrong side.

When his voice and Mabel Leonard's came through the speakers, Gil looked at him quizzically. While the tape kept playing, he explained to Gil about meeting Mabel Leonard and the sessions he'd taped starting three years ago. 'It's a front row seat in theatre history, man. She's got some great stories.'

A phrase from the tape recorder jumped out and caught Richardson's attention. 'She's talking about *Main Street*?' he asked Ben. *Main Street* was an unproduced Glenn Leonard show from 1960 that theatre aficionados still lamented never got off the drawing boards. It was to have been Leonard's salute to small-town America, but he and his producer decided the show was too similar to, and would be unfavourably compared to, *The Music Man*. Leonard had never published the music, and the show had been forgotten by all but the scholars of American musical theatre.

As Ben was sharing with Richardson his enthusiasm over Leonard's work, music playing in the background of his conversation with Mabel Leonard caught his attention first, and then Richardson's. As Ben's eyes widened and he sat back on the piano bench in shock, Richardson stepped to the tape recorder and turned up the volume.

What he was hearing was the music for 'Remember When', the big production number in act two of *Reunion*, a number that had worked spectacularly well from the first rehearsals. Only on the tape it was the 'City Slicker' number from *Main Street*, Glenn Leonard accompanying himself on the piano, on a demo tape that Mabel Leonard had played for him.

'Oh, my God,' he moaned. He hadn't listened to that tape since he'd recorded it, almost three years ago now. But the song must have stayed in his head. He'd unconsciously used Glenn Leonard's melody and, the more he listened, the whole structure of his 'City Slicker' number for 'Remember When'. Consciously or not, he'd plagiarized.

If word of this got out, he'd be ruined. No, first he'd be a laughingstock and then he'd be ruined. Too many people had already heard the 'Remember When' number from *Reunion* to hide its similarity to 'City Slicker'. Similar, hell! It *was* 'City Slicker'.

He leaned his elbows on the keyboard producing a bleat of sound as he put his face in his hands. 'I just got a note from Mabel Leonard last week,' he said to the director in a voice full of misery. 'She moved down to the Carolina shore year before last, but she said she'd be in the opening night audience, cheering *Reunion* on.' He looked up at Richardson, trying to find some humour in the grim situation. 'Well, at least some of the score will be familiar to her, won't it?'

'So you'll change it,' Richardson said with a shrug. 'Now let me hear what you've got for the love songs.' The director had dismissed it so casually, Ben could never have dreamed of the nightmare it would become.

It wasn't until after Richardson left that night that Ben realized the bastard had taken the tape with him. At first he tried to think that was accidental, but as he played the end of their meeting over and over in his head, there didn't seem any accidental way the tape leapt out of the machine and into Richardson's hands.

When he'd asked the director for the tape the next day,

Richardson's response chilled him. The director didn't confirm having it, but he didn't deny it either. He only said, 'Let's just see how good the replacement number is,' as though the tape were some damn insurance policy.

That was bad enough, to know that there was a tape out there proving that he'd plagiarized off a dead man. A revered dead man. But then Richardson started playing some weird kind of mind games on him, insisting in front of the whole company that 'Remember When' didn't need to be replaced, that the number was working so well it was foolish to replace it. Ben thought the world had gone crazy when he first heard Gil say that. It was as if he wanted Ben to get caught.

In fact, Richardson had turned into a different man in the last ten days. It was almost as though he'd had some fucking personality transplant or something. He seemed to enjoy torturing people. Ben, at least. He wanted to see Ben squirm.

And today, when the cops told him he couldn't get into Richardson's dressing room, he felt like his last ship had sailed. The tape being in Gil's dressing room was his only chance at getting it back. There wasn't any way he was going to get into the guy's apartment, for God's sake. As far as he knew, nobody had ever been there when the guy was alive, so it was much less likely he'd get in now that he was dead.

But Ben Wheeler wasn't going to rest until he found that tape and erased it. Then, for good measure, he was going to burn it.

The phone rang. It was Beverly, calling from the apartment. 'Listen, honey, you got a call from this Detective Stuart Beckman. He says you should call him back at this number, that he and this Lieutenant Buratti need to speak to you . . .'

225

Ben dropped the phone and raced to the bathroom again.

Howard Goldman got the call at the union council. The office still had a switchboard operator, although it was a large computerized phone system, not a switchboard that she operated. Her eyes lit up with curiosity when she told Howard as he was walking back from the men's room that a Detective Beckman of the New York Police Department was on the line for him.

Howard took the call, and listened carefully. They had some questions for him, the detective said. Would it be possible for him to come in for questioning? Since it was late in the day, perhaps he could come into the precinct house tomorrow, Saturday?

'Yes, Detective Beckman, of course,' Howard answered in an unsteady voice. 'And the address where I should come?'

He copied down the address and appointed time on his scratch pad. His hand was shaking enough that it made his usually neat handwriting look wobbly.

CHAPTER TWENTY-THREE

Simon made the walk to his office in record time and was slightly out of breath when he stopped at Janet's desk in the reception area.

'I'm sorry to pull you out of there—'

'Don't be sorry,' Simon stopped her. 'I should be thanking you.'

'—but I thought you'd want to see this right away.' She held up a letter on a law firm's letterhead, and the standard business envelope in which it had been delivered.

'What is it?'

'A notification about the Rowan property on Broadway. They've received an offer.'

Simon snatched the paper out of her hand, and read it, his heart racing now more than it had when he'd sped across 14th Street. Goddammit! Whoever said when it rains it pours must have had this week of his in mind. He looked at Janet, said, 'You're right. Thanks for getting the message to me.' And he retreated up the curving staircase to his office.

He walked into his office, threw the notice on his desk and shrugged out of his raincoat, which he threw over one of the guest chairs in front of his desk. He knew that he'd get a notice on one of the buildings one day. Hell, that's why he'd come up with the damn contract in the first place – he *wanted* to receive the notice. But did it have to be *today*?

Simon had been cash-strapped when he started on this Century project, and there was no way he could put together the financing for all four buildings that would make up the whole complex. When finished, it would not only be the theatre, but three other combined-use residence and office buildings that would surround the theatre. One on Broadway facing east, one on Fourth Avenue facing west, and one on 13th Street facing north. Quigley had come up with the same nineteenth-century look to them, although it was just the front third of the buildings that were limited to the four- and five-storey design of that time; behind the smaller streetfronts sat fifteen- to twenty-storey towers, but the materials of those facades would be the same as on the buildings that looked like they were fresh out of the 19th century. Quigley had done an amazing job on the whole design.

Quigley's design, as good as it was, was only a little over a year old, though. This idea had been Simon's baby for close to ten years now. And when he started, he knew that he couldn't afford to buy up the rights to four block fronts in Manhattan, even if it was an area then in need of restoration.

Instead of trying to buy out the properties or existing buildings, Wexler had researched the ownership of each of the properties and took a page from his experience in the theatre. He approached the owner of the buildings or the lots in question, and got an option on air rights. The mechanism of the deal was that he would pay a yearly option fee to the property owners. In turn, they would notify Wexler and Company if they received a bona-fide offer of purchase for the property, which, of course, would include purchase of the air rights. Wexler and Company would then have thirty days to match or exceed the offer for purchase of the property.

In a blockfront with more than one owner, he approached them one by one until he got a deal; one owner's agreement was all he needed to tie up the block. The options were payable by him yearly, and he'd poured hundreds of thousands into this over the last eight years, but it was the only way to tie up several million dollars' worth of properties without tying up money he didn't even have.

It had seemed a great plan to him. It gave him time to get the whole development moving, although he never thought it would take eight long years to get to this point. But it protected him from other developers stepping in and buying up the properties from under his nose. He'd tried to keep it quiet, of course. In fact, he'd put a confidentiality clause in the agreements, but the secrecy didn't last too long. While his contracts never became really public knowledge, the word that Wexler and Company was dealing got around to the owners, and the last two agreements were much more expensive than the first two.

As much as producing *Reunion* was a dream coming true for him, his real-estate mogul's heart started beating fast at the thought of the whole Century complex. This was the part of the development that would be fun for him, the part that was going to transform Union Square into one of the most desirable neighbourhoods in the city. It was the part that he had been hoping would start right after *Reunion* opened, when he'd be able to interest the money men again.

He looked at the notice on his desk from Rowan's attorney. The offer to buy had been received formally this morning. The thirty-day clock had already started ticking.

Damn! He didn't want to lose that Broadway property! One of those Queens construction companies might come in, put up one of their ugly, sharp-cornered, assembly-line apartment buildings and charge a higher rent than they might have gotten because of all the value Simon Wexler and the Century Theatre were bringing to the neighbourhood. And there was nothing that galled Simon as much as somebody else making money off of his ideas.

Simon moved to the bar and poured himself a couple of fingers of bourbon, and glanced at his watch. Almost four o'clock on a Friday afternoon. Not normally the best time to start initiating business dealings, but he didn't have much choice.

No, instead he had a show that was in trouble, a dead director, an asshole assistant who wanted to make a funeral the first show that played his theatre, and he had no money. The clock was ticking on the thirty day option for a piece of property that was probably going to cost him twelve million to buy, and right now he couldn't lay his hands on a tenth of that.

'Goddammit!' Simon said aloud to his empty office. 'Can't anything go right?'

He moved to his desk and tried to get his game face – and his game voice – on. He placed the call himself instead of buzzing Janet. After a few moments that he was on hold, the secretary put him through to the point man at one of New York's biggest investment banking firms. 'Barney!' he said in as energetic a voice as he could summon up. 'Glad I caught you before the weekend.'

Simon stood up and stared out the window, down toward Washington Square. 'Listen, Barney, I just want to put a thought in your head so it can gestate over the weekend. You know the Century Theatre opening I'm working on. Yeah, yeah, it's an incredible thing with Gil, but this show is going to be a testament to him, believe me.' He reached back to his desk to take another sip of bourbon then turned back to the window, listening to Barney. 'Glad you're looking forward to it. You and Harriet will be my opening night guests, of course. But before that, Barney, y'know things are going so well with the theatre, that the second part of my plan is moving ahead a little faster than I thought it would. The whole Century complex. The other three buildings.' He paused again while Barney remembered.

'Listen, Barney, I'd like to get you down here maybe Monday, show you the models, we'll walk around the property, because I think this would be a great opportunity for Heritage to get involved in.' Another sip, another question.

'Other funding? Well, I have my usual bankers, and I'll be expecting the construction loans from my usual sources. And did I tell you that Jonathan Humphries is on board with me now? Yeah, that Jonathan Humphries, and he has quite a bit of access himself, including that Humphries trust which I think he'll be drawing on quite a bit for his investment in the complex.'

When he heard the first words of agreement, Simon closed his eyes in relief. 'That's great, Barney. Listen, have a good weekend and I'll look forward to seeing you Monday. That's right, we'll touch base in the morning on the time, then we'll meet here and walk over together. Give my regards to Harriet.'

He slumped in his chair and replaced the phone in its cradle. One down, however many to go. He didn't even want to think of how many similar calls he was going to have to make before the three buildings went up. But at least he'd made it to first base with the initial one.

He drained his glass, put it back on the bar, and headed out the door. Janet was just returning to her desk, and she looked up the stairs, surprised to see him.

'You finished with Mr Humphries already?'

'Mr Humphries?' Simon repeated. 'Jonathan?'

'Yes, he came in just as I was heading to the ladies' room. I sent him on up. You mean you didn't see him standing in the door?'

CHAPTER TWENTY-FOUR

Saturday morning Mac's phone rang just after nine o'clock. Peter picked it up in the kitchen, where he was pouring Mac's third cup of coffee and his own second mug of tea. Buratti, not quite sure he had the right number, asked for Dr Mackenzie Griffin rather formally.

'May I ask who is calling?' Peter replied.

'Lieutenant Mario Buratti.'

'Hi, Lieutenant. It's Peter Rossellini.' Though he hadn't seen the man in almost two years, Peter remembered Buratti well from when he was the lead detective investigating the murders that were unfortunately related to Peter's early music videos. It was Buratti's early intuition, and the fact that he brought Mac into the case, that first saved and then changed Peter's life. 'How are you?'

'Peter! *Paisan!* How ya doin'? You taking good care of my friend there, right?'

'Believe it, Lieutenant.' He looked toward Mac, who was smiling at the half of the conversation she was hearing; she would bet that Buratti called Peter his *paisan* again. 'She's right here,' he finished, and pulled on the long cord to hand the phone to Mackenzie.

'Good morning, Mario. What's up?' Mackenzie said, reaching for the cup Peter was handing her.

233

'I just heard from Dr Christopoulos. We can't see him at his office because the building's not open today, but he says he'll be here around ten. Thought you might be interested.'

'Mind if I join you?'

'I was hoping you'd ask,' Buratti said. 'You doctor types can talk to one another easier than to us poor plebeian cop types, you know.'

'Plebeian cop types? A little early in the morning to be piling it on so thick, isn't it, Mario?' She said with a laugh. 'See you at ten.' Mackenzie handed the phone back to Peter. 'That means I have to walk out the door in about twenty-five minutes, and hope there are plenty of cabs on Third.' She squinted, as though doing a calculation in her head. 'Which means I have time to finish my cup of coffee, but I can't even look at the comics.'

Peter moved from the kitchen to his place at the table, opposite Mac. The spark of interest he'd noticed in her last night was still there this morning. Mackenzie was already home by the time he'd returned late yesterday afternoon, and after the latest drizzle stopped, they'd walked over to Hudson's for dinner.

He'd noticed the difference in her energy as they sat in their favourite booth in the back room of the restaurant. As she told him some of the revelations of the day, Mac was more animated than he'd seen her in a while. He'd even teased her about it. 'I don't know about you, Mackenzie,' he said with a shake of his head. 'Being around murder seems to cheer you up.'

'Well, I will admit to being intrigued,' she admitted as the waiter served their dinners. 'A dead man with a knife in his back, who apparently wasn't stabbed to death. That's interesting in and of itself. But I'm also fascinated by the difference between the public image of Gil Richardson and the private. This man that I was so excited to meet last week, who was so charming when I did meet him, and warm, and who lived in the coldest apartment I've ever seen. He had a wonderful reputation in the theatre, and apparently people were really eager to work with him. But nobody *liked* him very much.' Mackenzie tapped the base of her wineglass pensively. 'He's certainly not what he appeared to be.'

Dr Eugene Christopoulos was a handsome man in his late forties. His Greek heritage was obvious in his wavy black hair that was lightly salted with grey, and his strong cheekbones and bright dark eyes.

Buratti had taken over one of the interview rooms at the precinct and he and Mac sat on one side of the long table, while Dr Christopoulos settled in on the other.

Placing his raincoat on the chair next to him, the doctor started. 'I heard about Gil's death just as I was about to get on the plane in London. I hadn't heard any news there, but somebody had a copy of *USA Today*.' He shook his head, reliving that moment when he read the small box above the masthead, and read it again and again until it sunk in. He patted the pockets of his sports jacket until he found what he was looking for, and withdrew some folded papers. 'I had my office fax a copy of Gil's chart over to me,' he said by way of explaining the papers as he smoothed them out in front of him.

Buratti started pulling out the many prescription bottles he'd found in Richardson's bathroom, and was startled when Mackenzie Griffin didn't wait for him, but began with a question for Christopoulos.

'Do you specialize, doctor?'

'I'm an internist, yes,' he replied.

'Was Mr Richardson's death a surprise to you?' Mackenzie asked.

The man let out a long sigh. 'It should have been, but no, it wasn't.'

Maybe this guy *would* be able to clear up a few things, Buratti thought as he placed the bottles in front of Christopoulos. Maybe Richardson was dying already, or something. 'Can you take a look at these, doctor, and let us know which Richardson was taking currently? Some of the dates go back a bit. It would help the guys at the Medical Examiner's office sort through what they're finding in Richardson's blood if we knew what he was on.'

Christopoulos started picking up the bottles one by one, and his eyes grew larger and darker. 'Goddammit, I can't believe he went back to that quack!' he snapped, slamming one of the bottles down on the table.

'Quack?' Buratti looked up, surprised at a doctor using the term. At least in front of him. 'You talking illegal prescribing?'

'No, it's probably legal,' he replied, looking up at Buratti. 'Barely. It's just medically unsound. This jackass over on East 73rd,' he shoved the prescription bottle in question toward the detective, 'a psychiatrist,' he added with some contempt evident in his voice. 'He's been doing an updated Dr Feelgood routine on people, giving patients these,' he tapped the top of the bottle, 'as a follow-up to his once-a week "intensive vitamin therapy" injections. The goddam stuff is like speed.' He flicked the label of the bottle with his fingernail. 'I swear to God, some of these psychiatrists should have their prescription privileges yanked. They don't know what the hell they're doing with the medicines they're prescribing.'

'If Richardson had an injection of that on Thursday, do

you think it could have contributed to his death?' Mackenzie asked.

'Maybe. I don't know. Certainly no way for me to say so without having examined him.'

Mackenzie reached for one of the bottles Christopoulos hadn't looked at yet, and turned it toward him. 'Was Richardson suffering from depression?'

'Not clinical depression, no. He went through the same swings we all do, up at the beginning of a project, let down when it was all over. Why?'

Mackenzie leaned forward and tapped the bottle she'd just moved. 'This bottle is Hyperion. A few weeks ago I read a journal article on anti-depressants that a colleague had referred me to. It mentioned this specifically. It's pretty powerful, isn't it?'

Christopoulos picked up the bottle in question, a quizzical expression on his face. 'Hyperion? I can't believe it. This is *another* doctor he was going to? Damn, if Gil was pumping all of these into himself, it's a wonder he didn't implode before this.'

'Correct me if I'm wrong, doctor, but isn't Hyperion developing a reputation of doctors prescribing it for its side-effects? Mood elevation in non-depressed patients, for example? Weight loss in others?'

Christopoulos nodded his agreement, a look of disgust creeping over his face.

'But it could have some other effects, too, as I recall from the journal article,' Mac added.

'Yeah, that's right. I haven't prescribed it for anyone, partly because of the warnings I read in the literature about it. It can produce personality changes, paranoia. It also can cause a dramatic and rapid increase in blood pressure, as I recall,' Christopoulos said, lightly drumming his fingers on the table. 'And some of my colleagues are handing them out like breath mints.'

'Doctor, was Richardson sick?' Buratti asked. 'This is some assortment here for somebody who wasn't sick, I mean.'

Christopoulos shook his head. 'No, Gil wasn't sick. At least he wasn't the last time I saw him, which was about ten days ago. He thought he might be coming down with a cold, or maybe his sinuses were flaring up, he wasn't sure. He had a few ailments, of course. But anybody his age who led as physically active a life as he had would have some.' The doctor examined the bottles in front of him again and glanced at the fax sheets briefly. 'I'll show you. The medications in this array that I had prescribed for him are,' he reached for the bottles and lined them up as he spoke, 'a vitamin plus iron supplement, since Gil had a tendency to anaemia, an analgesic for when his dancer's knee started acting up on him, and a very low dose Valium, which he usually needed the week or two before a show opened.' He leaned back in his chair. 'That's it from me. That's three bottles out of – what – eight?' he finished with a shake of his head.

'Doctor, if Mr Richardson wasn't ill, then why did you say it wasn't a surprise to learn that he was dead?' Mackenzie asked. Buratti looked at her with a nod and an expression that seemed to say 'good catch'.

Christopoulos considered his answer but seemed almost reluctant to give it. 'Because Gil Richardson was convinced he would never make it to fifty. Apparently his father and his grandfather, and *his* father and grandfather before that, all died by the time they reached their late forties, and some kind of family story developed that the men of the family never lived past fifty.' He looked over at both Buratti and

Mackenzie. 'To be honest, I wish he'd developed some kind of normal hypochondria or something that I could have tried to deal with. But he had it set in his mind.'

Mackenzie tried to recall the details she learned of Richardson's life in the *Times* profile. 'His father who was the music hall performer? He died before he was fifty?'

Christopoulos looked at her with a strange expression in his eye, but before he could reply, they were interrupted by a knock on the door.

One of the precinct's young female detectives opened the door and leaned in. In the hallway behind her was an older woman who looked to be about seventy, dressed in a well-worn light green wool coat. As she removed her rain hood that was a folded piece of light-weight plastic with ribbons on the ends, she revealed the curls of her freshly permed grey hair. Looking at the woman, Mac could picture the small-town beauty parlour that produced this kind of hair-do.

'Can it wait, Morales?' Buratti said to the young detective, surprised at the interruption.

'I think you'll be wanting to talk to Mrs Rogers, Lieutenant.'

Buratti stood and walked over to the two women.

'Mrs— Rogers, is it? I'm Lieutenant Buratti. What can I do for you?'

The woman wasn't much over five feet, and Buratti towered over her. She looked up at him with a clear gaze. 'They say I need to talk to you to get my boy's body released.' Mrs Rogers had one of those sweetly flowing accents of the South, the type that made even the simplest phrases sound melodious.

'Your boy?'

'My son George.'

239

Buratti looked immediately apologetic. 'I'm sorry, ma'am, but somebody must have misdirected you, because I don't kn—'

'This last number of years he's been calling himself Gil Richardson.'

Hands still in his pockets, Buratti turned back to look at Mac and Dr Christopoulos, his eyebrows cruising his hairline. Composing himself somewhat, he asked the young detective to take Mrs Rogers down the hall to get her a cup of coffee or tea, and by the time they returned, he'd be ready for them. Detective Morales ushered Mrs Rogers out the door.

'Unless British accents have changed in the last twenty-four hours, I'd say a lot of what we know about Gil Richardson just went out the window,' Buratti said as he moved back to his seat. He looked over at Mackenzie, who, if she were less well bred, would have had her jaw hanging.

'What did I tell you about my intuition on this case, Mac? Hunh?' Buratti said. 'I think I just heard somebody yell bingo.'

Mackenzie nodded slowly, then turned back to study the man across the table from her. 'Something tells me that Mrs Rogers isn't quite as much of a surprise for you, Dr Christopoulos. Am I right?'

When Mrs Rogers returned to the room, Buratti expressed his condolences and introduced her to Drs Griffin and Christopoulos.

'Mrs Rogers, Gil – George – wasn't just my patient,' Christopoulos said as he helped her into the chair next to his, 'we had become friends over the last few years. While you're here in New York, my wife and I would be pleased to have you stay with us.'

'That's very kindly of you, Doctor, and I've a mind to take you up on that. I've been to New York City a few times, but I've never felt real comfortable here.'

Buratti started with a few questions. 'Mrs Rogers, we're looking into the circumstances of your son's death, and it would help if you could give me some more background.'

'Of course, Lieutenant. What would you like to know?'

'Could you start with when he became Gil Richardson?'

'Let me see, that was about twenty-four, no, twenty-five years ago.'

'And how did that name change come about?' Buratti continued.

'Just before George was to graduate high school, this touring company come through our town, of the Passion Play based on the famous one in Germany, what's the name?'

'Oberammergau?' Mackenzie offered.

'That's the one. George's high school music teacher, she was always very fond of George because he was such an enthusiastic student, well, she took him and a few other students to the first performance when these people arrived, and after that, George was a different person. He came home that very night and told his daddy and me that he'd found what he was gonna do with his life. The next day or the day after, his teacher, Miz Parsons, called and said the company was looking for a few volunteers to fill in the crowd scenes, don't you know, and would George be interested? Would he,' she said, with a tap of her hand to her purse. 'He was up on the stage with them the rest of the week, and when they were leaving the following Monday, he told us he was going with them. They'd offered him a full-time job.' She looked off in the distance, capturing a memory for a moment. 'They had the sweetest faced young man playing Jesus.'

'So is that when George changed his name, when he left with that company?' asked Buratti.

'No, he was still George Rogers then. He stayed with the Passion Play almost a year, I think, and, my, they played all over. Huntsville, Nashville, Jackson, Memphis, down to New Orleans, up to St Louis. Of course, they would play the small towns near those cities, not in the cities themselves, but George got to see them all.' She paused, and reached inside her purse for a tissue, and dabbed at her nose after finding one. 'The show closed in southern Illinois, as I recall, and George and another young man went up to Chicago, and auditioned for a musical there, and got the parts, and that's when he started dancing. Oh, he'd been dancing here in Mentone, studying with Miz Parsons, who was also the dance teacher, you see, but he said that nothing prepared him for that kind of dancing. But my George, once he put his mind to it, he could do anything.'

'When did he change his name, Mrs Rogers?' Buratti asked more directly.

'After George was in New York a few years, he came home and stayed a while.' Buratti sat back in his chair at that point in her story, realizing she was going to get around to telling him when George changed his name at her own pace. 'But he wasn't happy back home, like I knew he wouldn't be, and when he decided to come back here, he said he was going to make it work for him this time, and there had to be some changes. One of those was that he was changing his name and giving himself a new res—' her face looked puzzled as she struggled for the word.

'Résumé?' Mackenzie offered.

'That's it. His daddy was a little hurt by the fact that George was changing his name, but he never let on to the boy. After he got back to New York, maybe a month or two

242

later, we got a long letter from him that he was calling himself Gil Richardson now, and it was important that we not tell people who he was. It was always hard, pretending we didn't know where George was and all, but he was always real good about his daddy and me. When Mr Rogers died, George came home right away, and since then, he's always made sure I have enough money to live on. He's been a good son.'

'Did you talk to George – or Gil – often, Mrs Rogers?'

The woman shook her head. 'No, not as much as I would have liked to. When he first left, and then after Mr Rogers died twenty-one years ago, George would call every Sunday like clockwork. But in the last few years, it's been more on the order of once a month.' She looked at Mackenzie, and then looked down at her hands. 'Or maybe every other month,' she said quietly.

'Do you know of anyone who wanted to see your son dead, Mrs Rogers?' Buratti asked.

The question seemed to surprise her. 'No,' she paused. 'Of course I don't know much about my son's life, Lieutenant.' She looked him directly in the eye. 'Are you saying that you think someone killed my son?'

Buratti shook his head. 'No, ma'am, we're not sure of that. It's just that the . . . circumstances surrounding his death are questionable, and we're trying to do what we can to answer those questions.'

Mrs Rogers seemed mystified at that. 'I just never dreamed . . .' her voice drifted off. 'I just assumed it was because George was like the other Rogers men. None of them lived to be fifty, you know.'

Buratti had told Mrs Rogers that Detective Morales would help with the paperwork involved in getting her son's body released. While Christopoulos was helping her to the door, Mackenzie asked if he could stay behind for a few more questions. The request surprised both the doctor and Lieutenant Buratti, but they quickly made arrangements for the older woman to be escorted down the hall.

'What're you thinkin', Mac,' Buratti asked when he saw her moving some of the medicine bottles again.

'Doctor,' she addressed Christopoulos, 'if Richardson was taking this,' she moved the Valium to the centre of the table, 'and this,' she moved the Hyperion next to it, 'and he'd also received a Dr Feelgood special,' she moved the bottle related to that next to the others, 'and he took some over-the-counter medications, could that trigger a reaction that was potentially fatal? A reaction like heart failure?'

Christopoulos stared at the bottles she'd positioned, weighing her question. 'It's possible, I suppose. But I'd have to know what OTC medications we're talking about.'

'I'm thinking of the anti-histamines particularly. In the journal piece I read on Hyperion and the other anti-depressants, it mentioned the possibility that anti-histamines can block the elimination of some anti-depressants from the body.'

Christopoulos squinted in concentration. 'I think you're right. I remember something that common in the warnings in the literature. I remember wondering if people would pay any attention, because we treat OTC medications like they're harmless.'

'And am I right that if there was a build-up of the anti-depressants in the system, that could increase some of the side-effects we're talking about? Like the paranoia, the personality changes?'

'Yes.'

Mac turned to Buratti. 'That could explain some of the

comments we've heard about how Richardson wasn't himself.' Buratti agreed with a nod. Mac continued. 'Do you still have somebody down at the theatre?'

'Yeah. Beckman's here, but I think we still have someone down there.'

'Can you call and get them to pick up all those cold and flu medications in Richardson's dressing room, and read them off to Dr Christopoulos? They'll probably have to read the ingredients, too.'

'Sure,' Buratti said. 'I'll get that set up. Where you gonna be, doctor?'

Buratti and Christopoulos made the arrangements, and agreed that they'd do a conference call to the Medical Examiner's office as soon as Christopoulos had done his review. The doctor excused himself to go collect Gil Richardson's mother. Buratti was headed down the hall to get Beckman on the horn with whoever was still stationed at the theatre, but he paused before heading out the door. 'See what I mean about you doctor types communicating? You done good on this one, Dr Griffin.'

He returned to the room a few minutes later to find Mackenzie still studying the prescription bottles. 'So is this what it's come to, Mac? Now we don't know whether we got a murder on our hands or some guy dyin' from goddam cold medications. And of course, we find out today that we didn't even know who the victim was, for sure.' He sat down and moved one of the bottles in front of him to occupy his hands. 'I tell you one thing, if one of my sons came to me that he was changing his name and giving himself a new life story,' he paused, trying to think of what his reaction would be. 'I guess I don't know what I'd do.'

'I feel a little like the world has gone topsy-turvy,' Mac said. 'I can't believe that Gil Richardson got away with this incredible deception for so long, but he apparently did.' She looked at Buratti. 'Is it me, or is this incredibly sad?'

Buratti looked at her and nodded in agreement. Then he slapped the table, forcing himself to move. As they headed for the door, he turned to Mackenzie again. 'You know, after a case like this, a mob hit would seem nice and clear. 'Cause if one of those guys has a knife in his back, *that's* what killed him.'

CHAPTER TWENTY-FIVE

As they stepped into the hall, Mac spotted Dr Christopoulos and Mrs Rogers disappearing around the corner to the main hallway out of the station. Buratti, following her, greeted Beckman who was approaching them from the opposite direction. The younger detective had a puzzled expression on his face.

'Lieutenant—' he started, and there was an unusual plaintive note to his voice.

'What's goin' on, Stu?' Buratti asked. 'Your guys show up or no?'

'Yeah they showed up, and I think we got some surprises on our hands.'

Buratti looked at Mac. 'Just what we needed, hey, Doc? A few more surprises.' He turned his attention back to Beckman. 'Okay, whatcha got?'

Beckman began with a deep breath. 'Down in interview one, I got this Gregory Byers. The guy's practically in tears, begging me not to tell his wife that he's been here, begging me not to tell his wife that he's been boffing this actress – Rhoda, Rhonda—'

'Rhonda,' Mac interrupted. 'Rhonda Deveraux.' It took a good bit of will power not to add 'Doncha know?'

It was Buratti's turn to look a little puzzled now. 'Why

would we be interested in the fact that he was boffing this Rhonda Deveraux? Or is Mr Byers here confessing just because it's good for the soul?'

'Well,' Beckman continued, 'he says that Richardson guy walked in on him and the Deveraux woman ah, in the act, so to speak,' he glanced at Mac nervously, and she knew that his phraseology would be different were she not there.

'No kidding?' Buratti said with a hint of a smile. 'Actually in the—' he stopped himself before he finished the question, and deliberately straightened his face. 'And?'

'And he says Richardson was blackmailing him.'

'What?' Buratti said, noticeably louder than he'd been before.

'He's nervous 'cause he thinks that gives him a motive, but he swears he only talked to Richardson once,' Beckman continued.

Buratti looked interested now. 'What was the blackmail for? Richardson wasn't after him for money, was he?'

Beckman shrugged his shoulders. 'Sort of. Apparently besides Wexler and his partner, this guy's wife is the main financial backer of the show. Wexler needs more money for the production, and Richardson tells Byers to encourage his wife toward making the investment, or he – Richardson – will tell her that he – Byers – is *shtupping* the actress.'

'Blackmail, hunh?' Buratti said, turning toward Mackenzie. 'Just when it sounds like an overdose, we finally get a motive that sounds like murder.' Buratti smoothed his palms over his face wearily. 'Blackmail. I tell ya, this Richardson guy is not who we thought he was in more ways than one.'

Beckman held up his hand, signalling that he had more to tell. 'And then Ben Wheeler, the composer, I had him in interview two but I had to move him close to the men's room because he's upchucked twice now. I can't quite tell, because his story doesn't make sense yet with all the interruptions, but it sounds like Richardson was holding something over him, too. I'm waiting for him to calm down a little before we try again.' He looked down the hall toward the interview rooms. 'And now Morales just told me that Howard Goldman's here, and she put him in interview two.'

'Why don't you finish up with Byers, and then we go in and start with Goldman,' Buratti said, including both Mackenzie and Beckman in his statement. 'Maybe Wheeler will be through communing with the porcelain gods by the time we're through.'

Moments later, the three filed into interview room two, Beckman first, with Mackenzie and then Buratti bringing up the rear. The three moved to take seats on the side of the table opposite the older man.

Beckman made the introductions and then started with a simple 'Mr Goldman, can you tell us wh—'

Goldman cut him off with, 'I saw him dead.'

'What?' Beckman said, as Buratti overlapped him saying 'What was that?'

'Gil Richardson,' Goldman said in a calm voice. 'I saw him dead in his dressing room. Before the young woman came off stage.'

'Tell us what you saw – exactly.' Buratti said quietly, but the fact that it was an order was clear. 'As precisely as possible.'

'I got into the backstage area when there were some deliveries being made, late in the day. I wanted to talk to Richardson, ask for his help on the union recognition. I wanted to appeal to his conscience in person, you know.' The older man paused, remembering the details of those few minutes. 'The door to his dressing room – I think it's dressing room A he was using, was closed,' Goldman continued, 'but his young assistant had told me he was in there. I knocked on the door, but there was no reply. I knocked again, and finally opened the door. I went in and—' he shook his head at the recollection, 'and I saw him slumped over his make-up table. I called to him again, but when I looked at how he was resting there, I knew he wasn't asleep. I went over and felt for a pulse, but there wasn't any. He was dead.'

'You could see his back?' Beckman asked.

'Yes.'

'Was there a knife in it?'

'No.'

'What did you do?' Buratti asked pointedly.

'I did the cowardly thing,' Goldman replied, trying to sit a little straighter, 'of which I'm still not proud. I closed the door and walked out of the theatre and headed for the subway.'

'And you saw Miss Morgan?' Beckman inquired.

'She was still on stage when I left the stage door, yes.'

'Why didn't you tell anybody?' Mackenzie asked.

Goldman smiled in her direction, knowing she wouldn't understand the answer. 'Because I wanted to avoid scenes exactly like this,' he said, holding out his hands to demonstrate that he meant this whole police interrogation room. 'I thought someone else would find him, and that would be that. I never expected that young woman would be treated that way by her colleagues.'

Buratti started to move from his chair, but Mackenzie leaned forward, indicating she had another question for the man. 'Mr Goldman, if I remember correctly, you were in the theatre when they took Mr Richardson's body out. But you've told us that you left the theatre and headed for the subway immediately after finding the body. What made you come back?'

A pained expression passed over Goldman's face. 'I had a crisis of conscience on 14th Street, and I turned back to the theatre, thinking I would let someone know. But by the time I returned, they had found his body, and the police were already en route, or so I heard. And then I heard they were detaining this young actress, and I could have cleared it up then, but I knew my explanation would be suspect, because I had left the building already. And so I stayed silent again.' His remorse was evident in his face.

Buratti rose from his chair, arranging for Beckman to take Goldman's formal statement, and beckoning for Mac to follow him into the hall.

Closing the door behind her, Mac smiled up at the lieutenant.

'Well, that clears your friend.'

'She'll be pleased to know about Goldman's corroboration,' Mac replied. She was relieved, too, knowing that Sylvie was cleared now. Or she would be, as far as the company members were concerned, as soon as Goldman's statement became public knowledge. But that wasn't likely until the police could be definitive about the cause of Richardson's death. 'Am I right that this isn't going to be the subject of your next announcement on the case?'

'Let's see what help Christopoulos can be to the ME's office. But I think the big press conference will happen after we figure out who put a knife in this guy.'

'Thank you,' Ben Wheeler said a few minutes later as Beckman handed him a cup of tea. The two cops had decided they'd question him in the room normally reserved for lawyer interviews, since it was closest to the lavatories, and Beckman still looked on the pale side of green.

'You okay with us starting the questioning?' Buratti asked warily.

'Yeah, I think so,' Wheeler said. 'I don't think there's anything left in my stomach. Of course, I've been saying that for a few days now.'

Buratti turned to Beckman. 'You want to fill us in on what you covered with Mr Wheeler so far.' He looked over to where Mac was sitting, emphasizing the point that she was included.

'We didn't get to cover much before the first . . . interruption,' Beckman replied, glancing at Wheeler. Not really. 'I think he mentioned that Richardson seemed different in the last few days or so, and it sounded as if there might have been a threat of some kind. Is that the way you put it, Mr Wheeler?'

'Yeah,' Wheeler said, setting down the cup on the table in front of him and moving his hand over his stomach. Buratti consciously leaned back in his chair, putting as much distance as he could between himself and the composer.

'You gotta understand,' Wheeler looked at all three of the questioners, his posture tense and his expression earnest. 'I was thrilled to be working with Gil Richardson. My first musical, the guy who was the best musical director around. What's not to be thrilled about? And those first few months were incredible, I tell you. Watching the man work . . .' his voice drifted off as he remembered. 'And since California,' he began again, more energetically, 'when everything really picked up steam, it's been a crash course in theatre. I mean, if you were interested, you could learn about everything – a little producing here, a little bit about design there, about how the music works and why, how to deal with actors, what advertising you need, everything. And this was all from Gil. He was incredible.' He stopped and picked up his tea again. 'He was never that bullshit kind of friendly that you see around show biz so much. Nice enough, but not real personable, if you know what I mean.'

'But he seemed different lately? And there was some kind of threat?' Buratti prompted him.

Wheeler nodded resolutely. 'I first noticed the change after we got into New York, so it was a few weeks ago. At first, he just seemed tired. Snapping at people, losing his temper real fast. I thought maybe it was just that – that he was worn out. We'd put in a hellacious couple of weeks just before we hit New York. Then I thought maybe it was being back in the city, with the pressure building, whatever. Then I wondered if maybe it was because we're coming to the end of the process as far as he's concerned anyway – and some people get depressed over that.' He stopped, seeming reluctant to go on. 'Then, in the last ten days or two weeks, I don't know what had happened to him, but it was as though he'd turned into some evil parody of himself.'

Mackenzie recognized the reluctance in the man, and with her eyes, indicated to Buratti that she was going to ask a question. 'Mr Wheeler, you mentioned to Detective Beckman before that Mr Richardson was holding something over you.' She leaned forward until Wheeler was looking her directly in the eye. 'We've had some indication that he was blackmailing another person. Was he blackmailing you?'

Wheeler was obviously alarmed at the terminology. 'I don't know if you'd call it blackmail . . .' he said, and started to tell the police and Dr Griffin his embarrassing saga of accidental plagiarism, and Richardson being with him when it was discovered.

'Gil was perfectly calm about it that night, professional, nice even,' Wheeler said, finishing his story. 'I kept going on about how I'd be ruined if it ever got out, but Gil was calm as anything, saying "so you'll fix it". But after he left that night, I discovered Gil had taken the tape.'

Mackenzie glanced over at Beckman and Buratti. So that's what was being held over Wheeler: a tape that proved his plagiarism. 'Did he say anything to you when you saw him next?' Buratti asked.

'It was so weird,' Wheeler said, barely containing a shake that resembled a chill overtaking him. 'He wouldn't say that he had it, but he didn't deny it either. He said "We'll see how good the replacement is," like if mine wasn't good enough, we'd be using this plagiarized song from the Leonard archives. Like that was really an alternative.'

'Mr Wheeler, what was the name of the song you were replacing?' Mackenzie asked.

' "Remember When",' he said, a bit uncomfortable at even mentioning the title, knowing that these people knew it was not his original composition.

'I was there at the end of a rehearsal a little more than a week ago, Mr Wheeler. Is that the same song Mr Richardson was saying didn't need to be replaced?'

Wheeler sat up in his chair, alert to this change in the conversation. 'You were there? You heard him?'

'Yes.'

'Do you see what I mean about him, then? The way he was taunting me almost, as if he wanted me to blurt out to everyone just why it was that the song had to be replaced.'

'Knowing the context now, I'd have to say that that's the way it appeared,' Mackenzie said with a glance to Buratti and Beckman.

'That was the same night he went after Quigley the

architect, wasn't it? It was Gil getting his rocks off torturing people or insulting them in front of their peers. Yeah, that's what he was doing. Torturing people.'

Buratti turned to Beckman. 'We got the information on where Mr Wheeler was when Richardson died?'

Wheeler's head snapped up at that. Mackenzie realized that this man was so consumed by the thought that he might be accused of plagiarism, he hadn't even considered that there might be a more serious accusation in the wind.

'Yeah.' Beckman said leafing through his small notebook until he got to the page he needed. 'He's accounted for from the time Richardson left the stage. Nobody knows where he was just before that.'

Wheeler shook his head with an expression of regret. 'I was in the men's room upstairs – the one off the men's dressing room. Somebody may have heard me puking my guts out. For a change.'

Buratti sat forward, leaning on the table. 'Mr Wheeler, what were you trying to get out of the dressing room? The tape?'

Wheeler nodded. 'The tape. I still haven't found it. That *cannot* fall into the wrong hands; it just can't.' The man sounded perilously close to tears.

'Detective Beckman will let you know when you can get into the dressing room,' Buratti said, rising from his chair and beckoning for Mac to follow him out into the hall. 'No later than Monday, I think. Hope you find it.'

Once out in the hall and clear of the doorway, Buratti turned to Mackenzie. 'Hearing more about Richardson makes me wonder why nobody popped him off sooner.'

'I was there that night, as I mentioned,' Mac started, 'and I was surprised at his behaviour. But I chalked it up to nerves or fatigue or whatever. He was perfectly charming

255

when I met him a few minutes later.' She frowned in concentration. 'It's beginning to sound like the man had become pathological, though. It'll be fascinating to talk to Christopoulos or the Medical Examiner's office, to find out if there was a physical cause for this erratic behaviour. A drug-induced personality change.'

Buratti let out a small harrumph. 'The guy sounds like a bastard, pathological or no. And you know, I've been thinking about that ghost of the Century Theatre you mentioned.' That got Mackenzie's attention. She was amazed that Mario even remembered the ghost stories, and she looked at him with eyebrows arched. 'Maybe this ghost thing just didn't like the guy and decided to stick a shiv in his body. And it was probably annoyed it didn't get to him first.'

'Do let me know if you're going to try to sell that theory down at the commissioner's office. I'd pay Broadway prices to be a fly on the wall.' Mackenzie moved away from the wall, watching Beckman escort Ben Wheeler down the hall. She glanced at her watch. 'I have to get back downtown.'

'You around tomorrow if there's any late breaking news?' Buratti asked.

'I'm planning on a nice quiet Sunday at home,' Mac replied as they fell into step together heading for the door. 'By the way, Mario, you haven't told me. How are Gloria and the kids?'

For most of the members of the *Reunion* company, it turned out to be a quiet weekend. But even for them, it wasn't a particularly restful one, given the uncertainty about the production's future that hung in the air. Others didn't even have the respite of a day off.

Thomas Kinsolving, with the generous assistance of

Manny Erickson, was preparing a funeral service that would be a worthy remembrance of the esteemed theatrical personage that Gil Richardson had been. Even the rector of the church was impressed with Thomas's attention to detail and his selections for the readings. In addition to the usual Scriptures, Thomas had prepared excerpts from various English poets including Shakespeare, of course. The only drawback was that, with the exception of Curtis Leland, Thomas was having a hard time getting members of the *Reunion* company to agree to do the readings at the service.

Manny Erickson found new reserves of patience he didn't know he had. This Kinsolving kid was trying to make the church into a stage set, and while the rector was patient with a few lights that Manny brought in at Thomas's insistence, Manny finally had to take the young man aside after he made one particularly inappropriate suggestion. 'This isn't the memorial service we talked about, Tom.' Kinsolving's arch of the eyebrow reminded Manny that this person was always Thomas, never Tom. But Manny was past caring at this point. 'This is the funeral, not the memorial service, and this is a church, not the Broadhurst Theatre. I can't hang spotlights in the ceiling. You'll get all the lighting and all the set you want for the memorial service, but for now, just bag it.' Manny walked away, wishing he'd taken up Bruce Quigley's offer to use this time that the theatre was free to meet with him and the electrical sub-contractor.

They still had a problem with those damn lights off stage left. And he'd also discovered a problem with one of the curtain panels in the same area; in fact, that part of the theatre seemed to have a jinx on it. The curtain panel in

257

question almost looked liked it was hanging upside down; the nap of the fabric was different from the other surrounding panels. As a result, it was taking the light differently and Manny had spent too damn much time fixing the lighting problem to have another problem crop up. But that's what his life was in the weeks before a show opened; details and problems.

In fact, there were *lots* of other ways he could've used this time besides figuring out the best way to light the flowers at both ends of Gil Richardson's coffin.

That weekend, Rhonda Deveraux spent more consecutive hours alone in her subleased 20th Street apartment than she had since she'd moved in. She hovered near the phone, hoping Gregory would call any minute to tell her he'd be able to get away from his wife to meet her, even if it was just for a few hours. By Sunday it was three days that Rhonda had been a-sexual and she didn't think it was healthy.

Joan Henley Byers was enjoying the sight of Gregory playing the attentive husband. Except for a few hours on Saturday morning, he'd been hovering all weekend, asking what she'd like to do, where she'd like to go. Gregory could be an amusing man when he wanted to be, and those occasional glimpses of charm that surfaced over the course of the weekend reminded her of why she'd fallen in love with him all those years ago. Not that a remembered infatuation was going to make her change her plans.

Jonathan Humphries almost wore a rut in the Aubusson rug that covered the floor between his favourite reading chair and the window that afforded the best view of the New York skyline, trying to deal with the anger that was building inside him. He was trying to decide if he'd challenge Simon face to face about the reasons the older man had quote 'taken him under his wing' unquote. Was it as Simon had told him in their meetings months ago – that Jonathan had that fabled producer's instinct? Or was it because of Jonathan's easy access to his brother's trust fund? Of course, if he let on that he knew of Simon's reference to the trust fund, he'd have to explain that he was eavesdropping, and the impropriety of that disturbed him. But not as much as Wexler's duplicity did. Or had he misunderstood Simon? Was that a possibility? He walked back to the window again to listen again in his mind's ear to the half of the conversation he'd heard.

Simon Wexler spent the weekend running endless figures, trying to see how many different investment scenarios he could propose to Barney Ames at their meeting on Monday, and wishing he still had the whole staff of young financial whizzes who used to help him prepare such presentations. Thank God Quigley had given him some of the basic construction budget on the other three buildings. At least it would be enough to get him through this initial meeting with the bankers. If this went well enough, he'd hire one of those young financial whizzes again.

Bruce Quigley spent hours on the phone with the general contractor and some of the sub-contractors, trying to figure out how to cut down on the time they'd need for the final preparation of the exterior of the theatre. There was still some scaffolding on the rear of the building that should have been down a week ago, and he chewed out the subs in charge of that job. Now if Manny ever got his schedule freed up, they'd meet with the electrical sub-contractor about the lighting problem.

Actually, this unexpected free time was a bonus to him. No detail was too small for Quigley to attend to it himself, because this theatre was his baby. The constraints of time had gotten in his way over the last several days, and he was glad to be able to take his time and go through his checklist item by item.

After all, he didn't suffer from the same uncertainties that most of the company did. Bruce Quigley knew that his show would be going on. Delayed it might be, but it would open. His theatre would be introduced to the world, and then the rest of the Century redevelopment project would follow. His life was about to take off like a jet.

Duran Nadeem used her unexpected free time over the weekend to work out new choreography for the song Ben Wheeler had just added to the second act. She hated to say it, and she particularly didn't want to be the one to tell Ben this, but 'Like It Used to Be' just wasn't as good as 'Remember When'.

Ben Wheeler got some rest over the weekend, his stomach calming somewhat after his visit with the police. He was still distraught that the tape still wasn't in his possession. The new version of his nightmare was that the tape would fall into someone else's hands, someone who knew the show and had access to Richardson's dressing room, someone like that Thomas guy. And in this new scenario, Ben Wheeler was being blackmailed for real.

After two days of fielding calls about Gil Richardson's death, and after two days popping antacids almost continuously, Max Osgood decided his stomach lining was

260

non-existent. When he wasn't on the phone dodging yet another journalist's questions, Max was polishing his résumé. He'd decided that whenever this *Reunion* gig was over, and that could be tomorrow or after the show opened (*if* the show opened), he was going looking for another corporate staff position. No more of this freelance flack-for-hire life for him. Some nice and easy staff position – perhaps working public relations for a tobacco company – would be a comparative walk in the park after this experience.

Lenny Yarnevich sat at his desk taking notes on a story he thought had possibilities as a screenplay for television. It was about a theatre director who gets killed right before the show's opening. It was the old writers' room trick again: write what's in front of you.

Mackenzie had phoned Sylvie as soon as she returned home Saturday afternoon with the good news that Goldman's testimony would fully exonerate her. Sylvie's elation was cut short when Mac told her that his statement wouldn't necessarily be made public, and, in any case, not until the cause of death was determined.

Sylvie wasn't calmed by Mac's quiet explanation of how this was better for her, especially because Sylvie had never been identified as the woman the police had questioned. Sylvie declined Mac's invitation that she join them for dinner, but promised they'd talk again on Sunday afternoon.

Mackenzie tried to talk Sylvie into dinner again on Sunday, but Sylvie begged off this time as well, saying she was trying to get her head set for tomorrow.

'Then you're going to the funeral?' Mac asked.

'Yeah, I planned on it,' Sylvie replied. 'Are you?'

'Probably. I have to check on moving one appointment in the morning. But Buratti says it should be pretty interesting.'

CHAPTER TWENTY-SIX

By mid-morning on Monday, Mackenzie had re-scheduled
her day's appointments to later in the week, and she phoned
Buratti to let him know she would meet him at the funeral.
The service was set for twelve o'clock, and she left her
apartment at eleven-fifteen, intending to take advantage of
a day that promised to be dry if not clear and walk the eight
or nine blocks to the church.

As she was cutting across Union Square Park, she saw a
blue-uniformed figure waving at her from the west side of
the park, and within the next few steps she recognized
Eddie Lopes.

'Dr Griffin,' Lopes called in greeting as he approached
her. 'I thought Monday was one of your uptown days.'

'You're right, it usually is,' she replied as they fell into
step next to one another. 'But I'm headed over to Gil
Richardson's funeral.'

The young patrolman nodded. 'Boy, I hope this guy dyin''
doesn't mean they're gonna cancel that show opening.
People in the neighbourhood are pretty excited about it.
The new theatre and all, you know.'

Mackenzie glanced at him, impressed that he was tuned
into the concerns of those people in the neighbourhood,
and apparently shared them as well. 'How have you

been, Eddie? How was your weekend?'

'Been doin' okay,' he said as he waved to a hot-dog vendor who was setting up in the middle of the park in anticipation of the lunch time traffic. 'Got a letter Saturday from Sister Margaret. You know, the one from the subway.'

Mac had noticed in their group meetings that Eddie almost never referred to The 16th Street Bombing by that term or by any reference to bombing. He always referred to the events of that day or the people it involved as being from 'the subway'. The need for that emotional anaesthesia was still there. 'It must have been nice to hear from her,' Mac said.

Eddie nodded in rhythm with his step, indicating she was right. 'Yeah, I was happy to hear she was okay. She's been in a convalescent home down in Maryland that nuns from her same convent run. Her leg was banged up pretty bad, you know.'

'How is she doing now?'

'Good, she says. They've got her in physical therapy, but at least she's back at St Stephen's now, and she's happy about that.' He paused, but Mackenzie suspected there was more. 'She said she was worried about me.' He slowed his pace and looked directly at Mac. 'Can you believe that? All those kids to think about, and her own leg in a thousand pieces, and she's worried about me.'

'Did she say why she was worried?' Mac asked.

Eddie shook his head. 'Not in so many words. Just that some of the sisters had saved the newspaper articles from the days after, you know, and there were a couple of ones that mentioned me where I had talked to the reporters, and she thought I was being hard on myself. She said to remember that I'm a hero.' This last phrase Eddie said with a tinge of embarrassment, and his pace, which had slowed even more, came to a halt as they reached the west walkway of the park.

Mackenzie stopped alongside him. 'And do you?'

'Do I what?' he repeated, puzzled.

'Remember that you're a hero.'

'Nah,' he shrugged her comment off, his embarrassment more acute this time. 'I'm no hero.'

'I'm sure I could get any number of people to disagree with you, Eddie,' Mackenzie replied. 'The members of our group, the parents of those children you rescued, the children themselves . . .'

He shook his head. 'Nah. Down there in the subway I was either on automatic pilot, or I was so scared I was ready to freak. That's no kind of hero.'

'Haven't you heard?' Mac said in a lightly teasing voice. 'Heroes aren't people who are never scared. Heroes are people who are scared and do what they have to do anyway.' She reached out and patted his arm, her voice more serious now. 'By any definition, you're a hero, Eddie. I know it, those parents and kids know it, and Sister Margaret does, too. I guess the only one we have left to convince is you.'

Eddie Lopes looked down at his shoes, unwilling to look her in the eye. Eddie's unwillingness to recognize the value of what he'd accomplished in those dark and fearful hours down in the Union Square subway station was something they'd been working on in those quiet walking sessions after group, even if Eddie had been unaware of Mac's agenda. And she was thrilled to see it was working, too. A month ago, Eddie would never have told her that Sister Margaret had called him a hero.

She glanced at her watch. 'I've got to get a move on if I'm going to be at the church before the funeral. I'll see you, Eddie. Take care.'

'Yeah, Doctor Griffin,' he waved her off as she headed for the south-west corner of the park, and he headed north on his usual patrol, 'you, too. And thanks.' Mackenzie decided to walk across 13th Street, assuming that it would be, as usual, less crowded than 14th Street. As she wended her way toward Fifth Avenue, it dawned on her that she was feeling better than she had in ages. The fact that it wasn't raining was a factor, sure, but there was something more.

Her conversation with Eddie seemed to underscore a realization she'd come to in the last few weeks, an awareness that had, in fact, been building over the last few days. As reluctant as she had been to begin it, and as painful as those first sessions had been, her work with Eddie and with the police officers of the group had given her more of a sense of accomplishment than anything else in her professional life had afforded her in the last eighteen months.

Part of it had been the challenge: the challenge of dealing with a group of men whose training and mindset exaggerated the American social norm that men shouldn't feel too much, or, if they did, they certainly shouldn't let on that they did. These men had, in varying degrees, lived through the heart of one of the grimmest episodes of urban trauma in the city's history, yet when they began their regular meetings, those same men were reproaching themselves that they couldn't shrug it off. Mackenzie had seen improvement in every one of them; microscopic in some cases, but improvement nonetheless.

For as much of a change as she saw in the men of her group, she had been forced to acknowledge in the last several days that a change had occurred in her, as well. How different her feelings from those first meetings with the group, when she reacted only to her discomfort at being

266

around that much pain. Now her work with the group seemed alive, and her academic life seemed dry. When she'd started thinking about this, one of the first things she'd had to contend with was the fact that she hadn't missed the classroom as much as she thought she would. She'd missed her seminars, of course, but those had always been her favourites: they involved fewer people – professionals, mostly – allowed for closer contact and always presented an intellectual challenge.

There was something else she had to admit to herself, too. The last few days, she recognized how much she truly enjoyed working this case with Buratti. Maybe Peter was right, she thought with a smile. Maybe murder did turn her on. But she did know that she'd been more engaged, more productive, that she was using more of her faculties than she had in months involved in an academic study. And she loved the challenge of it – there was that word again – and the team work.

As she approached Fifth Avenue, she saw that 13th Street was closed to west-bound traffic. A blinking yellow light topped the sign that said 'All Traffic Must Turn'. The symbolism of it amused her: it appeared she was at an intersection, too. Maybe the route ahead wasn't blocked, but there was a decision to be made. Which way was she going to turn?

Mackenzie spotted Buratti leaning on a car parked just north of the church when she stopped to cross 12th Street. Sylvie was talking with him, and nodded at something Buratti said. They both greeted Mac as she approached.

Sylvie excused herself almost immediately when she saw a group from the *Reunion* company arrive. 'The lieutenant says I can tell them about what Goldman said, even if there's no public announcement yet,' she said to Mac. 'I can't wait to see their faces.'

With a nod to Buratti, Mac edged closer to where the group of six actors was assembled as Sylvie approached them. Their discomfort was evident at seeing Sylvie there, and the changing expressions on their faces gave a perfect visual accompaniment to Sylvie's monologue. 'So the Lieutenant here tells me that Howard Goldman – you know, the union guy – well, Howard Goldman corroborates my story completely.' The expressions on the faces of the assembled actors changed from discomfort to surprise. 'He found Gil in his dressing room, dead, just like I did, only without the knife in his back, and this was while I was still rehearsing. So this is all going to come out in the papers in a day or so, but I know how concerned you've all been about me,' the surprise turned to relief now, 'so I wanted you to know. And I wanted to let you know how much I appreciate your support through all of this,' the sarcasm in her voice was evident to anyone who knew Sylvie, and the relief on those faces gave way to obvious embarrassment.

Buratti tapped Mac on the shoulder and pointed out the hearse that had just turned on to Fifth Avenue. They worked their way to the edge of the assembly on the sidewalk. Mario indicated Sylvie and the other actors with a tip of his head. 'Your friend knows how to take care of herself, doesn't she?'

Mackenzie nodded her agreement. 'She always has.'

Mackenzie looked around the crowd of people as the hearse pulled up and the undertaker started to instruct the pall bearers on carrying the coffin into the church. Ben Wheeler and Lenny Yarnevich were standing together on the far side of the sidewalk, Wheeler looking less pale than he had on Saturday. Despite the fact that most of those gathered were in lightweight raincoats, Lenny Yarnevich looked to be bundled up against a chill that only he was feeling.

Duran Nadeem joined the group of actors that Sylvie was standing with, and they moved to the left side of the stairs to wait until it was time to file into the church.

Joan Henley Byers and her husband stepped from her limousine and made their way through the crowd toward the church stairs. Mac noticed Rhonda Deveraux staring holes in Gregory Byers' back, but he refused to look at her, keeping his eyes focused forward as if his life depended on it. Which, in a way, it did.

Manny Erickson stood off to the side, looking like a stage manager with a pad of notes in front of him. As the coffin was loaded onto the wheeled frame that transported it to the stairs leading to the church's front door, Manny checked off something on his list.

Simon Wexler, Jonathan Humphries and Bruce Quigley all waited together for the coffin to pass, on the opposite side of the stairs from where Mr and Mrs Byers were standing. The tension of the last few days was showing on all of them, Mackenzie realized. Though she'd only seen these men a few times, even she could recognize the strain evident in their faces.

The pall bearers lifted the coffin up the stairs and Thomas Kinsolving, followed by Curtis Leland, and another man and a woman Mackenzie didn't recognize, continued the procession into the church, almost as if they were the next of kin. Mackenzie knew she shouldn't be surprised – that's what Leland had promised the young assistant in the theatre on Friday, after all, that they'd be Gil's family – but she wondered where Mrs Rogers was in all this.

After the mourners had assembled in the church, Mac and Buratti slipped in the back to stand. Once she got into a spot with a clear view, Mackenzie perused the congregation carefully until she located where Mrs Rogers was. She was sitting with Dr Christopoulos and his wife in a pew in the mid-section of the church. Buratti turned to see what she was looking at, spotted Mrs Rogers himself, and turned back to Mackenzie with a shake of his head.

The service was conducted by the rector of the church, who apologized a few times for the fact that he didn't know Gil Richardson personally. 'Although I, like many New Yorkers, and lovers of the theatre from wherever in the world, enjoyed the fruits of his work,' he said from the pulpit, 'I wish I had had the privilege that so many of you had of knowing Gil Richardson the man.'

'This guy shouldn't feel so bad,' Buratti leaned over to whisper in Mac's ear. 'His friends didn't know Gil Richardson either.'

The rector introduced Curtis Leland as representing the company of *Reunion*, and two other actors who were from other Richardson companies, including one from the show currently running on Broadway. While the selection of readings was very well done, the overall effect of the service seemed cold to Mackenzie, and somehow lonely. Perhaps it was because most of the funerals she'd attended in her life had been in her hometown of Registon, and one of the advantages (and disadvantages) of small town life was that everybody knew everybody else. And she was acutely aware of how almost no one in this congregation knew Gil Richardson.

When it was all over, at about ten minutes to one, the coffin was escorted down the aisle with Thomas Kinsolving, Curtis Leland, and the other actors following behind as before. Mac and Buratti slipped out one of the side doors to wait out on the sidewalk.

The end of the funeral was awkward. There was to be no graveside service, since Thomas had decided Gil would be cremated. Nor had anyone arranged for a reception, so the mourners lingered outside the church, breaking into small groups.

Buratti saw Dr Christopoulos heading down the stairs, and gave a discreet wave to get his attention. Christopoulos saw him, and left Mrs Rogers with his wife to join the lieutenant and Mackenzie.

'Morning, doctor. Or I guess it's afternoon now,' Buratti started. 'I understand you talked to the ME's office this morning.'

'Yes, I've talked with them a few times since Saturday, actually,' Christopoulos replied. 'You heard about the heart?'

'Yeah,' Buratti said, nodding.

'I didn't,' Mackenzie said. 'What about the heart?'

'They found a thinning in the wall of the heart,' Christopoulos said. 'It's probably been there his whole life, and it's probably the same thing that killed his father and grandfather, but they never knew.'

'So are you saying it was a heart attack?' Mackenzie asked.

'No,' Christopoulos said. 'They're pretty sure it was the drug interactions – you were right on that one, doctor. At this point it looks like two of the medications he was taking – the Hyperion and the remedy from our friend Dr Feelgood – had really elevated his blood pressure, especially if the Hyperion had been building up in his system. Our theory now is that he took a larger-than-usual dose of one of the over-the-counter medications that were there,

271

probably one of the anti-histamines which can raise the heart rate anyway, and that started a reaction that in effect, blew out his heart. From my conversation with them this morning, they're pretty close to identifying the combination that did him in. They might even have it by now.'

'The way you refer to it, blowing out his heart. Wouldn't there have been some sense of struggle?' Mac asked.

'No, actually,' Christopoulos replied with a casual shake of his head. 'He probably would have felt a little light-headed at first, and maybe put his head down to rest. Close to the way they found him.'

'And it would have been that fast?'

'Yes. He would have lost consciousness pretty quickly, and he was probably gone within a few minutes.'

Mackenzie shook her head in wonder; sometimes the dividing line between life and death seemed amazingly fragile.

'I talked to the deputy commissioner's office this morning,' Buratti said, 'and she talked to the mayor's aides. The word is that even if we have all the information today, they said to hold it until tomorrow late.' Mackenzie looked at him questioningly. 'If we release it today,' he explained, 'then it's the drugs that make the headlines instead of his funeral.'

'That's true.'

'Helps to have friends in high places,' Buratti added.

Mackenzie stopped the doctor as he was ready to move away. 'Doctor, why wasn't Mrs Rogers sitting up front?'

He let out a long sigh. 'I asked, but she insisted on sitting back with Denise and me. She told me she didn't want to embarrass her boy – can you believe that?' he finished with an expression of regret. He looked over and saw that they were loading the coffin back into the hearse. 'Excuse me, but I've got to go talk to Gil's assistant and break the news that Mrs Rogers wants to take her boy home for burial.'

'Oh, this oughta be good,' Buratti said. 'I'm gonna hang around to watch this.'

From a distance, Buratti and Mac watched the little drama play out as Kinsolving at first listened attentively to Dr Christopoulos, then looked at him in surprise, his back arching up, and then looked at Mrs Rogers with widening eyes. He took in a deep gulp of breath and allowed himself to be led over to the woman, where Christopoulos performed what looked to be extremely awkward introductions.

'Do you believe this,' Buratti said. 'This is like watching our own play right here.'

As Mac and Buratti watched the private drama unfold, Simon Wexler glanced at his watch yet again. He couldn't believe how long it was taking to get this over with. Past one o'clock now and they still hadn't loaded the hearse.

He worked his way through a group of people from the *Reunion* company that included Jonathan, Bruce and Manny.

'This is embarrassing, but I've got an appointment over at my office, and I've got to get out of here,' Simon said to his young partner. 'I'm meeting a potential investor for the whole project, and then I'm taking him over to the theatre.' He looked at Bruce Quigley with a wink of his eye. 'This could be a big day for us. Wish me luck.' He leaned toward Jonathan again and asked, 'Listen, if anyone asks for me, be sure to tell them I was here, and cover for me, okay?'

The coolness of Jonathan's reply was apparent even to Manny and Bruce Quigley. What was going on between the two partners?

It was after three o'clock by the time Simon Wexler and

273

Barney Ames made it over to the Century Theatre. Ames had been putting him through his paces for over an hour and a half, and Simon realized he was getting too damn old to do this kind of dog-and-pony show on his own. As soon as he had the first infusion of cash into this next stage of the development, he was definitely going to hire one of those young computer whizzes with the spread-sheet programs. Then Simon could go back to giving orders to people the way God intended him to.

Simon escorted Ames to the main entrance on 14th Street. It was actually easier to use the Broadway stage door entrance, but he wanted to make an impression, and he knew that bringing the banker in through the front door was the way to do that.

Simon stood in front of the theatre, arms waving as he pointed out the sites where the models they'd just reviewed in his office would go. 'I tell you, this is going to be dynamite, Barney. This will transform this whole area. In fact, I think it's going to be so big, besides the three blockfronts I've got lined up, you might want to bring in your own.'

Ames nodded his head casually as they stepped into the lobby. He took a long look around the impressive, if still in-progress, foyer. Simon played tour guide as he rhapsodized about the detail in the flooring, the walls, the sconces, the lighting. 'So the financing you're looking for is on the other towers, not on the theatre,' Ames finally said.

'That's right,' Simon replied.

'So your financing on the theatre itself is solid?'

'As a rock,' Simon said. *Please, God*, he whispered a prayer in his head, *don't let him get a look at the books until I'm ready.*

Simon opened the door to the auditorium and waved

Ames ahead of him. The theatre was dark, of course, but the traditional work light on the stage would give them enough light to make their way down the aisle. Once they got inside the auditorium of the theatre, Simon became even more eloquent in his descriptions. By the time they neared the stage, he was winded.

'The financing on the towers. Have you got any leads?' Ames asked when he stopped at the base of the stairs and looked around the theatre.

Simon's stomach sank. Oh, Christ, it was going to be one of those deals. One of those where nobody wanted to be first, but everybody wanted to be second to jump on the bandwagon. He was going to have to play this just the right way. Even though he was frantic to make this deal, the last thing he could show was desperation. He had to make it seem as if he was doing them a favour.

'Well, as you know,' Simon finally said, just a hint of reluctance in his voice as he led Ames up the working stairs to the stage, 'with Jonathan Humphries on board, a lot of our financial problems are solved. His own investment banking background, his father's firm, the investments from the Humphries Trust that he represents. We have all that going for us.'

'Good, good. Glad to hear it,' Ames said. 'I tell you what, Simon. I like the area. It's convenient, a great neighbourhood, I think this whole development has a lot of possibilities. I only see one problem.'

'What's that?'

'I just don't see our investment analysis group going along with this old style design. Our experience with residential properties – rentals, condos, whatever, is that people are going for convenience, for ease. People want something modern looking, something that looks like it will give them all the conveniences they're used to. If we were to recommend on this, get in on it with you at this stage, we'd probably have to recommend a re-design.'

Damn! Didn't these people have any taste? Quigley's design was one of the best goddam things about this whole project! But Simon had to bite his lip to make sure that none of those thoughts escaped. Instead he said, as calmly as possible, 'Well, you know, we thought it tied in very well with the neighbourhood, and the history and all, and with the problems of dealing with the Planning Commission—'

'You've got the go-ahead from the Planning Commission already?'

'No, no,' Simon explained. 'Not on the towers yet. It's just that Union Square is what they call one of the special districts, and we got the theatre approved in record time, you know, so we thought we'd get a jump on things by seeing which way the wind was blowing, so to speak, so we've had a couple of people take a look at the models for the whole development.'

'But you don't have any official approval as yet?'

It galled him to say it, but Simon had to be honest at this point. 'No,' he said.

'Well, then, a change wouldn't present a problem.'

Simon knew he couldn't press the point. At least not now. 'Well, maybe I can see your point. Modern look, conveniences, all that's a real selling point. Maybe we can go for a revision of the design. As long as it's compatible with the theatre here, of course. Maybe you want to bring in your own architect.'

'Maybe,' Ames said with a smile. He glanced at his watch. 'Oh-oh,' he said. 'I've got to get uptown by four-fifteen. What are the chances of a cab outside at this time?'

'Should be pretty good. We can go out this door,' Simon

said, heading for the Broadway stage entrance, 'and if you head over to the other side of the theatre, the Fourth Avenue side, you should be able to catch one heading uptown.'

'I appreciate the tour, Simon, and you keep me posted about the progress of your other talks. Pending the changes that we talked about, I might be able to interest our group in investing.'

'That's great, Barney,' Simon said with more enthusiasm than he felt. He opened the Broadway stage door. 'Listen, I'm going to go check the doors out front, so I'll leave you here.'

'You'll have someone call my girl about those tickets for opening night?' Ames said as he stepped out onto the sidewalk.

'You bet. And thanks again for coming down.'

Thanks for nothing, Simon thought to himself. *What was this let-me-know-how-your-other-talks-are-going kind of crap?* He was looking for money from this guy, money that he needed now, and all he got was the promise of future conversations. Damn! And the sonuvabitch had the nerve to expect tickets for opening night!

Simon walked to the lobby, checked the doors, and walked through the auditorium again up onto the stage. He was just turning into the offstage area on the Broadway side of the building when he noticed the damn stage door was open. He was positive he'd closed it when Ames left. He'd have to talk to Larry about security in the theatre if the door was that easy to leave open.

Simon reached for the wide handle on the door to pull it shut, and was startled to hear footsteps behind him. As the door swung closed, the area dimmed considerably, and all he had left to see by was the working light on the stage, which was at the back of the figure that walked toward him.

'Who's that,' Simon said, moving so the light from the stage would help him see. 'Oh it's you. How did you get in here?'

'I have keys, remember, Simon?'

'I know that, I just meant that I was here a minute ago and you—' The figure approached him, blocking out the light again. Something was in his hand.

'What are you doing?!' Simon cried, alarmed when he saw the expression on the man's face. 'What the hell's the matter with you?'

'You're a weasel, Simon Wexler, and you lied to me. I don't like being lied to.'

The first blow stunned Simon and brought him to his knees, and then to his back. At the second blow, the pain exploded inside his head, and then all was blackness, and he felt nothing.

Mac had finally cajoled Sylvie into joining them for dinner when they met up again after Gil Richardson's funeral. Sylvie had agreed to come when she learned they'd be staying in for dinner, not going out to a restaurant. 'Not that your cooking's so fabulous, Mackenzie. I don't want you to get a swelled head or anything. I just don't want to be out and about tonight, if you know what I mean.'

'I'll take your remark about my cooking in the good spirit in which it was intended,' Mac replied. 'You say that only because you haven't had my chicken breasts with lemon and artichoke hearts.'

'Well, it sounds pretty good, Mackenzie.'

'It's one of the two dishes I still know how to make, so I've pretty much perfected it. Why don't you come over around six?'

★ ★ ★

At six-thirty, the two women were trading places in front of the stove, taking turns at sniffing the aromatic steam that drifted out of Mackenzie's large sauté pan, when the phone rang. Mackenzie was sure it was Peter, announcing again – for the third time – that he was just about to leave the studio.

It was Buratti instead. 'Hey, Doc. Sorry to interrupt your dinner if I did, but I thought you might be interested.'

'That's okay, Mario. What's up?'

'I'm over at the Century Theatre. We got a call about an hour ago. Simon Wexler was found dead.'

Mackenzie and Sylvie made it over to the Century in record time, considering that Sylvie was stopping every fifteen to twenty feet to yell out, 'I don't believe this. The biggest break of my career and first the director and now *the producer* gets killed! I don't fucking believe this!' Every third time she stopped, instead of yelling she'd start to tear up.

They walked around to the Broadway entrance, made it through the knot of reporters and television crews hovering on the edge of the sidewalk there, and found Buratti and the crime scene unit detectives not that far inside the stage door. Wexler's body was being loaded onto a gurney for transport in the morgue van they'd seen outside. The tears that Sylvie had been able to hold in on their walk gave way once she saw the body, and she moved toward the stairs that led to the dressing room and sat with her face in her hands.

Buratti was hunkered down on the floor next to a technician who was showing him what appeared to be a stain on the floor. He spotted the two women almost immediately, and rose to walk over to them. 'Mac, you

279

heard the phrase, we gotta stop meeting like this?' He nodded toward Sylvie. 'She okay?'

'A little shaken. What have you got, Mario?'

'Simon Wexler, Caucasian, male, aged fifty-nine. Dead presumably from a blow to the head – actually a couple of blows to the head, from what the guys are telling me.'

'What time was the body found?'

'A little after five. The designer, Erickson, is the one who found him. Wexler's secretary thought he was still in meetings with a Barney Ames until Ames called the office around four-thirty and that's when Wexler's secretary found out that their meeting broke up between three-thirty and four. We've got a pretty good time estimate from Ames so far as to when he left Wexler, and we figure it might have happened right after that. So he could've been here since three-thirty, four o'clock.'

'No possibility it was a slip and hit his head situation?'

Buratti shook his head with certainty. 'Nope. He got bashed in pretty good.'

'Well, there's something to be said for that,' Mac said ruefully. 'At least it's clear it's murder.'

'Yeah, at least it's clear it's a murder. And this time at least we know who the victim was. Unless, of course, he turns out to be some long-lost member of the royal family or something.'

CHAPTER TWENTY-SEVEN

Mac had to catch a cab to get Sylvie back to her apartment, even though it was just a few blocks. A combination of nerves, tears, shock and worry all hit her at once, and Sylvie was having a hard time getting hold of herself. Mackenzie walked her down the hall to her apartment and was thrilled to see Peter open the door to usher them in. She got Sylvie situated in the living room with a glass of wine and a box of tissues and joined Peter in the kitchen.

'This is unbelievable,' he said. 'I saw your note when I walked in and flipped on the local news. They showed them bringing Wexler's body out of the theatre. Talk about *déjà vu*!' He looked down at her and eyed her warily. 'You okay?'

'Yeah,' Mackenzie replied. 'Just thinking how those stories of the ghost of the Century Theatre are making more sense to me these days.'

After a dinner of reheated chicken breasts with lemon and artichoke hearts, Mac promised she'd get Sylvie back to her apartment, but Sylvie wouldn't hear of it. 'I'm over my diva stage for the moment, Mackenzie. Sorry about the dramatics earlier, but everything just got to me at once. But I'll just get in a cab and go home and contemplate my probable future as a temporary receptionist again.' Sylvie was sure that Wexler's death was the nail in *Reunion*'s coffin.

Mackenzie walked out to 15th Street with Sylvie and waited with her until a cab came along. 'I have meetings on the PEPSI study tomorrow, but I'll call you by eleven or so, OK?' she said, looking Sylvie straight in the eye. 'And you call me before that if there's anything you need, OK?'

'OK, Doctor Griffin, ma'am,' Sylvie teased as a taxi pulled up. 'And Mackenzie, thanks for dinner, thanks for everything, just – thanks.'

Her first PEPSI study meeting was briefer than she thought it might be, and she was free by ten-fifteen. She tried Sylvie first, but got no answer, so Mackenzie put a call in to Buratti. He sounded discouraged.

'I was hoping this was going to be an easy one, Mac, but it's not. Our guys finished up down there last night, and basically we've got nothing.'

'Nothing?'

'Nope. Well, we've got approximate time of death, we've got the weapon—'

'What was the weapon?' Mackenzie asked.

'A fifteen inch length of pipe, similar to other remnant pieces they found on the other side of the stage. No prints,' he told her before she asked. 'Wiped clean.'

'Anybody with a motive?'

'You know, I was just saying to Beckman here, this is where experience counts, Mac. 'Cause my years in homicide tell me that guys in real estate usually give you plenty of raw material to work with, motive-wise. We're heading over to his office shortly, to start finding out who hated his guts.'

'I'm not sure where I'll be later, but I'll try to catch up with you,' Mackenzie said with a smile. She did enjoy Buratti's attitude towards his job.

'Mac, before I forget. I got a call from the Deputy Commissioner. She's putting out the announcement on Richardson's death for tonight's news. We'll see if anybody notices, now that Wexler is dead, too.'

Mackenzie reached Sylvie at her apartment a few minutes later. Her voice sounded dreadful. 'Sylvie, what is it?' she asked.

'I got a call to get down to the theatre this morning, usual time. So I was stupid enough to think maybe it would be a rehearsal.'

'What was it?'

'Jonathan Humphries made an announcement, and he said he was – and I quote – speaking on his behalf, on Joan Henley Byers' behalf, and on behalf of Simon Wexler, and that he was suspending the production of *Reunion*.' Sylvie paused. 'There it goes, Mac. The ship has sailed. My big break in the theatre and it's gone.'

'Sylvie, I'm so sorry. Is there anything I can do?'

A big sigh came through the telephone. 'I don't know. Jonathan told us we have to clear our things out of the theatre by tonight. Some of the kids were standing around after he made the announcement, trying to figure out if suspended meant the same thing as cancelled, but I couldn't take any more just then, so I have to go back and clean out my dressing room.'

'Well, let me help you with that, anyway.'

'You don't need to, Mackenzie.'

'I know. But it will be easier this way.'

'Well, I'm planning on getting there around four o'clock. I'm hoping everyone will be gone by then. I don't think I could take any more emotional scenes.'

'Fine. I'll meet you there as soon after four as I can get there.'

★ ★ ★

Mackenzie stopped at her apartment to change into a sweat suit, since she suspected this job would involve carrying a carton or two. She also picked up her rain slicker again; even though it had been dry all day and fairly mild, the skies were threatening again.

She walked to the theatre, and when she turned the corner from 14th onto Broadway, she was surprised to see Sylvie and Curtis standing just inside the stage door waving to yet another camera crew that was just leaving. 'The last one,' Sylvie explained when Mac caught up to them. 'They got the shots of the chorus kids all piling out of the theatre with their dance bags over their shoulders, and then the crews started heading uptown. I think *Reunion* is officially yesterday's news.' She turned to the older actor. 'Well, Curtis, shall we?'

Curtis Leland extended his bent arm to her, and the two walked toward their dressing rooms as though headed for a ball. 'Mackenzie,' Sylvie said over her shoulder. 'You'll be shocked to hear this, of course, but I'm not ready.'

'You're right, I'm shocked,' Mackenzie said in a placid voice.

'I just got talking to all the people leaving, and you know,' Sylvie continued.

'You? Talking? I'm doubly shocked,' Mackenzie teased. She recognized Sylvie's too-cheery demeanor for what it was, but she also knew it was best just to go along with it.

'See how well we get along, Curtis?' Sylvie said as they entered his dressing room. 'That's the benefit of old friends. Or what's that phrase we're using now, Mackenzie?'

'Friends of long standing.'

'Right. Friends of long standing. Now, Curtis, what can we do for you?'

'Nothing too much, my dear,' he said. 'I just have this tote bag and one small box and my book bag.'

'And your make up,' Sylvie said looking at the counter.

'Oh, yes, I have to finish putting that away. But my make up case fits inside that box.'

'You do that while I head to the ladies' room and then Mackenzie and I can help you out.'

'There's really no need—' Curtis started.

'You might as well just go along with her,' Mackenzie explained as Sylvie disappeared down the hallway. 'When she gets like this, you can't talk her out of anything.'

As the older actor started putting the tools of his trade into the meticulously neat case he'd pulled from his packing box, Mackenzie started to tell him how sorry she was about the way things had turned out. 'I remember that night we met – it wasn't even two weeks ago – when you were talking about turning this building into a theatre. I'm just sorry for you – and for Sylvie and for all of you – that that's not going to happen.'

'Thank you. It is a disappointment, you know.' He caught her eye in the mirror. 'You know what surprised me? This building was so dead when we first came in here. It didn't even smell like a theatre. What amazes me is that even after only a week or two of rehearsal, it was beginning to acquire that theatre smell.' He finished putting his small items in the top tray and closed the case securely. 'I've never been in on the beginning of something like that. I do wish it could have lasted.'

Sylvie's heels clicked coming down the hall and she appeared in the doorway, holding her arms up with a flourish. 'See that? Perfect timing.' She moved to take the box for Curtis, and he insisted on carrying both the tote and book bags. 'Mac,' Sylvie started, 'I'll just help Curtis into a cab, and then we can pack up my dressing room in a flash, and then we'll get out of here, go to get some dinner and then get drunk. How about that for a plan?'

'We'll confer on the last step, but it sounds workable up to that point,' Mac said, extending her hand to the actor. 'Goodbye, Mr Leland. I hope we get to meet again someday.'

'It's Curtis, please, Doctor. And I'm sure we will.'

Curtis and Sylvie headed for the Broadway stage door.

He was watching from the opposite side of the stage, hidden deep in the panels of curtains that formed the whole side of the stage. Good! The old man and Sylvie were finally out of the theatre. They were the last ones, if his count was right. It had frightened him when he arrived and found people still in the theatre, but now he could begin. He moved to the control room, stepped in, closed the door behind him, and stepped directly to the panel controlling the power to the left side of the stage.

Mac heard steps out in the hall, but she knew they were too soft to be Sylvie's. She peeked out from Sylvie's dressing room to see Thomas Kinsolving heading from the back of the theatre toward the dressing rooms, carrying four empty cartons, two in each hand.

He stopped when he saw Mackenzie, startled by her presence. 'I saw you at the funeral with that Lieutenant Buratti. Are you police?'

'No, I'm Doctor Mackenzie Griffin,' she said and stepped into the hallway, hand extended. He didn't take it. 'Sometimes I'm a consultant for the police, but I'm just here in my capacity as a friend of Sylvie Morgan's.'

Kinsolving shrugged his shoulders, and headed for the

dressing room where Gil Richardson's body had been found. Within moments, Mackenzie heard him talking to himself. She stepped out into the hallway again, and moved toward the open door to the dressing room. From what she could hear, Kinsolving was not only talking to himself, he was punctuating every sentence by throwing something into one of the cartons.

'Lied to me for years!' Thud. 'Three years I worked for him.' Thud. 'And what does he do?' Thud. 'He makes me look like a fool!' Thud.

Mackenzie gradually worked her way to the doorway, just in time to see Thomas throw a tee-shirt on the floor. 'What's that that didn't make the cut?' she asked.

Kinsolving looked at her, deciding if he would answer or not. 'A tee-shirt one of the dancers gave him. He never wore it. Bad design. Bad grammar. And Gil Richardson was very particular, you know.' Mackenzie detected a bit of a sneer in this last phrase.

He put his arms around a number of items that had accumulated on the right side of the make-up counter and moved them all together toward the centre, where his cartons were. An audio tape became dislodged from the pile and fell on the floor. Mackenzie bent down and picked it up. The pencil written label said 'Mabel – September 7th'.

Obviously Ben Wheeler hadn't been here since the police released the room. She looked at Thomas. 'I think I know someone who was looking for this tape. Mind if I take it?'

Kinsolving stared at her again. 'Whatever,' he said and resumed throwing things into the cartons. 'Can't believe I wasted all those years.' Thud. 'Can't believe he fooled me. Me!' Thud. 'Damn him anyway! I should have let them find him like a junkie.' He was about to toss the item in his hand when he heard what he'd said, and realized he'd said it in front of this woman.

Mackenzie, still examining the tape in her hand, looked up. 'You're the one who did it, aren't you?'

Kinsolving's eyes flared as they heard the accusation. 'I didn't kill him—' he started.

'No, you didn't,' Mac agreed. 'Nobody killed him. But you're the one who put the knife in his back, aren't you?'

Sylvie had held the door open with her hip until Curtis got out onto the sidewalk, and when she moved, the door closed with a slam behind her. 'Oh, damn,' she said. 'That little wedge thing must have slipped.'

'Will you be all right getting back in?'

'Sure. I'll knock loud so Mackenzie will hear me.'

Leland hailed a taxi and waited at the trunk while the driver came around to unlock it. Sylvie handed the carton to the driver. 'Well, Curtis,' she said, turning to hug the actor, 'you can't say it hasn't been an interesting experience.'

'Ah, Sylvie,' he said, kissing her fondly on the cheek, 'if only I were twenty years younger.' He turned and kissed her other cheek. 'Make that fifteen.'

What was that noise? He thought he heard a vague muffle of voices. Damn! His plan had started already. Everyone was supposed to be gone. Nobody should be left in the theatre now. Nobody!

'You were the one who put the knife in Gil Richardson's back, weren't you?' repeated Mackenzie.

Thomas stiffened, still bent over the carton he was packing. At long last, he dropped the book he was holding

288

and it thudded into the carton. He nodded his head.

'Why did you do it?' Mackenzie asked calmly.

'I wish I hadn't now,' Thomas started. 'When I came in and found him, I knew it was the drugs. He'd been taking a combination of things in the last couple of weeks, and he'd gotten really weird a few times. I tried to tell him, but . . .' He paused, obviously recalling his conversations with Richardson. 'And I just didn't want him to be remembered that way, you know?' he said emphatically. 'I mean, a drug overdose. It's so *ordinary*. "Another show biz druggie bites the dust." I could already hear it on the news.' He turned toward the mirror, but he was seeing something other than his reflection. 'And this way at least it had a little mystery to it, some drama, a little oomph, you know? Gil always said you do what you have to do to get people lined up at the box office.'

Mackenzie didn't know how to react. She'd never before heard an untimely death described as a marketing opportunity.

Kinsolving looked back over to Mackenzie, sensing her disapproval. 'Gil Richardson was an extraordinary man, and I wanted for him to be remembered for what he was. Or for what I thought he—' he stopped himself and shook his head ruefully. 'What a fool I was—' He stopped himself again, and turned to Mackenzie, his expression suddenly alert. 'What's that?' he said to her.

'What's what?'

'Do you smell smoke?'

Sylvie waved Curtis off in the cab and headed to the stage door. She pulled on it, but couldn't get it to budge. She realized that Mac would have a hard time hearing her. Maybe she'd try the front doors first.

She trudged around to the 14th Street side, and couldn't get in those doors either. And just to help things along, a light drizzle started as she headed back to the Broadway door.

She started pounding on the door again, pounding as hard as she could, calling Mackenzie's name, but she got no response. What was going on here?

Mackenzie and Thomas Kinsolving came out of Dressing Room A to see that the whole glass-walled control room off stage left had filled with smoke. A thick, acrid smoke that was seeping through the partially opened door and permeating the entire backstage area. Within a few moments, Mackenzie could feel her nose and eyes starting to react to the fumes. 'Do you know where a fire extinguisher is?' she said to Kinsolving in a loud voice. She could hear a dull pounding nearby as well.

'No!' he replied, his fear evident even in one syllable.

'I'll go look for one,' Mackenzie directed. 'You go to the pay phone and call the Fire Department.'

'I'm afraid I can't let you do that,' a voice said as a figure stepped from the smoky shadows.

The fire had found what it first needed, a spark of ignition, in the control room. Tiny licks of flame, barely visible even if you were looking for them, found what they needed to thrive and began to move across the floor.

Sylvie was still pounding on the door, and now she was getting pissed off. The drizzle was really only a mist, but she was getting chilled. She'd been gone long enough that Mackenzie should be looking for her, for God's sake, and instead, she'd been pounding the door so long now her hands were pink.

Feeling temporarily defeated, she looked down, trying to figure out what to do next and that's when she spotted it. A wisp of smoke seeping from under the stage door. She couldn't believe her eyes. She leaned down to sniff at it, and jerked upright, alarmed.

Where was he – that patrolman who just went by? Where did he go? She saw him when she was walking from the 14th Street side of the building. There! There he was! Across the street in the park. She raced to the corner and saw him on the west side of Union Square, and she let out a bellow that her voice teacher wouldn't forgive her for years.

Eddie Lopes heard a roar and looked across 14th Street to see a woman flapping her arms wildly. He started to walk toward her, then picked up his pace when he saw that she was frantic. He recognized her as that Morgan woman that they'd questioned last week in the Richardson death.

Sylvie grabbed his arm as soon as he neared her and pulled him toward the door. 'She's in there, Mackenzie, she's in there, oh my God, and there's a fire and she must have been overcome by the smoke or something.'

'Mackenzie – are you talking about Dr Griffin?'

'Yes! Oh God, you know her! How do you know her? Of course, you're a policeman.' Sylvie knew she was babbling and couldn't stop herself

Eddie Lopes grabbed her by the shoulders and turned her, pointing out the fire call box on the south side of Union Square. 'Go call this in and stand by the fire box until they get here, OK?' Sylvie nodded. 'When they get here, you tell them where you left Doctor Griffin, and you tell them I'm heading in there, too, OK?'

'What are you going to do?'

'I'm going to find a way to get in there and get Doctor Griffin out.'

291

★ ★ ★

Mac was immediately alarmed at the man's appearance. She could tell from his posture, from the expression in his eyes, from an almost palpable aura of despair that seemed to surround him, that this man was dangerous. 'But we've got to get out of here,' Mackenzie said as calmly as she could. 'This fire could spread—'

'That's the intention.'

'You can't be serious – it's Mr Quigley, isn't it?' Mackenzie said, coughing. That stinging claustrophobic feeling of the lungs starting to shut down was hitting her already. The handsome face that Sylvie had pointed out less than two weeks ago was now drawn by tension and fatigue, and covered with a day's growth of beard. His flushed tone could indicate that he'd been drinking excessively or that his blood pressure was dangerously high. 'You expect us to stand here while this building burns down around us?'

'Not quite. I have to think about this for a minute,' he said agitatedly. 'You weren't supposed to be here. Nobody was supposed to be here.'

The smoke was coming out of the control room in larger billows. 'Isn't there a fire alarm or a sprinkler system or something,' Thomas Kinsolving interrupted, panicky.

'Not connected yet, I'm afraid,' replied the architect.

Thomas started to head for the door, but Quigley stepped into his path, fully emerging from the shadows for the first time. He was a bigger man, and a threatening figure. Even if he didn't have something in his hand. But he did. A pipe. Just like the one Buratti had described to her.

'I'm sorry. You weren't supposed to be here. I didn't mean for anyone else to die.'

'You mean Simon Wexler should have been the only

292

one?' Mackenzie said, finally giving into the impulse to cough. 'You're the one who killed Mr Wexler, aren't you?'

Finding the oxygen they needed and the fuel that kept them alive, the tiny flames danced in an elegant curve across the floor just outside the control room, following the graceful arc of the tiny stream of adhesive that had dripped across the stage when the carpet layer's tool gun developed a leak.

Eddie had watched this theatre going up, and he knew it well enough to know that there were no windows on the ground floor. But in the back, on the second and third floors, there were windows. And unless they'd moved it in the last day or so, there was still some scaffolding around on the 13th Street side of the building. He ran in that direction.

Eddie shinnied up the scaffolding and made it through a window up on the second floor into one of the costume rooms at the back of the theatre. He was trying to remember the rules about moving through a building on fire, but this was part of the reason he'd never become a firefighter. Fire – or more exactly smoke – scared the shit out of him.

He felt the door into the hallway. Nothing. He tried to open it. Locked. Then he reached down in the dim late afternoon light and saw that it was a lock he could turn from the inside. He opened it. The smell of smoke was noticeable in the hallway.

'What was it that Mr Wexler did that he deserved to die?' Mackenzie asked, as calmly as she could in between coughs and her eyes starting to water.

'He betrayed me. Utterly betrayed me. Just like before,'

Quigley said as he lifted the pipe and looked at it. He, too, started to cough as the smoke continued to build. 'I worked almost two years on this project, on this theatre, on the whole development. Like I worked six years up there and ended up with nothing. Nothing!' He tried to suck in air, and only started coughing more. 'Because I believed in this theatre, you see, and because Simon romanced me. I worked for a quarter of what I should have gotten, because I believed the bastard that I'd share in the long run. And the first chance he had, he sold me down the river. Gave it all away.' He slapped the pipe into his hand, coughing now as much as Thomas and Mackenzie were.

'But nobody's going to take my theatre away from me. Nobody gets credit for this except me! Nobody! I'll destroy it first.' He turned toward the door, then back to the two people in front of him. They all heard the sirens in the distance.

The fire's mission was to keep itself going, and to do that it needed more oxygen and more fuel. The flames licked across the floor, and shimmered around the bottom edges of the first curtain panel. No fuel here. The flames receded to the line of adhesive and started toward the second fabric panel.

Mackenzie saw something moving along the floor, almost elegant in its sinuous grace. Her eyes widened when she saw what it was.

Sylvie stood out on the corner, shivering. Even though it wasn't very cold, the combination of the mist and the circumstances chilled her. She'd been hearing the sirens for a minute now, but it took her a while to figure where they were coming from. Finally she saw they were coming around the park, and she ran into the middle of 14th Street, ignoring the traffic and the honking of horns to flag the fire engines down. The driver of the first one leaned out and she pointed them toward the theatre, then ran to catch up with them. If anything happened to Mackenzie, anything, she'd never forgive herself.

Eddie crept down the stairs that would bring him to the open area just inside the stage door. He was doing everything he could not to start coughing, because he knew once he started, he'd never stop. The three people below were now coughing almost constantly. The smoke below was building, and it was already affecting his eyes.

He made it all the way to the last step before the larger man spotted him. Eddie held his revolver out in a two handed position and pointed it at the man, who seemed to be holding some weapon on Dr Griffin and the young guy from the theatre company.

'Okay, drop it, whoever you are,' Eddie yelled, and started coughing. 'We're all going to get out of here, and we're getting out of here now.'

The flames worked at the edges of that second fabric panel, and were rewarded. This was fuel. Tongues of flames started to creep up the heavy material. The shock on Mackenzie's face was enough to make even the distracted Quigley turn.

'No, that's not possible,' cried Quigley, looking at the length of the fabric panel. 'These are all fire curtains!' He started to move toward the curtain, where the flames were now over his head. Mackenzie and Eddie both moved in his direction, and Thomas headed toward the door.

'No, stop I can't do it! I can't let it burn down!' Quigley cried, reaching for the curtain as though he would smother the flames with his hands.

Just at that moment, Thomas threw open the Broadway door, and a gush of fresh air rushed in. As Quigley pulled the curtain to him, the flames were fed with the fresh supply of oxygen, and he was engulfed. Eddie Lopes tried to get to him, but Quigley squirmed away from him, and pulled the fiery curtain down on himself. The sound he made was one Mackenzie knew would stay with all of them forever.

The firefighters rushed through the stage door. Another firefighter was still on the sidewalk, trying to restrain Sylvie from running into the burning building. Even though the man was well over six foot, it took all his energy to hold her around the waist as she screamed Mackenzie's name.

Buratti and Beckman arrived at the theatre not too much later, sirens and lights going full tilt. They had to leave the car on the west side of Broadway, since the fire trucks completely blocked the east side of the street near the stage door.

The car had barely stopped moving when Buratti bolted out of the passenger side. He found Mackenzie, Thomas Kinsolving and Eddie Lopes all sitting curbside, oxygen masks to their faces. 'Judas Priest, Mac, what happened here?' he asked, looking around.

In between sips of oxygen, Mackenzie filled him in on her conversation with Thomas, the incident with Quigley, and offered a vivid description of Lopes's heroism in coming in to rescue them. Buratti gave an approving nod to the young man, 'Good going, Lopes,' he said with a casual salute.

Lopes seemed to be embarrassed by Mac's description and tried to wave it off. Mackenzie, still holding her oxygen mask in one hand, reached out with the other and grabbed

Eddie's arm. 'Look, Thomas and I would have died in there if not for you. And you put yourself in danger for us. You felt the fear and you came in to get us anyway. Right?' She leaned forward until she caught his eyes with hers. He nodded his agreement, reluctantly.

Mac continued at full volume. 'You saved our lives, you saved *my* life, and that is my personal definition of a hero. It's apparently Sister Margaret's too, and a whole bunch of other people I can name. I'm beginning to think it's your definition we have to work on, because it seems a hero can be anybody *but* you.'

Eddie's reaction to her outburst was even more embarrassment. Buratti rescued him somewhat. 'I've known her longer than you,' he said. 'When she gets this way, it's best just to go along. She'll be happy if you admit that you're a hero.' He turned back to Mackenzie. 'Won't you, Doc?'

Before she could answer, the gurney bearing the gravely burned Quigley was brought out of the stage door entrance. He'd been pulled from the curtain fire alive, but the EMS driver shook his head when Beckman, inquiring about where they were taking him, also asked about his chances. 'Well, he's going to the special burns unit over on First,' the man said.

'Think he'll make it?' Beckman asked.

'I don't know,' the driver replied. 'I've seen a couple of cases like this. Enough to leave you hoping for the guy that he dies.' They finished loading the gurney into the back of the ambulance and pulled away from the curb, the wail of the siren echoing off the buildings around them.

In a brief, almost coded communication, Beckman signalled to Buratti that he was going to follow the ambulance. Buratti nodded and turned back to Mackenzie. Sylvie Morgan appeared with soft drinks and wet cloths that she had coaxed out of the deli across the street, attending to Mackenzie and Eddie first and then begrudgingly to Thomas as well. 'So did she tell you yet, Lieutenant? Did she tell you about the hell that this *putz* put me through?' She looked like she wanted to thwap Thomas in the head, but she was practising some restraint.

'I'm sure I'll be getting the full details from Mr Kinsolving here when we take him in for questioning,' Buratti said.

Kinsolving dropped the mask from his face. 'But I didn't do anything!' he cried and then started to cough immediately. The oxygen mask went back in place.

'Sure you did, kid,' Buratti replied. 'Maybe you didn't kill Gil Richardson, but you sure made my week hell, and that irritates me, you know? And if I look hard enough, I'm sure we can find something to charge you with.'

Mackenzie looked up at Buratti; her eyes, the only part of her face the lieutenant could see clearly, were crinkled at the sides. He knew she was smiling at him. He knew that she knew his bark was worse than his bite.

'What're you smiling at, Doc? Do you know what my *paisan* would do to me if anything happened to you?'

CHAPTER TWENTY-EIGHT

Bruce Quigley lasted only three days before he mercifully expired, but in those three days he managed to become the most infamous architect in New York since Stanford White had been shot and killed in the roof garden at Madison Square Garden by his lover's jealous husband.

The tabloids couldn't get enough of the story, and started portraying Quigley as a madman, an artist enamoured of his creation, a victim of an 'edifice' complex. From that kind of coverage it was a short jump to connect Quigley to the stories of the ghost of the Century Theatre. Rather than put people off, the idea of this modern-day 'phantom of the opera' (as one of the tabloids captured the story) seemed to titillate people, including, surprisingly, some investors.

Thanks to the expertise of the New York firefighters, the Century Theatre suffered minimal structural damage. Minimal enough that when approached by Jonathan Humphries and his father, the bankers holding the loans on the Century, intrigued not only by the story but by the prospect of recovering their money, agreed to increase the loans to repair the Century and prepare it for opening. Financial assistance also came in the form of an insurance settlement from the curtain manufacturer, who had neglected to fireproof an entire panel of the stage curtain.

It was the possibility of owning the theatre that had intrigued the senior Mr Humphries enough to explore the feasibility of going into business with his son. He still wasn't convinced of the stability of investing in a production like *Reunion,* but a theatre, at least a theatre building, was something he could understand.

Mrs Humphries had, of course, been appalled. When, in the days after the fire, her son's connection with the tawdry story playing out in the headlines of New York's newspapers became conversational fodder at her various luncheons, she was absolutely mortified. 'How could you, Jonathan,' she started when he entered the library one evening after receiving an official summons to his parents' apartment. She proceeded to excoriate him for his association with these 'theatrical types' and inevitably got around to her favourite refrain. 'Need I say that Paul, of course, would never have embarrassed me this way.'

Before Jonathan could even come up with a response, his father, who had been standing at the library bar, quietly adding ice cubes to his nightly Scotch, turned to his wife. 'Oh, shut up, Genevieve.'

His wife looked at him wide-eyed. 'Sampson! How dare y—'

'I'm sick of hearing you talk about Paul that way,' he interrupted. 'And sick of the way you've treated Jonathan all these years. And sick of myself that I've let you get away with it.' The library was absolutely silent; it was hard to tell who was the more shocked at the senior Humphries' words, Jonathan or his mother. 'You always favoured Paul because he looked like a Barstow. Well, he took after them in another way, too, because he was a drunk just like your father was.' Her rapid intake of breath let Sampson Humphries know

300

he'd made his point. He took a long sip of his icy Scotch, silently congratulating himself on finally saying something he'd wanted to get off his chest for the last fifteen years.

'Now, if you'll excuse us, Genevieve, I'm going to talk to my son about how we might be able to rescue this investment of his.'

After a frenzy of meetings that took place over the course of the next week, Jonathan gathered the company together, and with a delighted Joan Henley Byers at his side, announced that the production of *Reunion*, previously suspended, was on again. As soon as the theatre could be declared habitable, everybody would be back at work, and except for a few chorus members, who had already signed on with other shows, the entire company was reunited again. The opening was scheduled for the second week of June, as fate would have it, a few days before the presentation of the Tony Awards.

As Mackenzie arrived at the theatre that night, the excitement in the air was almost palpable. Because of the notoriety that the deaths of Richardson, Wexler, and then Quigley had brought to this production, every television crew, klieg light and satellite truck in the city seemed to be there, making 14th Street virtually impassable. Max Osgood stood on the sidewalk in front of the theatre, lord of all he surveyed, happy that he'd decided to stay on as the press agent for the show. He knew this would turn into a gold mine.

And the notoriety it had attracted wasn't the only reason the show was drawing this kind of press, either. Even though the official reviews wouldn't be out until tomorrow morning, a few of the columnists who had popped in for one of the ten preview performances had already offered their pre-opening comments, and the consensus was that *Reunion* was a smash. One woman, writing in the *Post*, pointedly mentioned that even if *Reunion* had opened on time, it wouldn't have been eligible for that week's Tony Award. 'How odd,' she noted, 'that the best new musical in years, an off-Broadway show actually playing on Broadway, isn't even eligible for New York's highest theatrical honour. Does this make sense to anyone?'

When Mackenzie had called Sylvie this morning to read the comments to her, they both decided that Simon Wexler would have been gratified to know that his instincts about using their Tony ineligibility as a publicity ploy were absolutely right. 'Well, whaddya know,' Sylvie crowed. 'Maybe they'll change the rules by next year, whaddya think? And maybe they'll remember us.'

'And then you can give the speech you've been practising, right?' Mackenzie teased. 'See you after the show. And break a leg.' Darn! she thought, hanging up the phone. She still hadn't found out where that phrase came from.

Jonathan and Sampson Humphries were among the first arrivals that the camera crews caught on opening night. It had been the topic of some conversation along Park Avenue in recent weeks that Mr Humphries seemed to appear these days only at functions where Mrs Humphries wasn't present. And vice-versa.

Ben Wheeler arrived not long after, with the long-suffering Beverly on one arm and Mrs Glenn Leonard on the other. He hoped the new medication Beverly had gotten for him worked. Given his record of the last few months, he might have spent half the night in the men's room throwing up, but Beverly promised him that the doctor said these new pills would work. Ben waved enthusiastically when he saw

Mackenzie Griffin in the crowd. He'd been so grateful when she'd given him the copy of the tape that Richardson had lifted, he almost threw up then, too. But he'd controlled himself that day, hadn't he? So maybe he could get through tonight.

Lenny and Mags Yarnevich hovered in the aisle next to their fifth row seats, both of them soaking up the excitement of a genuine New York opening night. Now that he'd achieved his dream, Lenny was looking forward to getting back to Beverly Hills and finishing up the screenplay he'd started just after Gil died. He couldn't wait to show it to Carl.

He really missed Carl; he really missed having breakfast at Nate 'n Al's and reading the trades and kibitzing with him. His new plan, he'd confided to Mags just that afternoon, was to surprise his old partner. 'I'm not gonna tell him when we're flying in, see, so I'll just walk into Nate 'n Al's and order my coffee and bagel like I haven't been gone for seven months. Whaddya think? Funny?'

'Funny, dear,' Mags had replied. 'Now you better get in the shower if we have to leave here by quarter to six.'

Lenny looked at his watch again. It was six-twenty and the opening night performance was scheduled for six-thirty, as usual for an opening. 'So whaddya think?' he said to Mags. 'Should we sit down?'

'I think you should look up the aisle and see who's coming.'

Lenny did. To his amazement, the ever-tanned Carl was strolling down the aisle to meet him. The two men wrapped their arms around one another in a bear hug.

'I thought you said you wouldn't come to New York,' Lenny said, almost overcome.

'And miss this? Besides, I figured it's June, I could risk

303

it. I know it's not gonna freeze or anything, but do you believe this humidity?'

Manny Erickson and Duran Nadeem arrived arm in arm. Nothing romantic going on between them, he assured one of the entertainment reporters off the record. It's just that neither one had seen anyone outside the company in at least two months, so neither of them could even get a date. As he looked around at the crowd, waiting for Duran to finish up an interview with one of the local television stations, Manny wished for perhaps the hundredth time that week that Gil Richardson could have been here. The old Gil Richardson. The one he wanted everyone to remember.

Duran finished up her interview and sought out Manny's arm again. He'd been such a help these last weeks, and he seemed to understand her nervousness. She was still wondering what the reaction would be when people read her bio note in tonight's programme. It was there, right after the posthumous note on Gil. *Duran Nadeem*, it read, *Co-Director and Choreographer*. She didn't know how many times she'd thanked Jonathan and his father and Joan Byers for this chance, for their trust in putting the show in her hands. But there had been another person she finally had to thank, and that was where the rest of the bio note came in. *Dorothy AnnWilson*, it read, *extends her long overdue thanks to Gil Richardson for setting his standards so high, for his lifelong pursuit of theatrical excellence, and for helping her change her life – even if he didn't know it.*

The performance was magic from the enthusiastically received overture on. Joan Henley Byers was happy to note that her instincts about sticking with this show were going to be amply rewarded.

Gregory sat next to her, applauding each performer generously, but applauding a little more enthusiastically when Rhonda whatever-her-name finished her numbers. He was so transparent. True, Gregory had stopped seeing the woman for a few weeks, maybe even a month, but recently they'd resumed their liaison. He still didn't realize that Joan knew.

Oh well, if the show was as successful as she thought it was going to be, and judging from the reaction of the audience, it would be, she'd have a little more money to pay the divorce lawyers. Over the last several weeks Joan had developed her own mental parlour game of planning in great detail just how she'd do away with Gregory without getting caught, but she'd come to realize that was just an amusement. She'd probably have to divorce him. But this time it was going to be at her schedule's convenience. And she'd be damned if she was paying any more in alimony.

Mackenzie walked past the phalanx of cameras and lights that night in the company of two gentlemen: Peter Rossellini on her right, and Eddie Lopes, the special guest of Sylvie Morgan, on her left.

Peter's appearance was met with a good deal of attention from the press and the photographers, as it usually was, but Mac was delighted when some of the press people recognized Eddie as well. After his rescue of Mac and Thomas Kinsolving from the Century, Eddie had been the subject of quite a few newspaper stories, lauding him for his second heroic rescue effort in less than six months. The photographers called out his name tonight, asking him to stop for pictures. Eddie's reaction, as Mackenzie knew it would be, was embarrassment. But at least he stopped. Eddie was gradually accepting the idea that somebody could, without being crazy, consider him a hero. Mackenzie was more gratified to realize that by the time their group ended, Eddie had accepted the fact that he bore no responsibility for little Francesca's death.

The group meetings had ended in early May, around the time when spring had blessedly, if belatedly, come to the city. The PEPSI study had been released the third week of May, and Mackenzie and her colleagues had generally received high praise for their work. Some spokespeople for the departments involved in the study took great exception to some of their conclusions, but that was to be expected. Word was that the same team was going to be approached about doing a regional or perhaps national study, but Mackenzie had already told Drs Parsons and Gershon that she would not participate. Not that she was sure what she was going to do as yet. It's just that she was sure another study like the PEPSI study wasn't it.

When spring had finally arrived, when she had the opportunity to start work in her small backyard garden that was such a luxury in this city, when the spring's longer days and warmer nights coincided with the end of her group meetings and the end of her participation in the study, Mackenzie had decided that it was a symbolic time for her, as well. The coming of this spring marked the end of a long dark period for her.

Sitting next to Eddie that night, watching his reaction to the play, reinforced Mackenzie's developing opinion that what she'd be doing in the future would involve more work similar to that which she'd done with the group, and an increase in the work she occasionally did with Buratti. While she hadn't formed a plan just as yet, she'd already started talking to Peter about it, generally phrasing it as 'what she'd do after this summer'. Peter, glad to hear her

306

talking positively about the future for the first time in a while, had some plans of his own to suggest to her.

As she sat and watched the premiere performance of *Reunion*, Mac was surprised to see so much of what she'd been through in recent months played out on the stage in front of her. More eloquently than she could have expressed, Lenny Yarnevich and Ben Wheeler wrote about feeling the march of time, the confusion of having your dreams change on you, the pain of wondering what was the point of so many of life's challenges. She felt at times as if it were her life up there on stage, and then she remembered an interview she'd read in the theatre section of the *Times*, which she'd been reading more faithfully of late. A playwright had remarked that, in her opinion, the point of theatre was to reflect the lives we live and in the reflection make things clearer to us.

Mackenzie still wasn't sure what she was going to do come autumn, but for now, this moment, this night, this spring, she felt good. By the time Sylvie and Rhonda finished their big duet at the end of the show, a song actually titled 'Dreams Change', Mackenzie felt her eyes misting up, both at the connection she felt to the song, and to the thrill of seeing her friend finally on centre stage in a starring role, where she was meant to be.

It was one of those nights in the theatre when stars were made, starting with Rhonda Deveraux, whom Mackenzie had gotten to know in the past several weeks. Rhonda might be dumb as a post, to use Sylvie's apt description, but tonight proved that the woman could move, the woman could sing, and the woman could command an audience with ease.

Curtis Leland was tremendously affecting as the Professor, and at the curtain calls, both he and the audience seemed to acknowledge the poignancy of the fact that he was being 'discovered' at the age of sixty-five.

Sylvie absolutely brought down the house with her Miss Goodwin. At the curtain calls, Peter leaned to speak into Mac's ear, trying to be heard over the din. 'This is great,' he said, genuinely glad for Sylvie's success. 'This is literally seeing a career born in front of your eyes. What a huge beginning for her!'

As they stood there applauding curtain call after curtain call, Mac's thoughts wandered to the men who weren't there. Gil Richardson and Simon Wexler, whose faith in the show had certainly been vindicated in the last few hours. And Bruce Quigley, whose theatre had been greeted with such kudos, kudos tempered in the press by the circumstances of his death. How odd that one show could represent so many lives lost and other lives, particularly those of the actors in front of her, just starting. So many endings and beginnings. Or, to put it in theatrical terms, so many finales and overtures.

Outside, Howard Goldman heard the bravos of the audience and he knew they'd been trickling out of the theatre soon. He picked up his sign and started walking his lonely protest vigil. He began again walking the loop he'd started tracing in the sidewalk in the minutes before the curtain went up, when there were only a few cameras left. 'Century Theatre Unfair to Labour' his sign read. No matter what anyone else did, Howard Goldman kept the faith.